Praise for ... and Her Books

The Forever Family

"I highly recommend *The Forever Family* to anyone who enjoys women's fiction."

—TheBashfulBookworm.com

"Such a lovely story...an emotional read with some very funny moments." —TheHappyReader.ca

The Marvelous Monroe Girls

"Adorable friends-to-lovers romance from bestseller Jump...This is sure to please."

—*Publishers Weekly*

"Perfect for readers looking for stories that feature both familial and romantic love in a small town."

—*Library Journal*

The Perfect Recipe for Love and Friendship

"In this heartwarming, sometimes heart-wrenching, story, readers are given a glimpse of the good, the bad, and the ugly sides to family and forgiveness."

—RTBookReviews.com

"There really isn't anything better than a book about family, friendship, and food, and *The Perfect Recipe for Love and Friendship* has all of this and more!"
—MargiesMustReads.com

The Secret Ingredient for a Happy Marriage

"Beautifully written and unflinching in its portrayal of the complexities of marriage, sisterhood, and long-held secrets." —Kristan Higgins, *New York Times* bestselling author

"Fraught with delicious tension, Nora's journey through loss, grief, and hope will resonate with readers."
—*Publishers Weekly*

THE
FOREVER
FAMILY

THE
FOREVER
FAMILY

SHIRLEY JUMP

FOREVER

New York Boston

Forever
Hachette Book Group
1290 Avenue of the Americas, New York, NY 10104
read-forever.com
twitter.com/readforeverpub

Originally published in trade paperback and ebook in January 2023
First Mass Market Edition: November 2023

Forever is an imprint of Grand Central Publishing. The Forever name and logo are trademarks of Hachette Book Group, Inc.

The publisher is not responsible for websites (or their content) that are not owned by the publisher.

The Hachette Speakers Bureau provides a wide range of authors for speaking events. To find out more, go to www.hachettespeakersbureau.com or call (866) 376-6591.

Forever books may be purchased in bulk for business, educational, or promotional use. For information, please contact your local bookseller or the Hachette Book Group Special Markets Department at special.markets@hbgusa.com.

ISBNs: 9781538720271 (trade paperback); 9781538740422 (mass market); 9781538720677 (ebook)

Printed in the United States of America

OPM

10 9 8 7 6 5 4 3 2 1

To my husband—the man I waited all my life to fall in love with and who makes my life complete.

CHAPTER 1

The morning sun blared through the floor-to-ceiling windows like a solar bonfire. Emma Monroe clutched a crisp white sheet tight against her chest, squeezed her eyes shut, and slid under the Egyptian cotton as if she were five and hiding from the imaginary monster in her closet. None of that, of course, erased the monster-size mistake she'd woken up to in a hotel room in Nevada.

Emma made major life decisions like some people bought uncomfortable shoes, without thinking or trying them out or even waiting for a sale. Last night, surprise-surprise, she'd made another one. But this time, the choice she'd made was bigger, more permanent, and...human.

The low rumble of snoring came from the right side of the bed. She closed her eyes tighter, but it didn't change a thing. Instead, the snoring stopped, and the bed swayed a bit with movement. Then a hand slid across and covered hers, fingers starting to interlace with her own.

No, no, hard *no*.

Emma scrambled out of the king-size bed, disentangling

from the sheets with a twist and stumble. "I…I have to go."

Luke lifted his head from the pillow. One side of his dark, wavy hair had flattened in his sleep, making him look like a two-dimensional version of himself. "What? Why?"

She had a hundred reasons for leaving, most of which started and ended with *because we never should have done this*.

"It was your idea. Remember?" He shielded his eyes against the sunlight streaming through the windows and grimaced. "It's so early, Emma. Go back to sleep, and we can talk about this later."

"It's after nine, Luke, and we…we can't talk about this. We are just going to forget it happened. Okay? I'm serious. This *never happened*." She started gathering up her clothes—faded jeans with tattered hems, a peasant blouse with tiny coral flowers, gold braided sandals—and avoided the floral headband sitting on the nightstand. The flowers had dried, and petals had begun to flake off, as if the headband were shedding its memories of the night before, too.

Smart headband.

Out of the corner of her eye, she caught a glint, a bounce of sunshine. A shiny gold circle sat on the fourth finger of her left hand, like a hallucination. She tried to wrestle the ring off, but it was good and stuck. Karma was probably laughing his butt off because Emma had long ago been voted the Monroe girl Most Likely to Never Settle Down. Maybe it was all some kind of waking nightmare. A hallucination. Yeah, and maybe the Easter bunny was going to waltz in here and hand her a Cadbury egg, too.

"Emma, they'll kick you out if you don't go through with the whole thing." Luke's voice held the huskiness of sleep, the kind of hypnotizing sound that lulled people into bad decisions.

"I don't care. I'll find another way to get into one of Yogi Brown's retreats." Except she'd been trying to go on one of the yogi's retreats for two years now. There was no rhyme or reason to the nearly secret getaways. He would announce one, it would fill up in a matter of minutes, and then he'd go silent until the next one. When the notice for the Renew Your Connection retreat came into her inbox, Emma clicked and paid without even reading the description.

Which was half the reason why she was standing in a bedroom in Nevada with a wedding ring and a six-foot problem.

If she stopped long enough to consider her decisions, maybe she wouldn't end up in situations like this. But stopping meant thinking—no, *feeling*—and Emma avoided the latter at all costs. It wasn't like she needed to have some kind of self-revelation, aha moment, or anything. She already knew she was the kind of person who flitted from relationship to relationship, job to job, and apartment to apartment, always in search of . . . something.

That something was definitely not a husband. Marriage was one of those semi-permanent things that Emma wouldn't touch with a ten-foot pole and a hazmat suit. Until now, apparently.

"They'll ban you for life," Luke said. "There's a clause in the flyer that says—"

"I know what it says. I know what we did. Can't you just forget all your stupid rules for one second, Luke? I need to go home. I need to think. I need . . ." Crap. Where was her phone? The little white wristlet she remembered dangling from her right hand last night was nowhere to be found. When it mattered, Emma rarely had her act together.

"You're really doing this?" he said.

We're really doing this? she'd said last night, in a giddy bubble composed of lies. There'd been something so . . . fun about pulling off the fake marriage. Undoubtedly fueled by the spiked punch that had been in abundance in the ballroom that had served as a wedding chapel for fifty couples. The only thing she hadn't planned for was the *real* marriage license.

Emma started moving throw pillows and sliding her hand into the couch cushions before finally finding her tiny bag under a stack of papers on the kitchenette counter. A foggy memory of celebratory champagne and stumbling back to their "Marital Reinvigoration Suite" on the other side of the resort danced in the back of her mind.

Marital Reinvigoration. That was what she got for not reading the paperwork packet for the retreat before hopping on a plane and showing up at the center. All she'd known was that she had to leave the suffocating envelope of her life. Do something that had meaning and impact. Prove to her family and the entire town of Harbor Cove that Emma Monroe had her shit together.

Except nothing said *my life is a total mess* more than getting shackled to a man she barely knew. God, how could she be so incredibly idiotic? She'd wanted an escape and an adventure, and she'd gone and taken the whole idea too far. There was spontaneous—and there was foolhardy.

"Listen, Luke, you're a nice guy and all, but I can't—"

"Already breaking us up before we've even consummated the union?" He propped himself on one elbow and watched her fumble with the buckle on her sandal. A look of amusement lit his features. "That's not exactly working on our marriage, Emma. You know that Yogi Brown would say you aren't listening to the Law of Correspondence."

"Don't go throwing universal laws at me, Luke…" Her voice trailed off into the void in her memory. "Whatever your last name is. That's not fair."

"My last name is now your last name, wifey, so you might want to learn it."

A year ago, Luke had unfurled his yoga mat beside hers in a canyon in Utah. They'd chatted between Sun Salutations and Downward Dogs, finding a common ground in their shared love of adventures and an uncle of his who lived in Harbor Cove, Massachusetts, only a mile from the house where Emma spent most of her childhood. Then she'd seen Luke again six months later at a weekend meditation retreat in Burlington, Vermont. They'd walked the serenity garden and the endless circles of the stone labyrinth as the sun crested over the mountains.

She'd liked him a lot and been happy to run into him again at the registration desk for the yogi's retreat. When he'd whispered, *Hey, we should pretend we're a couple*, she'd thought it would be a lark, until they'd ended up reciting vows with all the twosomes there to elope or renew their commitment. It was all fun and games—until it got super, super real. "Is all this funny to you? Because it's not even remotely funny to me."

"What happened to the Emma who jumped off the cliff at Navajo Falls and dove forty feet into a glacier pool? The

Emma who walked across hot coals, and who tried a little ayahuasca in a tent in the middle of the Pyrenees?"

"I'm not that person anymore." Geez, put all together, she sounded like the very definition of foolhardy. Or fun. Yeah, *fun* was a better adjective to go with.

And then a tiny part of herself, the part she tried never to listen to, whispered, *Aren't you already planning another risky venture in two months? One without a safety net to catch you if it doesn't work out?*

When are you going to get your act together, Emma?

"Anyway, as I was saying, I'm not like that. Anymore," she added.

"As of what, yesterday afternoon?"

She refused to rise to his bait. "This whole thing was a deal you and I made so we could get into the seminar. How was I supposed to know that Yogi Brown was going to *really* marry all the couples during the seminar? Is that even legal?"

He crossed his hands behind his head and leaned against the bank of pillows. "In all fifty states, apparently. So we are, for all intents and purposes, a married couple. And we're supposed to be at the"—he reached for a sheet of paper on the bedside table—"'Are You Attracting or Repelling Love?' seminar in seventeen minutes."

Repelling. Definitely repelling. If there was some kind of reverse magnet for whatever was happening between them, Emma would order a giant version right now. "I'm not going, Luke."

"And how am I to explain your absence, wifey?"

Wifey? The added note of sarcasm on the second use of that dreaded word added a little extra oomph of annoying punctuation. Emma parked a fist on her hip. Where did Luke get off questioning her choices? Her family did enough of that, thankyouverymuch. And maybe they sometimes had a point, but that was going to change. Right after she got out of this mess—the last mess, she swore—that she had created. Because Emma had big plans that were going to change her life and make a difference in the world. Then she could leave her screws-up-everything-she-touches reputation behind once and for all. "Why are you even here? You had to know about the whole marriage-required deal when you signed up for this retreat."

"You didn't."

She arched a brow. "The chance that there are two people who didn't read the fine print is slim to none. So what's your deal?"

"I don't have a deal. I wanted an experience, and I figured I could charm my way past the rules."

Emma didn't care about Luke's charm or his reasons or anything else about her *hubby* right now. All she wanted to do was leave and get back to her boring life in a small town. She had opportunities ahead of her that she refused to derail because of one stupid mistake after too much rum punch. "Tell Yogi Brown that I fell asleep during my meditation or that I got fatally entangled in my yoga mat. I have to get out of here."

"Fatally entangled in your yoga mat?" He laughed. "The worst part is, he might just believe that."

"Either way, I don't care, and we are done here, in every way possible." Emma grabbed the papers and the wristlet and then ran out of the room and down the hall, clutching the whole kit-and-kaboodle, as Grandma would say, to her chest, and whispering a quick prayer that the exterior doors would close before Luke... *What on earth is his last name?*...came stumbling after her.

The doors shut with a solid thud. Emma was now on

the outside of the resort, a sprawling eight-thousand-acre property with pools and waterfalls and vast views of Nevada in all directions. She'd checked in on the other side of the property, and all of her stuff was in the locker room right off the main yoga studio.

Emma stood on one leg while she slipped on her shoes, balancing against the stone exterior as she did. She needed a ride back to the main lobby. She had no idea how to navigate this gargantuan building, and she was not going back inside where she could possibly run into Luke again. She wasn't a fight girl. She was a take flight, avoid, then deal kind of girl.

She could handle this. No problem. She'd get back to the lobby and straighten out this entire mess. There was no way she'd really, legally, for sure gotten married last night, right?

Except she remembered standing in a room with white walls, white carpet, Yogi Brown in a white tuxedo, and dozens of couples filling the room while Emma sipped the unlimited agave nectar rum punch and laughed and wobbled and—

Oh. My. God. She'd said *I do*. She could hear the words in her head, caught on a laugh and the same devil-may-care, why-not impulsive whim that had been a part of Emma's personality since birth. Normally that trait made her dash off on adventures like a hiking trip in Yosemite or kiteboarding in Newport, or agree to upend her life for a chance to work with a start-up charity. Not this. Not doing the one thing she had long ago decided she would never, ever, ever do.

Get married to Luke What's-His-Name, or any other What's-His-Name man for that matter. No, not her. Impossible.

Emma went to fold the papers, and there, in black and white atop a colorful brochure for the Nevada Half Moon Restoration Resort, was a marriage certificate for one Emma Monroe and Luke Carter. Dated the night before, signed by Yogi Brown, an ordained minister from someplace with a URL.

An internet-certified minister couldn't marry people for real, could he? Even if he was the most sought-after retreat leader on the planet?

For more than two years, Emma had heard other people talk about Yogi Brown in soft, reverent tones and seen dozens of people in her Facebook groups rave about how Yogi Brown had transformed their attitudes and emotions.

And Emma—stuck in a job she hated, living in a town about as exciting as dish soap, and wondering what else the world might have to offer—felt like she was missing the one key that would turn everything around in her life and give her some meaning and substance, a purpose. She'd dabbled in this and that and jumped from thing to thing, looking for the answers that would finally ease the constant nagging feeling that she was failing at, well, everything.

Her mother, a person Emma didn't even remember, had been someone. Penny Monroe would have changed the world if she had lived, of that Emma had no doubt. People spoke of her late mother like they talked about a saint—maybe because that's what she'd been, at least from the stories Emma had heard. Her mother had been everything Emma wished she could be and kept falling short of achieving.

Emma shoved the papers under her arm and then dug in her wristlet for her phone. A dozen text messages filled

the screen. Her sisters and grandmother, worried that she
hadn't checked in for a couple of days. Plus three from
Diana, her best friend and the manager at the hotel where
they both worked, Diana at the front desk and Emma in
the wedding planning department. An irony to be sure,
given the situation Emma found herself in right now. *Call
me*, Diana wrote, *or I'll assume you've been kidnapped
by aliens and then I'm going to have to hop on a plane
and rescue you.*

Emma groaned and leaned against the wall. How on
earth was she going to explain this to anyone? She started
to type a reply to Diana and stopped. There were no
words to explain signing up for what she thought was a
yoga retreat—because who read the fine print anyway?—
then discovering the surprise-surprise marriage require-
ment, and waking up hitched to a man she'd met exactly
three times.

The resort flyer fluttered out of her hand, and as she
went to pick it up, she noticed a little note on the bottom.
*If you need assistance, just dial this number, and we will
help you find your center again.*

Emma dialed, and a friendly woman answered. "Half
Moon Restoration Resort. How can I help you become
more grounded and intentional today?"

"Um, can you get me one of those golf cart guys to
drive me back to the lobby? I'm standing out here on the
other side of the resort, and I think I got lost."

"All who are lost are easily found again," the woman
said. "Is there a number on one of the exterior doors?"

Emma turned around. "Um, A-235."

"Perfect. Someone will be there in a moment. Until
then, my dear, just breathe."

Yeah, easy for that woman to say. She wasn't married

to a near-stranger and stuck in the middle of the country. If she'd been smart, she'd have nama-*stayed* back home in Harbor Cove, and then she wouldn't be in this mess.

A few minutes later, the soft purr of an electric motor brought a golf cart around the corner. The man stopped and asked Emma if she was the one who had called for the ride. She climbed aboard, sank into the vinyl seat, and let out a sigh of relief. "Can you bring me to the lobby, please?"

The driver, a lanky older man in a green uniform and a ball cap emblazoned with the resort's logo, gave her a quick glance. "You one of those health nuts? My wife is always trying to get me to eat greens. I say, if God wanted me to eat vegetables, he would have made them look like steak."

"Uh-huh," Emma murmured as they began putt-putting around the endless building. All she wanted was the quiet of the locker room where she'd first stowed her belongings. Then a moment to collect her thoughts before she caught the first plane back to Massachusetts. Her head was pounding, clearly an aftereffect of the marriage-inducing punch she'd had last night…

And the bad decision that had followed. How much had she been drinking anyway? Whatever the amount was, it was a lot more than her usual couple of glasses of chardonnay. She'd stood in the ballroom with all the other couples—some with hope in their eyes that a renewal of their vows would change years of fighting, some with infatuation bubbling between them—and felt…

Alone.

For some reason, the thing she loved most—her freedom—had seemed like an albatross yesterday. "Who is ready to commit to changing their lives together?" Yogi Brown had asked.

A few minutes before that, Luke had made his way through the crowd and come over to say hello. Emma flashed him a quick smile, but her attention stayed on the tall, thin man with the long white beard, so much the epitome of a yogi that he might as well be a caricature. "You thinking of doing this?" Luke whispered.

"Maybe. I mean, yeah, I've been trying to get into his retreats for years. I've heard he's so life-changing. Whatever Yogi Brown has us do, I'm all in, because I need my life changed in the worst way possible."

"Anything?" Luke clarified, and Emma remembered wondering why he'd said that with a quirk in his grin.

"Anything," she'd replied, thinking it meant walking on hot coals or dropping into a cryo tank or holding the Lotus Pose for thirty minutes.

"Well, you should know that, this time, he has something different planned. Very different. I don't think"—his gaze dropped to her hands, clasped in front of her—"that you came adequately prepared."

"I have my yoga mat in the locker room, Luke." She shifted her weight. It had been a long day what with the flight, registration, and then waiting for the kickoff event. "I hope they assign us to our rooms soon. I'd really like to try to get in a quick meditation session before dinner."

"I don't think there's going to be time for that today. In fact, Yogi Brown only has one event on the schedule today, and frankly, I'm kinda surprised you're at it, Emma." He looked at her askance. "You did read the schedule, didn't you?"

"Shh. I'm listening." She shot him a glare. Yogi Brown was talking again, and Luke's whispering was distracting. And no, she hadn't read the schedule but now she was beginning to worry that maybe she should have.

"You need a lot more right now than a yoga mat, Emma. You're going to need—"

"Partners! Grab hands with your love match and stand before each other," Yogi Brown said. The crowd began moving and re-sorting itself, like fish dropped into a pond. Several women dressed in long white muumuus began making their way through the room, dropping floral headbands on the crowns of every female they saw.

"My what?" Emma asked, just as Luke came around to stand in front of her. "What are you doing?"

He leaned down and whispered in her ear, "Saving you from getting kicked out of the retreat."

"Why would Yogi Brown do that to me?" A woman placed a headband on Emma's hair and moved on to the next female attendee. Headbands? Partners? Love matches? What the hell was going on here?

"Because this retreat, Emma, is a marriage retreat. For building, repairing, or renewing relationships. And look at us here together. I'd call that an opportunity for a little fun." He brightened. "Hey, we should pretend we're a couple."

She spun a long, slow circle in the room and saw that yes, indeed, couples of all kinds, ages, races, and orientations were standing together, holding hands, waiting for Yogi Brown's next command.

"But I...I..." She turned back to Luke. "What am I supposed to do?"

"Two choices," he said. "Play along with me because I'm kind of in the same boat as you, or pack up your yoga mat and head back to Massachusetts."

Whatever crazy marital repair thing the yogi had going on this weekend was surely just a theme or something. She could pretend to be with Luke and take advantage of the spa day, the meditation seminar, and the hatha yoga sessions, then go back to Harbor Cove all recentered and recharged.

"Partners, are you ready to begin or renew your commitment?" Yogi Brown asked. "Are you ready to transform your relationships?"

A collective *yes* went up from the room. Luke tipped his head toward Emma, and she nodded in return. He took her hand, gave her a quick grin, and then shouted, "Yes!"

And that was how she found herself getting swept down a set of category 5 rapids that led from a ballroom in a fancy resort somewhere in Nevada to the wedding band on her finger. *It wasn't my idea after all, Luke Carter. It was yours.* She turned on the vinyl golf cart seat and glared at the building in the distance where she'd left her husband-mistake.

"Rough morning?" the golf cart driver asked as he stopped at a crossing and let several pairs of people meander past.

"That's an understatement." So no, it hadn't been her idea to get married, but she'd gone along with it, which was just as bad. All for a seminar. Was her life really that awful that she'd get married to escape it? Apparently... yes.

That alone was a sign she couldn't leave Harbor Cove fast enough. She had an opportunity to be part of a new charitable foundation that paired traveling volunteers with children in underserved corners of the world. In exchange for working with the kids, Emma would get free room and board and a trip around the world. It was essentially skills-based social work, but with airfare and hostels. And to Emma, it was the opportunity she'd been looking for all her life, one she believed in so much, she'd poured her entire savings account into the foundation. In a few months, she'd dust off her passport and take her life in a new, far more responsible direction. Finally officially going after a career she'd never dared to speak aloud.

Her phone rang, and Emma jumped, nearly dropping the cell on the floor of the golf cart. "Hello?"

"Thank God you're not dead." Diana laughed. "Seriously, I don't want to do your job, and if you died, I'd be stuck in the bridezilla department until Larry opened his wallet wide enough to hire a replacement."

Emma laughed. "I haven't quit yet." Soon enough Emma would leave her job and travel the world. No nine-to-five, no husband to tie her down—

Well, *technically* that last part wasn't true. At least right now. She'd get an annulment or a divorce, or whatever it was that people did after such a stupid mistake. Wasn't her cousin George a lawyer in Dover? He could help her figure out what to do.

"So tell me all about the retreat," Diana said. "Any yummy guys there?"

"Uh…" Luke was yummy. He had a toned, muscular body, a sharp wit, and a hell of a One-Armed Compass Pose. When she'd first met him, he'd become a friend of sorts, and yeah, Emma had thought about dating him down the road if he ever got to Massachusetts to visit whatever family member he had there, but not marrying him. Or anyone.

"Uh-oh," Diana said.

"What's uh-oh?"

"Usually when you're speechless, it means you've done something spontaneous and are possibly regretting it. Spill. What does he look like? Did he ask you out? Where does he live? Or is he just going to be one of those what-happens-at-the-yoga-retreat-stays-at-the-yoga-retreat guys?"

"Uh..." She didn't have an answer for half of those questions. It was easier to picture Luke in her mind and describe him like he was some kind of retreat fling that she was going to forget as soon as she got on the plane. And that was exactly what she was going to do. Forget him and this whole ridiculous thing. *I really need to get my life on track.* "It's complicated."

"Honey, they all are. So what's he look like?"

She closed her eyes, and she could see Luke standing before her with a grin that could melt steel. And damn it, she almost let out a little sigh. "He's tall, like six feet, and he's got super-broad shoulders. He used to play tennis competitively back in high school and does something like working on houses now, so he's in pretty good shape." *Pretty good* was like saying crème brûlée was an okay dessert. Luke was in incredible shape with muscles that popped and flexed every time he did a yoga pose.

"And...did he get your number?" Diana asked.

"Technically, no." Emma glanced at the ring, nothing more than a plain band that had oh-so-big, lifetime implications. "I might have...uh...accidentally married him yesterday."

"Happens all the time, especially up at this crazy place," the driver said, catching Emma's eye. "You can get a quickie divorce in Alaska for a buck-fifty. Just so you know."

"Thanks for the tip." Emma shifted away from the man, facing the grass rushing past her at a whopping ten miles an hour, and lowered her voice. "I mean, I think I did."

"Did you say you got *married*?" Diana said. "This

from the girl who thinks marriage is the equivalent of being sent to death row?"

"I'm not sure. I have to…" She was going to say *ask Luke*, but she had already decided she was never, ever going to talk to him again. What was she going to say? *Hey, you wanna get divorced? How legal do you think this piece of paper is anyway?*

"Although, if you never consummated your union," the driver went on, "an annulment might be faster. I don't know if it's cheaper, 'cuz I've only been divorced myself."

Emma gave him a nod and a quit-talking-to-me smile. "Listen, Diana, I gotta go. I'll call you when I get to the airport. I'm heading back on the first flight."

"Three times," the driver continued, oblivious. "Number four seems to be the one that's sticking. She told me there's nothin' more romantic than being married by Elvis."

"I'll keep that in mind," Emma muttered as she tucked her phone away. Not that she was ever getting married again. Or keeping this husband, for that matter. *Husband.* Even thinking the word felt weird. And the worst part?

She wasn't going to get to go to any of the workshops or sessions today. That was Luke's fault, she decided. If he hadn't come up with this ludicrous idea—

Well, truth was, she would have had to leave anyway. Yogi Brown had made it very clear in the papers that she now had in her hand that the whole thing was for couples, not singles. Would have been helpful to have read that before she showed up here. Either way, she wasn't going to get the retreat she had paid for. *And whose fault is that?*

Finally, the golf cart rounded the building, and the

front entrance came into view. "Thanks," Emma said, not even waiting for him to come to a complete stop before she fished a five out of her purse, left the money on the dash, and then hurried inside and down to the locker room, avoiding everyone she saw.

The resort itself was gorgeous with wide oak floors shined to a high gloss and mossy-green walls that made the rooms seem like secret dens in a forest. Calming music played over the sound system, while the water fountain outside gurgled a slow beat. The locker room was empty because everyone was probably at the retreat, figuring out if they were attracting or repelling. It was a minimal space—a wall of metal lockers, a couple of wooden benches, and a sauna on the far end. Normally, Emma would love coming back to a near-empty space like this because it gave her busy mind a chance to quiet.

But not this time. Right now, all she could hear was the panicked cacophony of her need to leave. She yanked her backpack out from inside the locker. Eighteen hours ago, she'd stowed it with such hope and anticipation. Never in a million years did she think the "life-changing" retreat would harness her to a husband whom she was now doing her best to run away from. A Google search told her there was a flight at two this afternoon back to Massachusetts, and she'd rather wait in the airport for five hours than run into—

"Emma?" There was a soft knock at the door and a familiar voice. "Can we talk?"

Luke. Damn it. How the hell did he get back here so fast? Would it be cowardly to pretend she wasn't here? She stood stock-still, her heart hammering so loudly that she was sure he could hear it in the hall.

"Listen, I know you're in there and probably avoiding

me," he said, "which is totally understandable, but we do have to talk about what happened last night."

She yanked open the door, and there he was, all six feet of him, with that crooked smile and dark wavy hair. Her pulse did a little gallop. "Nope, nope, nope, Luke." She spun away, threw the last of her things into the bag, and zipped it shut. "I can't deal with this. I need to go home."

"Or... here's an idea." He held up his hands in a don't-shoot-the-messenger move. "You could stay here, and we could get to know each other more, Mrs. Carter."

"Ugh. Don't ever call me that. The last thing I want to be is married to you." Then she brushed past him, ignoring the flicker of hurt in his features as she hurried down the hall and out the door. A taxi was waiting by the valet station, a gift from the heavens that Emma was so, so, so grateful to see. She climbed inside and shut the door, and for the first time in twenty-four hours, she let out a calming breath.

As the taxi pulled away from the curb, Emma hit FaceTime and her grandmother's number. If anyone would know what to do about this mess, it was Grandma Eleanor. She'd been the Harbor Cove advice columnist for decades and a surrogate mother to Emma and her two older sisters after their mother died. Grandma had always been the one with all the answers, and if there was one thing Emma needed right now, it was advice.

But when the phone connected, it was her sister Gabby's face that she saw, not Grandma's. "Hey, Em! How'd it go?"

"Uh... I think I accidentally got..." Emma paused. She couldn't seem to figure out a lie that would work, not right now while her mind was a muddled, hurried mess. "Married."

Grandma moved into the frame, so close to the phone that all Emma could see was her ear. "Uh, Emma, what did you just say? I think our connection's poor. Did you say you were in an accident?"

"No time to explain. I'm heading home right now," Emma said. If no one had heard the word *married*, maybe Emma could just keep the whole thing secret, go see her cousin George, and settle this idiocy with Luke before it got any further out of hand. "Gotta go! Love you!" Then she hung up the phone, laid her head against the back of the cab's seat, and tried not to cry.

CHAPTER 2

Luke Carter had done a lot of foolish things in his life. The truant officer at his old high school surely had a list, as did his parents, who'd washed their hands of their only child a long time ago. In truth, it had been a mutual unraveling of a relationship that had always been fragile at best. An alcoholic father with an anger management problem and a mother who loved her son but chose to preserve the peace rather than stick up for her child. He'd left home as soon as he could, and except for occasional visits around the holidays, he'd never looked back.

And never intended to have a child of his own. Hell, he had no idea how to raise a kid. He'd barely raised himself. Then along came his daughter four years ago, an event that should have made Luke slow down but instead made him move faster and farther because he was scared as hell to screw up his own kid.

For most of those four years, he had worked sixty

hours a week and traveled three weeks out of the month. All of which meant he hadn't had to step up and become the man he should have been a long time ago until he was literally forced into it. Now he lived every day trying to be better than his own parents because Scout was counting on him.

Two months ago, he'd realized his ex-girlfriend had begun drinking heavily. He'd called her mother, and together, they'd given her the ultimatum—rehab or lose custody of Scout. A teary twenty minutes later, Luke was holding a Paw Patrol suitcase in one hand and his daughter's tiny hand in the other. In an instant, he'd had to rearrange his life.

He'd given up his grueling, travel-heavy job working for a custom renovation company and instead taken the offer his cousin made him. *Come work for me, and I'll give you a respectable job and a steady paycheck.* His cousin had forgotten to mention that the stress factor was multiplied many times over because Luke was stuck in a four-by-four cubicle crunching numbers under soulless fluorescent lights eight hours a day.

But he kept clocking in, day after day. Because every time he left work and pulled up to the daycare's front door, the little pixie face waiting for him would light up with so much joy that Luke swore his daughter's energy could power three states.

Scout had come along when Luke least expected it, but she had been the greatest thing to ever happen in his life. He'd barely been dating Kim when she got pregnant, a relationship that had been more rocky than smooth. Long before Scout was born, they had agreed to go their separate ways. So he'd shared custody for the first three and a half years of Scout's life, with Kim taking the lion's share of the parenting because he'd buried himself in work.

When he'd seen those bottles piling up at Kim's house, he'd ignored them until he couldn't any longer. That intervention with Kim had been the wake-up call that told him he needed to get his act together and become a steady parent in Scout's life. There was no way in hell he was going to let his daughter live through the same hell he had as a kid.

Parenting, however, had not been the easy road he'd expected. Scout had acted out—a lot—after Kim went away, and Luke, who had never had so much as a potted plant, was left frustrated and at a loss for how to build a relationship with his daughter.

A few weeks ago, cousin Jimmy had asked him to fly out to Nevada and do an on-site evaluation of the resort's water systems. Luke had seen the Yogi Brown retreat on the resort's schedule and decided a few days away— with Scout staying with his uncle Ray in Harbor Cove— would help ease the stress of his job. As a temporary staff member, Luke could go to the yoga sessions without having to be part of the marriage retreat. Sounded like a good deal to him. And if he happened to soak up some information about how to deal with a four-year-old who was having a hell of a time adjusting to the shock in her life, so much the better.

As he'd passed by the lobby, he'd seen Emma, a woman he'd met a couple of times before and who had lingered in his mind both times. She'd looked lost and beautiful, and so he'd proposed posing as a couple. The next thing he knew, they were sporting wedding bands.

Almost six weeks had passed since that crazy night, and he'd been unable to forget her. The whole thing had been impetuous, and a mess he needed to clean up. But like most things in Luke's life so far, he was doing a damned fine job of ignoring the mess.

He glanced around the office, didn't see his manager, and fished out his cell phone. He pressed Kim's number and waited for the connection to be made. Three rings, four, five, and finally voicemail. "Call me, Kim. I haven't heard from you in a couple of days. Scout misses you."

His last conversation with her had been tough. Kim was emotional, missing Scout like mad and talking about checking out early and against medical advice. Luke had spent a solid hour talking her down and helping her see the big picture. She'd finally agreed to stay for as long as the rehab staff wanted her to because they both knew the best thing for Scout was stability, and this was her best—and maybe only—shot at having any of that.

The clock on his office desk ticked at a snail's pace toward five. Luke sighed and tried to focus on the mind-numbing spreadsheet in front of him. The Windsor knot around his neck threatened to choke him, no matter how many times he tugged at the buttoned collar of his shirt and the silk paisley fabric of the tie.

If Luke had his choice, he'd be working with his hands, outside, maybe high on a roof while the sun beat on his shoulders or down in a valley with the heft of stones and mortar in his hands. Not sitting in front of a computer calculating water densities for a softener company in Amherst.

His cell phone buzzed, and the familiar number of Brandon, his old boss, lit up the message app screen. *Hey, you interested in a job?*

Very, Luke texted back. *Where and what kind?*

As soon as he sent the text, he regretted it. He couldn't go back to that job, not now. Working with Brandon had been great and something he would have stayed at forever—until he became a full-time parent instead. Brandon was an up-and-coming developer who took existing and run-down neighborhoods and completed full, custom renovations that immediately raised the values and created hip communities near struggling downtowns. The company had been wildly successful, which had kept Luke traveling more often than he'd been home. Luke already had an apartment in New Hampshire that he'd barely seen for five years and a daughter who barely knew him. Going back to that kind of life was no way to be a good parent to Scout.

The buzzing fluorescent lights above his head chided him for checking his phone. He shouldn't even ask about a job that would undoubtedly involve a lot of travel. He had it made here, a nine-to-five with benefits, steady pay, and a Boring Quotient of ten million. Then the messages screen lit up again, and Luke's attention went straight back to the phone.

I know a guy who just got a subdivision contract out in Newburyport, up in Massachusetts, Brandon wrote. *Probably a yearlong gig, if you're up for it. Company housing is shitty, but if you can tough it out, might lead to a long-term thing. The owner of the company is looking for a guy to manage the project, and you're the first one I thought of. He said the job is yours if you want it.*

"You got that report for me yet?"

Luke jumped and pushed his cell phone to the side. His manager's voice, nasally and loud, grated on Luke's nerves. Stewart Whitley was a short man who wore a toupee that everyone thought looked like a runaway rabbit. He stood beside Luke's cubicle, fists on his hips, a look of irritated expectation on his face.

Ever since Luke had taken the job, he'd hated nearly every second he spent in this office. Actually, sometimes *hate* was too mild a word for how he felt about the tie, the lights, and Stewart.

"Yes, sir. Give me a minute." Luke scanned the numbers on Excel, checked the columns and rows, then hit the x button in the corner. A little question box came up, but Luke clicked on CANCEL before he realized what he'd done.

Forgotten—again—to save his work before closing the file. It wasn't that he didn't understand technology; it just wasn't second nature like laying a tile floor or installing a new sink. This job was so far from Luke's comfort zone that it might as well be another planet. "Uh, I accidentally deleted it."

His manager's face flushed crimson. "What is wrong with you? Are you a total idiot? Count on working all weekend to get that done, Carter."

"I can't. I have my . . ." He didn't want to mention Scout to this dictatorial guy wearing fake hair. "I can't."

"Either you finish that report this weekend," Stewart said, leaning so close to Luke's face that he could see one gray hair curling like a runaway from the other man's eyebrow, "or don't come back at all."

A few inches away on his cell phone, Brandon was waiting for an answer. Yes, moving to Massachusetts would mean uprooting Scout again, but Uncle Ray lived in Mass, a couple of towns away from Newburyport, which would make Luke's commute pretty short. A subdivision project meant staying in one place until it was done. A year was plenty of time to give Scout some roots.

The cookie-cutter sameness of subdivisions sure wasn't the challenging fun of a whole-house renovation, but it was steady work that beat sitting at a desk any day. Plus Newburyport was just over the border from New Hampshire, if Kim got sober and wanted to be part of Scout's life again. Either way, maybe a little family time would do everyone some good. And if it led to permanent work again in the field Luke loved, well, maybe this was a chance worth taking. Either way, it was better than one more second under these lights.

"Fine." Luke pushed off from the desk and got to his feet. "I won't come back at all."

"I knew it. I told Jimmy you'd screw up this opportunity, just like you've screwed up every other opportunity in your life. That's what Jimmy gets for hiring family. A whole lot of trouble from a whole-lot-of-nothing cousin."

Anger boiled in Luke's veins, but he kept it tightly leashed. He didn't owe this man an explanation about choosing to put his daughter and career satisfaction ahead of water hardness testing. "Do me a favor, Stewie, and mail my final paycheck."

"You're going to regret this, Carter!"

Luke was already striding out of the office, loosening his tie as he walked and then undoing the top button of his shirt. He was halfway to his car when a man in a short-sleeved mustard-yellow shirt hurried over to him. "Luke Carter?"

"If Stewart Whitley sent you after me..."

"I'm a process server, and these"—the man handed him an envelope—"are for you."

"What the heck?" But the other guy was already walking away. Luke tore open the envelope and tugged out the papers inside. Complaint for Annulment.

It took a second for the words to click in his brain. *Annulment.*

The end of his marriage to Emma, contained in a single sheet of paper and a court date. It made sense. After all, the whole marriage had been a spur-of-the-moment thing that neither one of them had thought through. There wasn't any reason to keep it going because there wasn't anything to build upon.

After Emma had rushed back home, he'd texted and called a few times, but she hadn't responded. He'd realized then how little he knew about Emma Monroe. Like what she ate for breakfast. Whether she liked roses or daisies. What she did for a living. Whether she had thought about him even once in the weeks since their hasty wedding.

For some reason, the word *annulment* felt like a failure to Luke. He'd failed so many things in life—left home at seventeen, dropped out of college, fathered a kid with an alcoholic, and now walked away from a job that anyone else would consider a good future—and today he could add *failed at marriage* to the list.

He flipped through the pages and found one from the family courts of the great state of Massachusetts, setting a hearing date for the annulment in a month's time. There was a note saying he didn't need to be present, that if the annulment was uncontested, he would be notified once the judge granted the end of their marriage.

He could walk away from this, just like he'd walked away from almost everything else in his life. Easy-peasy, over and done, just another memory in his rearview mirror. All he had to do was pretend it never happened.

Or, he thought as he pulled his phone out of his pocket, he could take the job Brandon had offered him, a job that would bring Luke very close to a second chance.

CHAPTER 3

Emma told herself to breathe. Two counts in, four counts out. Two counts in, four counts out. A little spur-of-the-moment, surreptitious mental meditation exercise while she sat in the worn leather chair in the overly decorated office of the Harbor Cove Hotel wedding planner.

Then maybe she wouldn't lose it with the bridezilla sitting across from her. Thirty-two days and counting until Emma quit her job and headed off for anywhere but here. And to work that offered a lot more fulfillment than this position.

When she first took the job at the hotel, she'd been the assistant to the main wedding planner. It was a hectic, stressful job that paid well, and Emma had decided she would take it—but hand in her resignation before she hit her one-year anniversary with the hotel. Then the head wedding planner left to work at another hotel, Emma earned an instant (and not necessarily wanted) promotion to sole wedding planner, and her one-year flight plan was in its second year of being delayed.

There was no way in hell Emma was going to spend her third year here dealing with panicked, demanding brides and their impossible expectations. Which was why the opportunity with the Atlas Children's Foundation sounded perfect. Okay, yeah, it was a start-up that still wasn't fully funded or fully organized, but when Emma had heard about the program from the father of one of her brides, she'd seen the potential in it. Karl Jensen, the creator of Atlas, had said that Emma had skills that could be valuable to the foundation. Coming on board as it was launching would allow her to be part of not just helping kids—a cause that grew more and more dear to Emma's heart as she got older and realized what a difference the people around her had made in her motherless childhood—but also creating something. Something that had way more meaning than a floral arrangement.

"Sharon, I assure you, our chef knows how to make chicken cordon bleu," Emma said, although she'd never tasted the dish. She'd been vegetarian for a year, a choice that made Grandma hover and worry about whether Emma was getting enough protein. "We serve it daily on our restaurant menu. Our chef is also well versed in the art of the salad. You won't—"

"Everything has to be perfect. Do you understand that?" Sharon's voice rose, and she leaned across Emma's desk. Her little white Pomeranian, a spoiled dog named Marshmallow, yipped in agreement. "This is my wedding, and I'm only going to get married once."

If you're lucky or, like me, a little unlucky, Emma thought. "I totally understand, and I can reassure you that the Harbor Cove Hotel is just as committed to perfection as you are."

Sharon's lips pinched. Doubt twitched in the vein on her forehead. "Let me see the linen choices again. I can't decide between the eggplant and the lilac. My bridesmaids are wearing aubergine and lavender, and Marshmallow, my little ringbearer baby, has a lavender harness. I don't think they'll match with the linens."

"Of course." Emma pasted a fake smile on her face and wondered how on earth other people did this job all day, or frankly any job in customer service. Diana worked the front desk and often voluntarily pitched in to help Emma with big weddings and never complained. Diana, however, was a hopeless romantic who read romance novels and was a sucker for any movie on Hallmark or Lifetime. Emma wasn't even sure she had those channels on her streaming service, never mind watching them.

She opened the heavy binder containing the fabric swatches and turned it to the exact same colors she had shown Sharon last week, last month, and last year. "If you compare the fabric of—"

"I know how to do that." Sharon yanked a square of material out of her voluminous Kate Spade bag. The purple leather purse was like a clown car—it could fit half the town of Harbor Cove inside, as evidenced by the leather-bound wedding planner, multicolored pens, fabric swatches, and multiple copies of *Bride* magazine she'd already unearthed.

A half hour of comparing and contrasting and hemming and hawing and Sharon had once again convinced herself that the colors were a match. She went over every single item on the list Emma put together, for the hundredth time since Emma had started planning the wedding with this overbearing bride, before finally deciding she'd had enough. "I'll be back next week. If I don't stay on top of this, someone is going to miss something, and my whole wedding will be ruined."

At her feet, Marshmallow started prancing around, yipping and jumping on Sharon, who shooed the dog away with a distracted hand. "I know, baby, but Mommy has to call the florist and make sure they know what kind of flowers Mommy likes."

Emma's smile hurt her cheeks. It had been almost two years of difficult brides and impossible requests, the monotony of that mitigated a bit when Emma had proposed the idea of the hotel offering children's events over school breaks. Larry had talked about expanding the hotel's footprint in the lucrative family vacation market, which had spurred a mini kids program for vacationing parents. That had been a hit, and Emma had volunteered to expand that by creating any other kids' events the hotel hosted. Over the last year, that had morphed from a once-in-a-while offering to a monthly kids' club for Harbor Cove and neighboring towns. They'd done a summer camp last year, a holiday craft party, and a Mother's Day gardening project, all of which had helped elevate the Harbor Cove Hotel's profile, thanks to Jake, her sister's fiancé and a local photographer, and the *Gazette*.

Larry was thrilled with the increase in business, but Emma had found something unexpected in working with the kids—kindred spirits. There were so many children in the middle of upheavals like divorce, death, or moving, just like Emma herself when she was five. She understood these children and their struggles to figure out life, and maybe that was why she enjoyed those events so much.

It was one of those events that had led to her conversation with Karl about the Atlas Children's Foundation. Karl had made his money in tech and told Emma he had been looking for a way to give back. He'd grown up in foster care, which had made children's causes important to him. Emma had leaped at the opportunity to be part of Karl's first volunteer group and donated her savings to the cause without a second thought. All she was waiting on was the details from Karl on where and when her first assignment would be. Sometime in the summer, he'd said, and Emma had started marking her calendar for a July 1 departure from Harbor Cove.

Finally leaving behind all these nightmare brides. "If that's all, Sharon...?"

"Actually, could you take Marshmallow?" Sharon gave Emma an apologetic-yet-not smile. "I have to take this call with the florist, and Marshmallow is supposed to be at the groomer's right now. It's just next door. Surely you could go the extra mile for a customer and just"—she held out the leash and shook it—"trot on over there for me? Thanks. You're a sweetie." Then she swiveled away and barked a hello into her phone.

Emma took the leash and Marshmallow, who was dancing back and forth, clearly in need of either a pee break or a quick escape. If taking the dog to the groomer meant getting away from Sharon five minutes earlier, then Emma would definitely do that. Sharon gave her a distracted wave as she walked away, yelling at the florist about the scent of her calla lilies.

"Mommy's a bit grumpy today, huh, Marshmallow?" Emma whispered to the dog. "Come on, let's go outside."

Marshmallow yipped and jumped, prancing alongside Emma with steps so excited that Emma was sure the dog was going to relieve herself on the hotel's carpet. But they made it outside, much to Marshmallow's relief, who promptly squatted on the first square of grass she saw.

Emma texted Diana that she was going next door and then answered a text from her father asking her if she was getting excited about working with Atlas. Emma smiled. For all his faults, her father was also Emma's biggest cheerleader, and right now Emma needed a little of that. *Can't wait*, she texted back. *It's going to be a challenge, though.*

If anyone can tackle a challenge, it's you, Emma, Dad wrote back. *Let's make a plan to grab lunch this week.*

She replied with a heart emoji before tucking her phone away. Although Davis Monroe hadn't been there when the girls were little, he had come around when Emma was a teenager, eager to build a relationship with his girls again. Gabby and Margaret were still a little distant from Dad, but he and Emma had grown close. Maybe because they had a shared appreciation for travel and adventure, and a little feeling of being the outsiders in the family.

Done with what she had to do, Marshmallow popped up and started bounding like a deer on speed the whole way down the sidewalk, tugging the leash surprisingly strongly for such a small dog. Emma stopped walking and gave Marshmallow a stern look. "Listen, I can't walk you if you're bouncing off the walls."

Marshmallow just blinked and wagged her tail, tongue lolling.

"You have no idea what I'm saying, do you?" Emma sighed. "Okay, let's try this again. Marshmallow, heel."

Marshmallow sat down.

"No, heel." Emma gave the leash a little tug, and Marshmallow bounded up to her. "Or something resembling heel. Close enough." She laughed and gave the dog an ear rub. Marshmallow pressed her little body tight to Emma's leg, clearly in heaven with the attention.

The bright-blue-and-white awning over the Dogs 'n Suds Grooming Parlor was crisp and new, installed just last month when Cassie Wallace opened her little shop. The bell over the door tinkled as Emma walked inside with Marshmallow. "Cassie? I have Sharon's dog here for her appointment."

Cassie poked her head around the corner. "Just one sec."

Marshmallow plopped down beside Emma's foot, and the two of them waited together. "I love the new place."

Cassie stepped over the baby gate separating the back part of the shop, with the tubs and clipping stations, from the front part. Emma had known Cassie in high school, and it was nice to see one of her friends running a successful business in Harbor Cove. "Thanks. It's been super busy, too." She peered around Emma. "Is Sharon coming?"

"No. She had to go scream at the florist or something."

"Thank God. She'll talk my ear off for an hour about which clippers to use on Marshmallow." Cassie bent down. "Hey, fluffball. Nice to see you again." Cassie glanced up at Emma. "I don't think I've ever seen this dog so calm."

"We had a little conversation on the way over here about manners. Right, Marshmallow?" Emma gave the dog another pat. Cassie was right. The dog was calmer, and when she was calm, Marshmallow was almost lovable. "Anyway, I have to go back to work." She handed the leash to Cassie. "We should grab a glass of wine sometime and catch up."

"I'd love that. See you, Emma!"

Once she was back at the hotel sans-Marshmallow and without Sharon hovering over her, Emma shut the door to the office and dropped into her chair. She pulled up the calendar on her PC and counted the days again. Yup, still thirty-two days until her last day working here. Then she'd sling a backpack over her shoulder and take off. The whole idea made her grandmother panicky, so Emma had learned to stop talking about her still relatively un-planned and open-ended adventure. The foundation's first venture was in the planning stages, and Karl kept saying he'd have something firm to tell her soon. Didn't matter. Emma was game for about anything—except winding up married again.

Either way, *that* little mistake would be undone soon enough, and she could put Luke Carter in her box of Bad Decisions that she kept shoved inside an overstuffed mental closet.

Her cell rang, and her eldest sister Margaret's face lit up the screen. Emma could count on one hand the number of times Meggy had initiated contact—much less a phone call—in the course of the last year. All the other Monroe girls, Grandma included, had made numerous overtures to the oldest Monroe daughter, but she'd dodged nearly every get-together. "Margaret? What's wrong?"

"Can't I just call to see how you are without you thinking I'm in the hospital or something? Geez. I just wanted to ask if you wanted to grab some lunch at the diner," Margaret said.

Emma pulled the phone away from her ear. Yup, that was Margaret's name on the screen. Their usually solitary and always workaholic oldest sister was asking Emma to take time off in the middle of the day and join her for lunch? Maybe the time the three of them had spent together when Gabby was struggling with her business had made Meggy miss the old days when it was the three Monroe Musketeers against the world. Or maybe Margaret was just hungry and bored. Either way, it was a break Emma desperately needed. "Uh...sure. See you in twenty?"

"Perfect." Margaret hung up, and Emma went back to making a plan for her escape from Harbor Cove.

She surfed over to the Atlas Children's Foundation Facebook page. No updates for the last week. Not unusual—Karl was building a volunteer organization from scratch, after all, and was undoubtedly busy. The website still had the UNDER CONSTRUCTION notice across the homepage. *Hey, Karl,* she texted. *Any news on our start date and location?*

It wasn't that she didn't love this town—she always had and probably always would—it was the expectations of everyone in her family and nearly everyone in town that made her want to run for the hills. From the time she was born, Emma had been expected to be a young lady. To sit quietly at the table and not climb trees or catch frogs or get mud in her hair. Grandma had called her a wild child, which she supposed fit, given how different Emma was from her two older sisters.

She'd always been the one looking for answers, a way to quell the yawning need to be something else. Yoga and meditation had helped some but weren't a lifelong purpose. That hunger had led her to go on adventures, take chances, live with abandon. She could die young, just like Momma, and she sure as hell didn't want to do that sitting at a desk debating aubergine versus eggplant.

Emma found Margaret at a table in the back, far removed from the other diners. Her sister had the look of a lawyer in every outfit she chose—tailored pantsuit, sensible heels, and her hair newly cut in a bob that never seemed to be out of place. For ten years, Margaret and her husband had owned the jewelry shop downtown, but the truth was that Margaret did the majority of the work there while her husband kept his accounting practice running. For a long time, the dual-entrepreneur partnership had seemed to work, but in the last few months it seemed as if the two of them were anywhere but together.

"So...what's the special today?" Emma asked as she slid into the booth.

"I have no idea. I didn't look." Margaret sipped at a cup of black coffee. "I'll probably just get the wedge salad."

"Same thing you get every time. You should change it up, Meggy."

"I like things the way I like them." Margaret set her coffee cup back on the table and wrapped her hands around it. She paused for a beat. "So...I wanted to ask you something that might sound weird."

Emma arched a brow. "You're never weird. You're the most predictable person I know."

Margaret scoffed. "Yeah, I know. And you're completely the opposite."

"I wonder if Earl has that vegan banana cream pie today." Emma ignored her sister's dig and craned her neck around the table, trying to see the pie case at the front of the diner.

Just then the door of the diner opened and a young mother and her daughter entered. The little redheaded girl spied Emma and ran down the aisle. Emma put out her arms and caught her in a hug. "Hey there, Macy!"

"Miss Emma!" Macy McArthur hugged Emma tight. "I missed you! When are you doing book club again?"

"Soon, I promise." She gave the little girl's pigtail a tug. Twelve months ago, Macy's hair had been sparse and patchy because the troubled little girl had pulled one strand at a time whenever she was upset. At the first book club meeting, Macy had hidden the bald patches under a cap and sat in a corner, barely speaking to anyone. Then Emma had asked Macy to pick her favorite book, and as the pages turned, the little girl began to open up more and more. She stayed after every week, talking to Emma about books and, later, about her life. Her mother had gotten Macy into therapy, which had gradually brought the little girl back to her normal self. "I see your hair is all nice and long again."

Macy nodded. "Mommy said I get pretty hair things because I've been so good lately."

A harried, breathless Betty McArthur came hurrying up to Emma. "I'm so sorry if she's disturbing your lunch."

"Not at all. I love seeing my favorite reader." She tapped Macy on the nose. It was so gratifying to see the change in Macy, who'd always been one of Emma's favorite kids. And if book club was a small part of that, Emma was doubly grateful. "A little bird told me you have completed the entire library challenge already."

"Uh-huh. And I got a T-shirt and a poster." Macy patted the image of a pile of children's books splayed across the front of her bright-blue HARBOR COVE LIBRARY CHALLENGE T-shirt.

"She's so proud of that. I swear she wears it every day." Betty ruffled her daughter's hair. "Why don't you go grab us a seat at the counter, Macy? I'll be right there."

"Okay! Bye, Miss Emma!" One more hug, and then Macy crossed to the dinette stools a few feet away and climbed onto one near the end.

Betty glanced over her shoulder and then lowered her voice. "I just want to thank you again, Emma. Macy was in such a bad place last summer, and the time you spent with her at the kids' book club made such a difference. It's been so hard since Reggie died, and I…"

"I completely understand." Emma covered Betty's hand with her own before the other woman started crying. "Macy is a wonderful girl. I'm glad she's doing well."

"Keep on doing what you're doing," Betty said. "It makes a difference." Then she joined her daughter.

"What was that about?" Margaret asked.

Emma shrugged. "Nothing really. Just a little girl who was in one of the hotel's children's programs last year. Her dad had just died, and she was struggling at home."

"Seems like you helped her out a lot."

"I just did my job."

"Well, good job," Margaret said.

Emma gaped. "Did you just pay me a compliment?"

"Oh good Lord. If you're going to make a big deal out of it, forget I said anything." Margaret flexed her menu and pretended to study it. "It's like that thing Momma was working on."

"What thing Momma was working on?"

Margaret looked at Emma over the big plastic menu. "You don't remember?"

Emma arched a brow. "I was five when she died. I don't even remember what my favorite color was back then."

"I don't remember much about it, to be honest. Grandma might know more. Momma had her teaching degree but never got to be a teacher because she had us and then…" Margaret's gaze went out the window for a moment. "Anyway, she was working on some kind of community program for kids. I don't think it ever got launched. She was the leader or something and I guess, without her, people lost their enthusiasm. Or maybe I'm wrong and it was something else."

"That sounds like something she would do." In all the photos of her mother with the girls, Momma always looked like she was having the time of her life. Gabby and Meggy talked about art projects and nature walks they remembered doing with Momma. Maybe a part of her mother had been passed on in Emma's DNA, and maybe that was a sign that she was meant to do the work with the Atlas Foundation.

Margaret dropped her gaze to the menu again and then said quietly, "What made you do it?"

"Do what? My job at the hotel?"

Margaret shook her head. "Marry a stranger."

"Pretty sure Captain Morgan and his friend Jim Beam talked me into it." Emma shook her head. There'd been so much more that had gone into that spontaneous decision than a couple of glasses of spiked punch. In that instant, with dozens of people professing their love, Emma had felt oddly more alone than at any other time in a life where solitude had been a treasured gift. She'd been seized with this weird craving for what those other people seemed to have, and so she'd leaped without looking. "It was a wild night."

An understatement, to be sure, even if her family had taken it all in stride. When she'd arrived back in Harbor Cove, clever Gabby had quizzed Emma about her "married" slip of the tongue on the phone. When she explained the rash decision to her family, they'd chalked it up as an "Emma Move." Just another impulsive escapade for the youngest Monroe. Something about that term grated on her nerves. Almost as if the whole family expected her to do something stupid. Just because she'd done a lot of rash things didn't mean she couldn't make smart choices, too. At least some of the time.

"Yeah, but something made you agree to that when you were at the retreat," Margaret said. "I've never done a single thing in my life that I didn't overplan and overthink. I just...I guess I want to know how you do something that big without thinking it over."

"I got bored doing all those Sun Salutations." But the joke fell flat, and Emma sobered. "Honestly, Meggy, I don't know. I just did it."

She thought of that moment of envy she'd felt in the ballroom at the retreat. A flash of craving that had disappeared almost as quickly as it appeared. It was just that, she told herself, a flash. Didn't mean Emma wanted the stereotypical two-point-five-kids fenced-in future.

"Did you like him?" Margaret asked.

"I didn't know him. Not really." Emma glanced out the window. The world of Harbor Cove moved along, tourists filling the streets more and more each day as spring warmed toward summer. People traveling, exploring, untethering. Emma longed to be one of them, if only for a little while. "I did like Luke a lot when I met him."

"But marry-like? I mean, that's a huge decision to make with someone you only met, what, twice before?"

"I didn't consider emotions in the equation." At least not her own emotions when it came to Luke Carter, who had merely been a placeholder during a moment of weakness. That was all. Emma had gotten a little envious of the couplehood all around her, and Luke had been handy and offering to pair up with her.

Margaret stared at her like she had mutant DNA.

Emma's face heated under her sister's scrutiny. "You know me," Emma said with a little laugh. "I never think anything through. We all know I don't really want to get married. This was just a lark, and I didn't even know it was legally binding until later."

"Except you *did* get married. Why do something you say you don't want?"

Geez. Where was the waitress when Emma needed a good interruption? "Yeah, I noticed that when I saw the marriage certificate, but it doesn't matter now. Cousin George got the annulment papers sent out. In just about thirty days, I'll be a free woman again, and the whole thing will be erased. Why are you so interested?"

"I just..." She drummed her fingers on the table. The pillow-cut diamond on her left hand glittered under the lights. "I'm not spontaneous like you, and I guess I want to figure out how to be more impulsive, not so..."

"Buttoned up like a winter coat?" Emma covered one of Margaret's hands with her own. "I'm just kidding. I'm the one with no career and no direction, remember? Grandma is always telling me I need to settle down and grow some roots or whatever. You have an established business, a mortgage, and a husband. Like a grown-up."

"Being a grown-up isn't all it's cracked up to be."

Emma studied her oldest sister. There were shadows under her eyes and a heaviness in her tone. "You and Mike still struggling?"

Margaret drew in a deep breath. "Yeah. Tax season didn't help because he was gone so much, and it seemed like we argued more than we said hello. Anyway, we're talking about maybe going on this couples getaway thing in the Poconos in the fall. Sort of a Hail Mary pass."

Margaret was taking time off and admitting she needed

help? Things definitely had to be rocky between them. "It's that bad?"

She glanced out the window, avoiding Emma's inquisitive gaze. "It's been better."

"I'm sorry." Emma had no words of wisdom, nothing that she could offer besides a lame apology. This was definitely not Emma's area of knowledge. Hell, she'd barely had relationships, so she couldn't tell anyone else how to have one.

"It's okay." Margaret straightened her shoulders and smoothed the front of her jacket. "And if it's not okay, it will be eventually."

"Are you sure?" Emma asked. "Because I think maybe you guys should go get a counselor or something. I mean, a couples' retreat sounds good, but that's sometime off in the future. Maybe you need something, like, now." She fiddled with the plastic edge of the cranberry vinyl menu. She didn't want to say aloud what she was thinking: *if Margaret and Mike don't do something about this now, there might not be a couple to go on that retreat in the fall.* "Have you tried just spending some time together? You both work so much, and surely don't see each other a lot."

Margaret unfolded her menu and studied the list of sandwiches. "You seem to be doing really well at work. The last two events at the hotel were big hits with the town. An Easter egg hunt paired with a history hide-and-seek? Brilliant."

The change of subject didn't fool Emma, but she went with it because she wasn't the one who would push Margaret into a confessional booth, not when Emma didn't want her own life under a microscope. "Thanks. That one was my idea."

"You're so smart," Margaret said. "I think you should do this event planning thing for a career."

Emma was already shaking her head before Margaret finished the sentence. "I'm not staying at this job. I'm taking off and traveling the world in July. I told you I'm going to work with that foundation, helping to build their children's program. It's all new and unknown and exciting. Who knows where I'll be in a few months?"

"Of course you're doing something like that. I bet you barely know anything about this supposed foundation." Margaret scoffed. "Why not stick with something and actually build a career? Save something for retirement? Maybe finish school, get a degree, and for Pete's sake, settle down. You're twenty-eight. Practically thirty already."

"Who says I have to settle down? Last I checked there weren't any grown-up police checking to make sure I did what everyone else is in such a rush to do."

"I'm just saying..." Margaret fiddled with the edge of the menu. "Maybe it would be better to stay here, spend a couple more years at your job—"

"A couple more years? I'm having trouble lasting a couple more *days*." Emma shook her head. "That's a definite no."

Margaret rested her arms on the table and leaned forward. "Emma, you've never stuck with anything in your life. Not a job, not an apartment, and certainly not a guy. This marriage thing was over before it even started. For Pete's sake, you can't even keep a goldfish alive."

"That fish was like a hundred years old when I won him at the fair. And I was seven, Margaret, not exactly a responsible adult."

Margaret scoffed again. "And you're one now? You've never even had a long-term relationship, Em."

And there was the critical, bossy Margaret she knew and loved. The one who had tried to tell them all what to do—and how they were failing some invisible Monroe standard—for most of their lives. And just as she always did, Emma reacted on the defense instead of offense. "I have too. I dated Robbie McLaughlin for…well, three months."

"That was in eighth grade." Margaret shook her head. "That's not long-term. Hell, for two months of that he was in Indiana working on his uncle's farm for the summer."

"It was Ohio." The detail didn't matter, but it was the only point Emma could defend. Okay, so maybe she didn't date long-term. That didn't mean there was something wrong with her or that she should upend her future plans just to find a guy she could tolerate for more than a few weeks. "And why are you suddenly so interested in what I'm doing with my life? Last I checked, yours was kind of a hot mess, too."

The waitress passed by the table with a load of plates in her arms. "Great to see you two in here. Crazy-busy this afternoon. I'll be back in a sec with some waters and to get your orders."

"No problem," Margaret said before lowering her voice and focusing her verbal offensive tackle on Emma. "I'm just worried you're going to have to be rescued. Again."

"That was one time, Meggy." Every time Margaret disagreed with what Emma was doing, she trotted out every mistake her little sister had made. Okay, yes, there were some moments that were better off forgotten or buried in a closet, but Emma wasn't that impulsive teenager anymore. Mostly.

"You skipped the entire first month of freshman year

to go hike the Appalachian Trail with some friends, and when you came back, you and your buddies raided the chow hall and had an ice cream party on the school lawn," Margaret said.

"I didn't steal the ice cream." At the time, it had seemed like a good idea, though Emma couldn't remember why now. She'd gone along with them, swept up in the adventure and excitement of it all, a party to celebrate their successful hike. An insomniac dean had caught them and called for all of them to be kicked out of UMass Amherst. "But I might have eaten...a lot of it."

"You're lucky that I saw the letter from the school before Grandma or Dad did. *I'm* the one who drove up there and talked the dean out of banning you from that school for life. *I'm* the one who told Grandma you just needed a gap year to get your act together." Margaret tapped her chest like it was some kind of badge of honor. "It's been like nine years, Emma. That's not a gap. That's the Grand Canyon."

"I'm not that person anymore, Margaret."

"Really? Because five seconds ago, you were talking about quitting your job, and you just married a total stranger."

Well, put like that, it all sounded like a bunch of reckless decisions. It wasn't like Emma was leaping out of airplanes or robbing banks. She was just living sort of impulsively. "One, I still have a job, and two, I knew Luke...some."

"Semantics, Emma." Margaret let out a sigh chock-full of disappointment and frustration. "I can't be your mother anymore."

"I never asked you to be. You just elected yourself to the position." Emma bit her lower lip and took a minute to breathe before she lashed out at her older sister. Margaret had, indeed, rescued Emma from her poor choices more than once when she was young, but that had all been a long time ago, and things were different(ish) now. "I appreciate what you did my freshman year. Yes, it was a stupid thing to do, and you're probably right that I wasn't ready for college. But like you said, it's been nine years, Meggy. A lot can change in that period of time."

"Has anything changed, Emma? Are you different now?"

Another deep breath, a second, and then a third, for good measure. "More than you know," Emma said finally, thinking of all the moves she had made over the last two years to get herself closer to where she was meant to be. Not every move had been the right one, but Emma preferred to think of those wrong choices as detours on a road trip. Sometimes the best memories were found on the side roads and U-turns. "Can we call a truce and get some lunch? I'm starving." Emma glanced around the diner, saw the waitress, and waved her over.

"Fine." Margaret picked up the menu and studied it again. The distance allowed the tension between them to ease until Emma felt like she could breathe again.

There was just something about Margaret's judgment and well-meaning advice that made Emma feel claustrophobic. Like she was being suffocated into conforming with the world's version of the perfect life.

The waitress brought over two glasses of water, one plain for Margaret and one sparkling with a lemon and a lime wedge for Emma. As she squeezed the fruit slices over the water, Emma glanced out the window. And promptly dropped both slices into her glass with a loud plop and a splash.

She blinked twice, sure she was seeing things. It was as if merely thinking about her impetuous marriage had summoned Luke Carter from wherever he lived. Yet there he was, all dark-haired, muscular six feet of him, standing on the sidewalk across from the diner. "What the hell is he doing here?"

CHAPTER 4

W hen Luke received the annulment paperwork from Emma's lawyer, her address had been right there on the forms, and he'd known that the decision to move to Massachusetts would undoubtedly mean seeing more of his wife. Maybe that was a bad idea, but to Luke, the whole thing felt...unfinished. So maybe this move was a little bit of serendipity. While he was here in Harbor Cove staying with Uncle Ray, maybe Luke could get some sort of closure. And answers to burning questions like, *Why marry me and then never talk to me again?*

But as he saw his wife emerge from a diner and cross the street in his direction, he realized that maybe she wasn't so interested in closing up anything.

"What are you doing in Harbor Cove?" She had a fist on her hip and annoyance written all over her frown. Even with that, she was beautiful as hell.

"I got a job managing a new development in Newburyport, just a few miles from here." He wasn't going to get into the specifics, or how complicated his life was right now, or how he doubted every second of the day whether he had made the right choice. Not while he was standing in the middle of downtown with two elderly women sitting on a bench gaping at them.

"Since when?"

A couple passed by, chatting about the weather and the chances of getting the lawn mowed before it rained later. Harbor Cove moved at a sleepy pace with just a handful of cars on the streets and no one rushing to get to anywhere in particular. Maybe here Scout could feel like a kid again. Maybe.

"Is this just some big practical joke and some guy with a camera is going to jump out from behind a telephone pole?" Emma continued. "Because this isn't funny, Luke."

He couldn't resist the opportunity to poke the bear. Just a little. Just enough to see those blue eyes flash the way they had the first time he met her. "My dear wife," he said, lowering his voice and closing the distance between them, "I'm so touched by your interest in my career."

Her cheeks pinked. "I don't have any interest in what you do, Luke Carter. And we are no longer husband and wife."

"For thirty more days we are, Mrs. Carter." Oh, she was good and annoyed now. He had no doubt she would have stabbed him with a fork if any such implement was available. Then he saw movement behind the counter of the hardware store, reminding him of his number one responsibility. One that had nothing to do with his spontaneous wedding. "I have to go."

She bit her lower lip, something he'd noticed she did when she was thinking or nervous. She'd done it a few times in class when the instructor gave them a particularly difficult pose to try. He found it endearing and sweet, but everything about her right now was as prickly as a porcupine. "Listen, if this is some crazy attempt to make our marriage work—"

"Would that be so bad, Emma? Because I seem to remember us getting along really well."

"Of course it would be a terrible idea. My life is a mess right now."

So is mine, sweetheart. You have no idea how big a mess it is or the havoc a three-foot tornado can wreak. The door to the store opened, and a familiar blond head skipped onto the sidewalk, followed by the shuffling steps of Luke's uncle. The only time Luke saw Uncle Ray smile was when Scout was around, but still, too much depression lingered on the war vet's shoulders, and Luke worried about how he could make that better. "Anyway, despite how it might look, I'm not here for you, Emma."

Before he could say anything more, he saw Scout break away from her uncle and charge down the sidewalk. "Daddy!" She plowed into Luke's legs and clutched the seam of his jeans to steady herself. "Uncle Ray got me a birdhouse but he says we gots to put it together. I want to have baby birds 'cuz I can feed them and pet them."

"That's great. But we might have to wait until tomorrow to put it together because I have a lot to do today." He hoped like hell they stayed here long enough for his daughter to see some baby birds born, because the last thing Scout needed was one more change in her roller-coaster life.

"But I wanna do it now." Scout broke away from him, crossed her arms over her chest, and shot him a glare he'd come to know very, very well.

"We'll do it, Scout. Later."

She stamped her foot. "No, Daddy. Now!"

Luke's uncle stepped up to them and caught his breath. He was only fifty-four but moved like an eighty-year-old. His injuries from a bomb blast during the war had been extensive, and he'd spent the ensuing years as a veritable hermit. Keeping up with a preschooler wasn't something he had done in a long, long time. "Sorry. She's as fast as a roadrunner."

"It's okay, Uncle Ray." Luke shouldn't have left him with the rambunctious, four-year-old Houdini anyway. In the months since his daughter had come to live with him, Scout had managed to dart off five times because she didn't like his answer or she wanted to chase a butterfly, or she just plain didn't want to be there. Luke swore his blood pressure was never going to recover. "Uh, Uncle Ray, this is Emma, my..."

"Friend," she supplied, thrusting her hand in Uncle Ray's direction. "Nice to meet you. Luke said he had family who lived here. I think I've seen you around town before."

"Maybe. I'm more of a recluse than a socializer. It's nice to meet you, Emma." In Uncle Ray's rare smile, Luke could see that he was utterly enchanted with Emma.

Well, who wouldn't be? Her long dark hair ran in a waterfall down her back, swinging with her every movement. She had on a spring-blue dress with dozens of tiny buttons running down the front, making him wonder if he would have to unbutton all of them to—

"Daddy!" Scout stomped her foot again, and the glare deepened. "I want my birdhouse now. The birds need to sleep. And you promised."

"I can help you," Uncle Ray put in, but Scout was already shaking her head.

"I want Daddy to help. Daddy promised."

"I did, and I promised later," Luke said, "which means—"

"No later!" Scout let out a scream that could have been heard in Wisconsin. "Now, Daddy! Now!"

Then she went into a full-on, writhing-on-the-ground, *Exorcist*-worthy tantrum. It was the third tantrum of the day, and it was only eleven thirty in the morning. God help him.

Luke looked to his uncle for some kind of miraculous answer to the outburst, but Uncle Ray just gave Luke an I-don't-know-what-to-do shrug. Uncle Ray had never had children. He'd been a lieutenant in the army, but leading well-trained soldiers was a whole other ball of wax compared with Scout. Luke had no real parental role model to call upon, no grandparent to reach out to for advice. His own parents had been a codependent, toxic combination. Luke stood there, helpless, debating whether to bribe his daughter with ice cream—again—and start a lifelong process of rewarding temper tantrums with dessert. Some psychologist would have a lot to say about that, he was sure.

Then Emma bent down beside Scout, the skirt of her maxi dress spreading in a puddle of sky blue around her feet. "Hey, kiddo," Emma said, as calm as an ocean on a windless day. "I have something that can help with your birdhouse and make it irresistible to every single bird."

A handful of words and a miracle happened—Scout stopped screaming. Silence descended over their little corner of the sidewalk for one blissful second. Scout sniffled and swiped at her nose. "But I don't have a bird-house yet."

"That's right. Because you don't have the magic piece that tells the birds this is where they want to live."

Magic piece? Luke glanced at Uncle Ray, who gave him another shrug. Whatever Emma was talking about, it was charming the Tantrum Beast better than this morning's vanilla ice cream with sprinkles.

Scout pushed herself off the ground and sat up. She brushed her sweaty, tangled hair off her face. Her cheeks were red and puffy, but her eyes were bright and riveted on Emma. "Magic piece?"

Emma nodded. "When I was a little girl, my momma gave me something to put on my birdhouse, and you know what?"

"What?"

"There were baby birds there *all* spring. I got to hear them chirp every day. And once"—Emma lowered her voice and glanced around as if she were about to share a state secret—"I climbed the tree and looked inside and saw all these tiny, hungry little mouths."

"You did? I wanna see tiny baby birds."

"Well, first, the momma and daddy bird have to find your birdhouse. And when you hang this"—Emma dug in the pocket of her maxi skirt and pulled out a long white-and-gray feather—"on the front of the birdhouse, all the birds know that this is a good place for them to live."

Scout pinched the shaft of the feather carefully between two fingers. She wobbled to her feet and then held the feather out to Luke. "Daddy, can we put the magic feather on my birdhouse?"

Hell, Luke would hogtie an entire ostrich to the front of the birdhouse if it got Scout to stop screaming like a banshee. "We certainly can, Bean."

"And Scout, while your daddy is busy today, you can

go find sticks and yarn and more feathers," Emma said. She was still at Scout's level and had the preschooler's undivided attention again. "Because the birds are going to need those to build their beds. Find as many as you can and put them in a pile near the birdhouse so the birds can just pick them up and start moving in."

"I'mma gonna do that when I get home. Can we hurry home, Daddy? I gots to find lots of sticks."

"Uh, sure. We absolutely can."

"I'll get her buckled in," Uncle Ray said. "Come on, Scout. Let's go get in the car and let your dad talk to the very nice lady."

Scout slipped her hand into Uncle Ray's and skipped off to the car. Luke watched her go, convinced his child had been replaced by someone else's. "What are you, a kid whisperer?" he said to Emma.

She laughed, getting to her feet and brushing the dust off her skirt. "No. I just run some programs for kids at the hotel and learned how to deal with them so I'm not doing crowd control all day."

"Well, I think you're the one with the magic touch because I can't get her to be that excited about anything. I've never seen her so...calm."

"You just have to pay attention to what she needs to hear or see or feel in that moment. Because when the other person feels heard, they stop feeling hurt." Emma gave him a smile. "Anyway, I should let you go. I'm sorry for misinterpreting why you were here. I...well, I'm glad you don't want to make this spur-of-the-moment marriage into something real."

Probably not the best time to mention that he'd been thinking about her and closure and second chances a few days ago. It was clear she wasn't interested in that

anyway. Even if a part of him was still very interested in
her. "Maybe not the marriage, but what do you say to a
job as a kid wrangler?" he said, only half joking.

"I have a job, Luke." She met his gaze, but she must
have seen the desperation in Luke's face because her
stance softened. "But...there is a kids' workshop this
weekend at the hotel, if you want to bring Scout. It's
two weeks before Father's Day and a way for the kids to
make something for their dads. She'd probably have a lot
of fun, plus make some friends."

"And you'll be there?" Even he could hear the notes
of hope and anticipation in his voice. It had been over a
month since she'd run out of that hotel room and a million
times since his mind had circled back to that wild night.
"I mean, working it? Because, well, Scout gets along with
you, and I...I'm just flabbergasted at how quickly she
went back to being a normal kid."

She smiled, and when Emma Monroe smiled, it was as
if the sun had been turned up a notch. "Yes, I'll be there."
She fished in her pocket and pulled out a business card.
"Email me, and I'll send you the details."

He took the card and thanked her. She turned to go and
had made it all the way to the diner door before he called
out to her. "Emma?"

Emma pivoted back. "Yeah?"

"How did you know about or even have that feather?
Seems like a weird thing to carry around."

"When I saw Scout start to melt down, I thought of
the movie *Dumbo* and how he needed something else to
focus on rather than his fear, so I grabbed a feather off the
ground. The rest..." She shrugged. "I just kind of made
up on the fly."

He cocked his head and studied her. He'd married this

woman, barely knowing anything about her, and now he was more intrigued than he had been when he had said *I do*. "Are you always this surprising, Emma Monroe?"

She let out a little laugh. "I'm not what anybody expects, Luke. Least of all me."

"No, you're not." He shifted his weight, nervous like he used to be in middle school when he had first realized girls existed. There was something...ethereal about Emma that seemed impossible for any man to capture. Didn't mean Luke wasn't going to try. "Before you go, I have one more thing to ask you."

"Sure. What is it?"

He crossed to where she was standing on the step that led to the diner's entrance. The seven inches of concrete brought her eye-to-eye with him. He inhaled the light scent of her perfume, watched the way her pulse ticked in the curve of her neck, and wished all over again that their wedding night had lasted longer than a few hours. He'd wanted Emma Monroe since the first time he saw her doing Warrior Pose, her face a mask of concentration, her muscles tensed, and her stance so confident and strong. "You still owe me something from Nevada."

"Were we charged for that room? I thought it was part of the marriage package thing. I can Venmo you some money."

"That's not what you owe me, Mrs. Carter." Then he leaned forward and cupped her face in his hands. Her eyes widened, and her lips parted, but she didn't move. Her skin was soft, her perfume a light floral, and everything inside him leaned closer, wanting, needing, dying of curiosity. "I'd like to kiss my bride. The first time was kind of a rush, and we were both a little drunk."

"Luke, this is getting annulled. We aren't going to be

married much longer." Her gaze met his and held. A beat passed between them, unfurling something warm and tempting. "It's almost over."

"All the more reason for this." Then he bent down and kissed her. From the second he'd met Emma, he'd seen a fire and passion inside her that he envied and craved. Kissing her was like stoking that fire with a blowtorch. She was soft in his arms, warm beneath his mouth. She was still for a second before a soft gasp escaped her. She stepped closer to him, clutching at his back, kissing him with the same hunger. Then, just as quickly, she jerked away and stumbled back a step or two. "That...shouldn't have happened."

"But it did." And Luke for one was damned glad it had. "The question is, what do you want to do about it?"

"I'm already doing it, Luke. See you around town." She turned and, a second later, disappeared back inside the diner.

❦❦❦

Eleanor Whitmore brewed a cup of English breakfast tea, took a single gingersnap from the plastic container on the counter, and was just sitting down at the kitchen table when the front door opened. Some people locked their doors, preferring to keep their peace and quiet to themselves, but Eleanor missed the days when her three granddaughters were in and out, the wooden screen door slamming in their wake, her house filled with laughter and arguments and love. Her three-story Victorian was altogether too quiet these days, so she left the door unlocked until she went to bed, hoping for the patter of feet and the clap of the door.

"Grandma? You home?" Emma's lilting voice carried

through the rooms. Emma was impetuous and smart, fierce but loving. She had been the wildest of the three, almost impossible to tame, and had tested Eleanor's patience more times than a saint could count. But she was also the most like her mother in spirit, and for that Eleanor absolutely adored her.

"In the kitchen!" she called out.

A second later, Emma poked her head around the corner. "And if you're in the kitchen, I assume that means you made cookies?"

Eleanor laughed. "Of course I did. Vegan ginger cookies, for my youngest granddaughter."

"You are too good to me." She grinned as she popped off the lid and pulled out two cookies.

Her granddaughter was as petite as a sugar snap pea, shorter than her sisters but a willowy girl with long dark hair that nearly hit her waist. True to her inimitable spirit, she had on a coral maxi skirt with gold threads woven among the panels, giving it a sheen that matched the gold lamé tank she'd paired it with. Her gold gladiator sandals had long straps that wound their way around her ankles and calves. She was as different from her sisters as an orange was from an apple, but Eleanor loved her just the way she was.

"There's hot water on the stove if you want tea." Eleanor got to her feet and pulled out a second china teacup, setting it beside the box of tea bags. "If you want, we can take it out to the porch just like we used to do."

"When I'd make you play tea party because Gabby and Meggy were too old to?" Emma laughed as she fixed a cup of blackberry tea and set the cookies on the saucer before slipping into the opposite kitchen chair. "Nah, we can stay here. Besides, you look like you're working."

She nodded toward the papers sitting to the side of Eleanor's notepad.

"Just working on this week's column." Eleanor had been the anonymous Harbor Cove advice columnist for more than two decades. An eon in this age of Insta-that and Face-this. Some people still read the weekly *Gazette*, however, which meant Eleanor kept penning her Dear Amelia column, a job that gave her a sense of purpose and kept her busy when most people would have retired from work.

Just this morning, Leroy Walker, the editor of the *Gazette*, had called Eleanor into his office to propose that she think about taking the column digital. "People just aren't reading print like they used to," he said. "We need to keep up with our demographic or they'll go some-where else for their news and entertainment." Which meant there could be a day when Dear Amelia was no longer in the paper, a thought that saddened Eleanor.

Going digital sounded so clinical and cold. She missed the days when hearing the mailman's truck pull up meant the joy of letters from far-flung places and distant relatives. Today the thunk of the *Gazette* landing on the front porch was the equivalent of a letter from home or, in this case, a well-meaning grandma dispens-ing sensible advice. How could a computer deliver that same rush of anticipation?

Eleanor loved her column and the secret that she was the person behind Dear Amelia. A couple of months ago, her granddaughters had discovered a trove of the letters up in the attic and pieced together their grandmother's identity, but as they had since they were little girls, they kept any information in the family. They also got involved by working behind the scenes to try to get all of Dear

Amelia's advice to come true. A few family machinations had ended well, thankfully.

"And who needs advice today?" Emma rose on her tiptoes and peered over Eleanor's shoulder and read a few lines of the letter waiting to be answered. "A dispute over a lawn gnome? I was hoping for something juicier, like a secret affair or a love child or something."

Eleanor swatted at Emma. "This town is not some kind of soap opera. And you should be grateful that the worst thing people can complain about to Dear Amelia is a stolen garden ornament."

Emma plopped into one of the chairs and rested her chin on her palm. Every time she did that, she reminded Eleanor of the little girl she had once been. Sitting at a counter stool, her chin in her hand, watching her grandmother bake or sighing over math homework or wondering aloud about what she would be when she grew up. "Which is exactly why I want to leave this town. I can't think of anything more boring."

Eleanor had no idea what her granddaughter expected to find in those far-off places of the world she wanted to see. Sometimes it seemed more like Emma made plans to leave Harbor Cove because she wanted to run from something rather than toward something, though what that could be, Eleanor didn't know. Her granddaughters didn't have perfect lives—Lord knew they had been through more than enough when their mother died all those years ago—but they had good lives. "Sometimes, my dear granddaughter, what you call boring is peaceful to others. Home can be a sanctuary if you look for the beauty in it."

"Peaceful? All I do is deal with bridezillas day after day." Emma dunked half of her cookie in her tea and then took a bite before the soggy end dropped into the cup. "That is the exact opposite of peace, Grandma."

"I disagree about the chaos. I've had more than enough of that for my life, thank you very much." Eleanor skimmed the letter before her. She hated to admit it, but Emma was right. There wasn't anything exciting about a missing gnome. "Leroy tells me that people are ready for a change in the way Dear Amelia gives advice."

"Change? What kind of change?"

Eleanor waved a hand in a vague dismissal of something she didn't understand. "He says he wants to take it digital. Create an interactive portal behind a paywall, whatever all that is, where people can ask Dear Amelia questions in real time."

"That sounds cool. It's basically what you're doing now, just on a computer."

Eleanor sighed. "To me, there's something about the written word that is so much more eloquent and meaningful. Writing to someone through a computer seems so...impersonal."

"Uh, Grandma, the entire column is anonymous so it's already somewhat impersonal." Emma grinned. "I think you just don't like change."

"You may be right about that." Eleanor shrugged. Progress could be a good thing, she reminded herself, even if it didn't seem so right now. "You, my dear, are the only one in this family who loves change and chaos and spontaneity. Speaking of which...where do things stand with your own little impromptu major life change? Has cousin George given you an update?"

That surprise wedding had been completely out of character for Emma, the headstrong, commitment-phobic granddaughter. Emma claimed the whole thing had been an accident, but to Eleanor, accidents often had hidden secret truths at their core.

"Yes, but…" Emma's voice trailed off. She dunked her tea bag before squeezing it out and setting it on the saucer.

"But what?"

"But the guy I kinda married is kinda living in Harbor Cove for a little while."

Well, well, that was an interesting development. Far more so than the pilfered gnome and Eleanor's day-to-day life, which consisted of the column and her pesky neighbor, Harry Erlich, who seemed to have the mistaken idea that he should be courting Eleanor.

Perhaps Emma's husband wasn't so anxious for an annulment after all, and there might be a chance he could convince Emma to stay right here in Harbor Cove. "Has Luke Carter come to win you back? I think that's so romantic. I should write about that in my column." She picked up a pen.

"Whoa, whoa, don't you dare." Emma put a hand over her grandmother's. "He's not here to win me back or do something romantic, thank God. He's here for work. He got a job in Newburyport, and he's living here with his uncle Ray."

"Ray? Ray Carter? I know him. He used to be a member of the VFW back when I used to volunteer there. Nice guy, although I think he got terribly wounded in the war. I didn't know he was related to your betrothed."

"Grandma, Luke is not my be-anything. The annulment will be final in thirty days, as long as Luke doesn't contest it." She dunked her cookie and took another bite. "I don't see any reason why he would anyway. It's not like I told him I was interested in him or anything. Not really."

"What does *not really* mean?"

"It means nothing's going to happen between us so don't be trying to fix us up." Emma wagged a piece of cookie in Eleanor's direction. "I know you are a big softie when it comes to everyone's love life but your own."

"I do not have a love life."

"You have Harry."

"He is... a friend." Eleanor stacked up her papers and set them to the side, avoiding Emma's inquisitive gaze. Harry was nothing more than a friend, even if he sometimes thought they were more. Eleanor had already had, and lost, her one true love.

Russell had been gone for more than two decades now, but there were times when Eleanor swore it felt like yesterday. For so long, she'd clung tightly to his memory. She'd set a place at the table for him every single night, slept on the far side of the bed, and left his favorite book and glasses on the nightstand.

But then the book and glasses kept collecting dust, and she'd tucked them away, preferring the uncluttered wooden surface. She'd wake up sometimes in the middle of the bed, as if her body was slowly reclaiming Russell's space. And as their family grew to include Jake and sometimes Harry, that space at the head of the table was no longer empty.

But dating again? That seemed like such a ridiculous, and frankly terrifying, idea. Eleanor didn't know if she had it in her to have her heart broken again. Far better to spend her time fretting about her granddaughters' problems and making sure all three of them were happy and settled in their lives.

Maybe Emma just needed a nudge in the right direction. Gabby was happily engaged to Jake now, and

Margaret...well, that was a problem for another day. Lord only knew what was going on with her eldest and most private granddaughter.

"Did you see your Luke?" she asked. "Did he look morose and lonely without you?"

"Ugh, Grandma. Stop trying to turn this into a love story. I assure you, it's far more ordinary than that. I ran into Luke when I was downtown having lunch with Meggy and ended up meeting his uncle and his daughter."

"You saw him today? And you saw Margaret? My my, dear granddaughter, I better pour you another cup of tea." Eleanor got to her feet to retrieve the teakettle. A small curl of steam slipped out of the spout. "Seems we have a lot to catch up on."

CHAPTER 5

Ear-curdling screams filled the bathroom, so loud that Luke swore the sound popped at least half the bubbles foaming on the top of the hot water. "I don't want to!" Scout wrapped her arms around herself, grabbing a T-shirt sleeve in each hand, in a life-and-death grip against having to get into the tub.

It was a battle Luke had had every single night for over a month. He didn't know if it was the change of parent, or the upset in her schedule and where she lived—or maybe Scout had been this difficult for Kim, too—but bath time with his daughter was akin to descending into the fourth level of Purgatory. Half the time, she won the battle and went to bed still sweaty from playing outside, and the other half, Luke enjoyed a moment of victory against a temperamental child who would then fight him tooth-and-nail about bedtime.

He should have been more involved when Scout was a little girl. More hands-on. Instead he'd spent too much of his time living out of a suitcase, following one job after another. He'd pop home for a weekend visit, descending like a fairy godfather with presents and trips to the zoo. Then he would be off again, leaving 99 percent of Scout's care in Kim's hands. He'd thought he was doing the right thing—or at least that was what he had told himself until he noticed the empty vodka bottles in the recycle bin and the growing disarray in Kim's house that only seemed to multiply between visits.

Now he was feeling disconnected and clueless, like an actor playing the role of a father with no real experience in how exactly to pull that off.

He had no choice but to figure it out. He had a million and one things waiting for him to do for work, and he didn't have the time to make this into another drawn-out-fight-to-the-death battle.

"Scout, the water is getting cold," he said. "You need to take a bath so you can get your pajamas on—"

She shook her head so hard that little blond tendrils whipped against her cheeks. "I want ice cream! Now!"

Every night, it was something else. To play with a favorite toy. To watch one more episode of *Paw Patrol*. To go outside one more time. Tonight it was ice cream. Tomorrow it could be anything. He needed to hold firm or she was going to walk all over him until the day she went to college. "We don't have any ice cream. You need to take a bath and—"

"But can't we go to the store, Daddy?" Scout's voice shifted into sweet and cajoling, like a reverse scene out of *The Exorcist*. With all these tactics for arguing, his daughter was undoubtedly going to end up a lawyer. "I want some ice cream. And you should have some, too"— she patted his shoulder and gave him a very serious look—"'cuz you've had a very bad day."

He couldn't help but laugh. He'd just said that very thing to his uncle fifteen minutes ago, and now here was his four-year-old parrot, feeding his own lines back to him. "Just because I've had a bad day doesn't mean we go get ice cream," Luke said, trying to stifle the chuckle at the end of his words. Wasn't that what he was supposed to say? So his kid didn't grow up into some comfort-seeking sugar addict stuffing doughnuts in her pocket just to get through morning rush hour?

"No, but . . ." Scout twirled the end of her hair and gave him an innocent who-me, I'm-just-trying-to-help look, "we can sit on the spinny chairs and have fun, and . . . and then your bad day won't be so bad and . . . and you're gonna be happy."

"Spinny chairs, huh?" He could still see the rotating seats at the ice cream parlor in Belleview, New Hampshire, where he'd grown up. He'd get a cookie dough cone and then twirl back and forth on the seat while the ice cream dribbled down his hand. "I gotta admit, Bean, that sounds fun. But you need a bath."

"I can take my bath later." Scout nodded, as if this was a done deal. "It's not even dark out, Daddy, and you said I go to bed when Mr. Sun goes to bed."

"You go to bed when I say it's time to go to bed," he said in his sternest voice. But he couldn't hold the hard line against the earnestness in her face. Luke sighed. "Fine. Go get your shoes."

"Yay! Yay! Ice cream!" The child who had just been screaming like she was about to be beheaded now skipped out of the bathroom and dashed down the hall toward the mudroom.

"You know you're spoiling that kid," Uncle Ray said as Luke crossed to the hall closet to grab his coat and keys. "And spoiling leads to rotten, leads to a living hell when she's a teenager. I should know because I was that teenager. The army was the only thing to keep me straight."

"Maybe I have a little dad guilt." *A little* was an understatement. He'd been too busy with his own life to realize Kim was slipping deeper into her alcoholism. If she hadn't gone into treatment, who knows what would have happened? If Luke had been there maybe he could have caught it sooner...

Well, he was here now. Maybe he could make up for all the playdates and bedtime stories he'd missed.

"Never parent out of guilt." Ray leaned forward in his chair, a threadbare armchair he'd had for as long as Luke could remember. The fabric had faded from a deep maroon to a soft red, and the stitching was fraying on the armrests, but Uncle Ray didn't seem to care. The chair was as old and reliable as Uncle Ray himself. "You make the wrong choices when you let guilt be your guide. I should know." His face softened, and his gaze went somewhere in the distance. Maybe to some memory, maybe to a regret. Then he shook it off and refocused on Luke. "Anyway, just be stern with her, and she'll learn that she has a routine and she needs to stick to it."

"I know, I know. That's what I should do but..." Luke ran a hand through his hair. Everything about this move had been ten times more exhausting than he'd expected, and dealing with Scout's tantrums only made him more exhausted. Sometimes it was easier just to cave because a man needed to sleep, not argue.

He was supposed to visit the job site tomorrow morning with his new boss and then have a meeting first thing Monday with the different subs to see where everyone stood on the phases of the project. Berry Circle was already at least a month behind because of the last project manager's mistakes. Luke couldn't afford to waste a single hour if he wanted to get it all back on track. He had reports to go over, budgets to create, timelines to finagle, and he needed a clear head that wasn't pounding because of someone screaming in his ear. "Sometimes I just can't be the bad guy, Uncle Ray."

"I get it, you old softie," Uncle Ray said with a chuckle. He sat back in his chair and propped his feet on the ottoman. "Just make sure to bring me back a mint chocolate chip. If you do that, I'll help you with bedtime."

Scout adored her uncle, and two against one always had better results than a mano a mano between Luke and Scout when it came to bedtime. "And this is why you're my favorite uncle."

"I'm your only living uncle so it's not like it's much of a competition, and I'm not that great of an uncle, so that's not saying much." Uncle Ray wagged the remote control at Luke. "Two scoops. In a waffle dish. I'm feeling fancy tonight."

Scout came skidding to a stop, her beat-up old sneakers squeaking against the hardwood floor. She needed a new pair of shoes, but that was a battle Luke was saving for a day when he'd had more coffee. "I'm ready, Daddy."

"Don't run in the house, and wear your coat." Now he sounded like his own parents with their rules and expectations. They'd both been so hard on him, their only son. Maybe that was another reason he couldn't put boundaries around Scout. He'd had enough of that himself and had grown up way too fast. He wanted more for Scout—more fun, more hugs, more laughs—but had no idea how to give her that.

A kid deserved a chance to be a kid because, all too soon, she was going to be an adult with a car payment, a job, and a kid of her own. If a little ice cream helped her stay a kid longer, then he'd buy out the whole damned shop.

Harbor Sweet Treats sat on the end of the boardwalk in downtown Harbor Cove in a little white building with a bright-pink awning. Outdoor furniture awaited the summer crowd, who could sit under the shade and watch the ocean roll in and out while they ate their waffle cones and brownie bite sundaes. There were only a handful of cars in the parking lot and a few people seated at the tables.

Luke unbuckled Scout's car seat. She ducked under his arm, scrambled out of the car, and dashed inside before he could tell her to wait. "Scout!" Luke slammed the door shut, took a step, realized his coat was caught, unlocked the car, opened the door, and then tried it all again. By the time he got inside, he could see Scout talking to someone. His heart began to race, because if his daughter thought it was okay to talk to strangers—

"Hi, Luke." Emma's friendly face peeked around Scout's body. She was seated at one of the tables with two other people, their dishes nearly empty. "Scout here said you're getting her an ice cream because she wouldn't take a bath."

Gotta love the honesty of kids. "Well, that's . . . precisely the truth." He took his daughter's hand in his but she resisted, trying to tug him toward the counter and away from Emma.

Luke, however, was cemented to the tiled floor. All he could do was stare at Emma and picture her in his arms. He'd spent one night with her, with her curled against his chest most of the evening, and shared two kisses, and now he couldn't get her out of his head. He wanted more of her touch, more of her smile, and definitely more of kissing the woman who would soon be his ex-wife.

That seemed to pretty much sum up every screwed-up relationship Luke had ever had. Either he was falling for the wrong girl or he fell for the right girl at the wrong time. And this was, hands-down, the worst time to fall for anyone, especially the woman who was divorcing him.

"Come on, Daddy." Scout tugged hard. "We gotta get some before it's all gone!"

Luke still couldn't take his eyes off Emma. She had her hair swept up into some messy bun thing that left tendrils cascading down her neck and back. The bright pink of her V-neck shirt offset the darkness of her hair and the blue of her eyes, drawing him like a magnet. A smile quirked up one side of her mouth as she caught him staring. Busted.

"Uh, Luke? This is my sister Gabby, and her fiancé, Jake."

Luke yanked his attention back to the present. "Sorry. Nice to meet you." He put out his hand and shook with a woman who could have been Emma's twin and a guy who looked like the kind of guy Luke would invite over for beers and barbecue, if he ever settled down long enough to make friends and set up a grill.

"And who's this?" Gabby asked.

"I'm Scout. I'm four." Scout tugged on Luke's hand again. "Come *on*, Daddy."

Luke could see an elderly lady at the counter, hemming and hawing over what flavor she wanted. There was no sense rushing up to the counter to stand there with an antsy preschooler. That's what he told himself anyway, as he lingered at Emma's table.

"What kind are you going to get, Scout?" Emma leaned over toward Scout. "They have the best ice cream in the whole world here."

"Cookie Monster." Scout nodded. She'd already had Cookie Monster twice this week, part of the bribe-reward system Luke had perfected. "It's my favorite."

"Because it makes your tongue all blue?" Emma stuck out her own tongue. "My favorite is cherry for the same reason."

Damn. Now Luke was thinking about kissing Emma all over again.

Scout giggled. "Your tongue is red."

Across from Emma, Gabby and Jake were talking to each other, their gazes locked. They looked like a couple out of a movie, all moon-eyed and happy. Luke didn't feel one bit of envy. Not one bit.

But for a second, he did imagine having Emma look at him like that. Having her next to him, her hand in his or her head on his shoulder, the two of them sharing a bowl of ice cream. Those were the kind of ordinary couple things he'd never really had and only rarely seen. Every woman he had dated had been someone who needed rescuing or saving, like a bird with a broken wing. Emma was the opposite—she was a bird who was determined not to be caught under anyone else's roof and who made it clear she didn't need anyone else's help, either.

"Want to try a bite, Scout? You might like cherry ice cream, too. Then you'll have to get some of each." Emma winked and then scooped up a taste of her ice cream. Scout took the bite without questioning it—which wasn't how she handled green beans or mashed potatoes or meat loaf—and immediately pronounced it *yummy*.

"I want cherry, too, Daddy."

"Two scoops? Kid, you're going to have a sugar high that will keep you up until three in the morning, and I need to work tomorrow."

"They do mini scoops for kids, if you ask. And as for work, you can always bring her to the event at the hotel," Emma said. She lowered her voice and cupped her hand over her mouth. "Free babysitting for three hours."

Luke smacked his forehead. "I forgot to sign up for that."

"Don't worry. I've got you covered, Mr. Carter."

"Thank you, Missus—" He glanced at Gabby and Jake before chopping off the sentence. She wasn't going to be his wife for much longer, and he had no idea if she'd even told her family about their impromptu marriage. "Uh, sorry."

"Oh, we know all about you, Luke. You're the only one who's ever managed to corral my wild little sister. You're like this mythical creature we've all been dying to meet and drag to a family dinner sometime soon." Gabby grinned. "There are two other Monroe girls who would love to know your secret."

Emma's face pinked. "Uh, Luke, you better get in line. They're closing soon."

"Yeah, yeah, sure." Luke headed for the counter, basically just a wallet at the end of Scout's leash. He was tempted to glance back at Emma, but he kept his gaze front and center, reading a list of flavors he didn't remember. *You're the only one.*

He shouldn't care about that or wonder why no other man had come along and stolen Emma's heart. He had no business thinking about anything other than taking care of the little girl whose life was literally in his hands.

Scout ordered her cone, and Luke came out of his

stupor long enough to order his and his uncle's. When he finished paying, he saw Emma and her group at the door, getting ready to leave.

"Tomorrow, nine a.m., at the hotel," she called back to him. "I'll see you then, Luke and Scout."

"I'm looking forward to it," Luke said, and for the first time that day, he felt optimistic and happy. And then Scout dropped her ice cream on his shoe.

CHAPTER 6

E ven at nine in the morning, the noise in the recreation center was a constant, loud roar. Fifty kids from Harbor Cove and surrounding towns had come to the "My Dad Rocks" craft event put on by the Harbor Cove Hotel on a warm Saturday morning in late May. It was one of two Father's Day–themed events at the hotel that Emma had put together. The weekend after next would be the Father-Daughter Dance on Father's Day itself, something that hopefully would turn into an annual event, given how many people had already signed up.

She'd started the kids' program at the hotel as a way to break up the frustrating tedium of working with brides, but after the first event, she'd realized she related to the children who were struggling because their parents were getting divorced, or their favorite pet had died, or they were simply having a hard time getting through life. She'd barely started kindergarten when her mother died,

and even though her sisters and grandmother had been
there, Emma had felt a little lost and scared for so many
years. She could see those same feelings in the eyes of
many of the kids who came to the events, and even though
Emma was no parenting or psychology expert, she hoped
that the warm, fun environment the hotel created was an
oasis in the middle of a difficult time.

Once she was with the Atlas Foundation, she could
start doing the same thing on a much bigger scale. She'd
not only escape this coastal suburb but hopefully be able
to change a child's life in the process. And give her own
some kind of meaning and depth.

Like Momma had done. Emma had heard over and
over again how amazing, generous, and compassionate
Penny Monroe had been. It was a high bar to live up to,
and as much as Emma wanted to do that, she had a track
record of failures and mistakes. And if she'd allowed herself a moment of vulnerability in the diner with Margaret,
Emma might have admitted that, deep down inside, she
was terrified of failing again.

Like she had when she'd married a stranger, filed to
annul the marriage, and then sent out a colossal mixed
message by kissing him on Main Street in broad daylight.
There'd been plenty of questions from Margaret about
that when Emma came back into the diner. "I thought you
were divorcing him," she'd said. "Pretty sure kissing the
guy says the opposite. Do you even know what you really
want, Emma?"

Did she? The honest answer was no. She could barely
think after Luke kissed her well and good, the kind of kiss
that lingered on the fringes of her thoughts, the kind of
kiss that stirred something all the way to her toes. What
did she really want?

More of that, so help her. If she had known Luke could kiss like that, maybe she wouldn't have dashed out of the room so quickly.

They'd exchanged one brief kiss after the wedding ceremony that she barely remembered. Then they'd stumbled to their Marital Reinvigoration Suite and fallen asleep. She had vague memories of curling up against his body and leaning into his warmth sometime in the middle of the night. To say she hadn't wondered about what would happen if they'd done more than exchange a brief peck on their wedding night would be an outright lie. Because she had wondered. More than once.

Last night in the ice cream parlor, he'd had that scruff of a beard that she loved on a man, and resisting that overwhelming urge to touch him had been almost impossible. The only thing that stopped her was the fact that they were in a public place with half her family and his daughter watching them.

Do you even know what you want?

Yeah, she wanted him to kiss her again. And again.

Oh, this was not a good path for her thoughts. Not at all. She was getting her marriage annulled and leaving this town, in that order, with no detours for flings or reunions.

"This was a great idea," Diana said, handing Emma an apron emblazoned with the hotel's logo and thankfully interrupting Emma's thoughts. "I can't believe what a hit it's been."

"I thought it was a great idea until I got here." She let out a sigh. "That is a lot of kids." Each of the children had been assigned a table when they had first gotten in the room, but instead of going to the table that matched the number on their wristband, they were running around the room and scrambling under the chairs as if they'd just been released from the zoo.

"Yeah, but look at Gregory Hawkins." Diana nodded at a nine-year-old who was talking to a group of other kids. "The first time he came to one of these things, he was so shy and scared, he sat in a corner and didn't talk to anyone."

Gregory's mother had left the family six months ago, and the sudden departure, coupled with an abrupt move back to Dad's hometown of Harbor Cove, had made the little boy retreat into himself. His father had started bringing him to the kids' events at the hotel so he could make friends. Emma had seen Gregory by himself, wearing a T-shirt with a *T. rex* on the front. They'd struck up a conversation about which dinosaur had the best chance in a *T. rex* battle. She'd brought over the Lego bins, and they'd sat side by side, building a mini Jurassic Park out of the multicolored pieces and then filling it with the plastic dinosaurs in Gregory's backpack. Ever so slowly, Gregory began to open up to Emma and the other children. "I didn't do much, Di. Just helped him build a skyscraper out of blocks."

"You did a ton. I talked to his dad when he brought Gregory in this morning for registration. He had tears in his eyes because he was so happy that his son is making friends again." Diana put a hand on Emma's shoulder. "You are really, really good at this. You have a knack with kids, without a doubt. Maybe you should go to school, get a degree in social work or therapy, and do this full time."

"I will be working in that area when I meet up with the Atlas Foundation. Karl's starting a bunch of programs overseas that are all about helping underserved children in poorer countries."

Diana made a face.

"What?" Emma asked. "What are you not saying?"

She sighed. "I should have said something sooner but I didn't think you were serious. Now you've put in your notice, and you're talking about ending your lease on your apartment and…"

"Just say it, Diana."

"I've met Karl Jensen, and I just find him a little… squirrelly. Are you sure his plans are legit?"

"They have a website and everything. Of course he's legit." Just like Yogi Brown and his internet officiant's license that meant he could perform real marriages. *And look how that turned out*, the little voice in her head said. "I have a call with Karl and the team in a few days. They're on it, Diana, and I'm so excited to be part of the beginning of something so cool."

Diana waved at a mother she knew and then directed the woman's daughter toward the right table. "You're right, Emma. I'm sure you checked them out and know what's going on far better than I do. And the whole thing does sound like a perfect match for you." Diana gave her a hug and then drew back. "So, not to change the subject, but… I have some news."

Emma had started sorting through the paints, making sure each table would have the same amount of colors. "What?"

"This." Diana thrust her hand in front of Emma, showing off a gorgeous one-carat solitaire with a halo wrap. "Aaron proposed."

"Oh, wow. Congrats!" They were engaged already? Diana and Aaron had been dating for just over a year, and the whole thing felt so fast to Emma. Like Emma was one to talk because she'd known Luke for like two-point-seven seconds before she married him. "I'm so happy for you."

"Me too." She sighed. "He's such a wonderful guy."

"Did you set a date?"

Diana nodded. "December twenty-fourth. I've always dreamed of a snowy Christmas wedding with white and red, and now you can help me make that happen."

"December? Diana, I'm leaving Harbor Cove in July. I won't be here in December."

"But you're my best friend and a better wedding planner than me. I can't plan my wedding without you, and my mother drives me insane, so there's no way I'd ask her." Diana rolled her eyes. "She'd be covering my dress with crystals and hanging a dreamcatcher over the priest."

Emma laughed. "True. Your mom is a little quirky. But listen, Diana, you can plan this. You know everything I know."

"Promise you'll think about it? Look at it this way—if this whole thing with Atlas doesn't work out, your sister's wedding and my wedding give you a perfect excuse to return to Harbor Cove." Diana grinned. "Oh look, there are our volunteers now, so it's not just you and me trying to round up all these little ones."

"Thank goodness," Emma muttered, both for the change of subject and the help, as she crossed the room to greet Gabby, Jake, and Grandma. The three of them had signed up to supervise a table and help the children paint rocks that they could give to their fathers for Father's Day. After they finished the ones for their dads, Emma had a bucket of extra rocks for the kids to paint and leave around town, like little painted and cheery surprises for residents to find and as a project for the kids without anyone they considered a dad in their life. Every Mother's

Day after Momma died had been bittersweet and a reminder of what the girls had lost, which was why Emma
tried to incorporate something for kids who didn't have a
parent to help them feel included.

"Good morning, Emma," Gabby said with a wide
smile. Emma's middle sister Gabby radiated happiness
whenever she was around Jake. All of the Monroe girls
had known the affable graphic designer and photographer
for most of their lives, and now that he was marrying into
the family, they loved him even more.

Jake ambled up beside Gabby and raised the trusty
camera around his neck. "I figured I'd take some pictures
for the hotel website and social media," he said.

"Great idea. The parents will probably share them, too,
which gets us more publicity." Emma grinned. "Thanks,
Jake."

"It was all Gabby's idea." He beamed at his fiancée.
"She's the smart one in this relationship."

"Of course I am, because I chose you," she quipped.

"I think you have that backward, my wife-to-be." He
grinned and then kissed her. "But you look so pretty, I
don't care who's right."

"Suck-up," Gabby said as she gave him a good-natured
jab. Emma watched them and felt that same weird craving for another person that she had felt back in Nevada.
Her life wasn't empty. She didn't need someone teasing
her and kissing her. Maybe she was just extra hormonal
this month or something because that kiss she'd shared
with Luke—okay, it had been a hell of a kiss—and this
moment with her sister had her feeling all *verklempt*, as
Grandma would call it.

"My goodness, you two still act like you did when you
were in first grade and all silly and smitten, and I have to

say, I love it." Grandma stepped forward to draw Emma
into a hug that was fierce and strong. "My dear youngest
granddaughter, you look well."

"Thanks for coming, Grandma."

"Thank you for asking me. I love volunteering at these
events. All these kids make me remember what it was
like when you girls were little. Plus, this is such a good
thing you are doing." Grandma greeted a towheaded girl
who came whizzing by. "I've heard many parents in town
say this program you started has been really beneficial for
their kids. You always did have your mother's heart."

"Thanks, Grandma. But it's really all the hotel. They
supported my idea."

"Well, someone had to have the idea to get the ball
rolling, and that someone was you." Grandma turned and
took in the waves of chaos careening around the room.
"Which table am I at?"

"Table Five. You'll be with the five-year-olds." She
grabbed another apron and handed it to her grandmother.
"But if they're too much for you—"

"I raised you three. I'll be just fine." She gave Emma a pat
on the cheek before she headed for her table. Like the pro
in parenting she was, Grandma clapped her hands together
and the hubbub stopped for a second. "Table Five! Are you
ready to have some fun? Then let's get started painting!"

Several kids scrambled over to the table and into
the plastic chairs. Emma did a quick wristband check
to make sure they were all at the right place before
corralling Table Four and Table Six for Gabby and Jake.
Diana was already sitting down with Table One, which
left Table Two, full of antsy, chattering four-year-olds,
for Emma.

She'd seen Scout's name on the registration list, which

meant Luke had signed her up last night, but the little girl wasn't among the crowd of children. Disappointment flickered in Emma's chest. Only because she knew Scout would have loved doing this, not because she cared about seeing Luke again. She was, after all, annulling him in a little over three weeks.

"Okay, guys, let's all pick a rock," Emma said as she put a basket filled with washed, smooth river rocks into the center of the table. The kids made a mad grab for the basket, but Emma put a hand over it. "One at a time, like you're picking out a roll at dinnertime."

"My mommy doesn't like rolls," said one little girl. "She says they stay on her tummy."

Emma bit back a laugh. "Well, these are rocks, and we're not going to eat them, so I think you'll be just fine." She handed off the basket just as the door to the ballroom opened with a squeak.

And there he was. Tall and too good-looking for his own good. Luke had on jeans and a T-shirt, which showed off muscular biceps, broad shoulders, and a very fit chest. And there went Emma's hormones all over again. Thank goodness for dozens of little kids to distract her from fantasizing about that man. Again.

Scout broke away from her dad and ran toward Emma. "Hi, Miss Emma!"

"Hi, Scout. You want to paint rocks with us?"

The little girl nodded, all solemn and serious but practically shaking with barely contained excitement. "Uh-huh. Can I paint a bird on mine? 'Cuz my daddy made the birdhouse, and I want to give it to the birds."

"Sure, we can do one with a bird. But first, take a seat and wait your turn for the basket. Then you can pick out a rock to paint."

Scout did as she was told, eager and happy. She started squirming when the boy next to her looked at one rock, put it back, took out another, and put it back, but she didn't say anything. She just did as she was told and waited for her turn. The tantrum Emma had witnessed a few days ago was nowhere to be seen.

"See? You're a kid whisperer," Luke said, his breath warm against her cheek. "Thanks for this, by the way."

He was so close and smelled so good that she nearly forgot what she was doing. "Oh, yeah. Of course. You're welcome. And for the record, I didn't set this up just for you." She grinned. "It is a town-wide event."

"And here I thought you were going the extra mile to impress me." He shot back a grin of his own. "Anyway, I have a job to get to. I'll be back at noon to pick her up. After that, can I buy you some lunch? As a thank-you."

"Oh, well, I'd love to but I can't." It wasn't a date, obviously, because he'd have Scout with him, and they weren't dating, even if they were married and the whole situation was weird. Which meant she probably should have said yes, but for some reason the words she needed were nowhere to be found in her vocabulary, especially whenever Luke talked to her. "I have to stay after and clean up, but maybe another time."

"Why don't we help you? I hear they say six hands can do the work of two in half the time."

"Wouldn't it be a third of the time?"

"Not when one of them is a four-year-old and the other one is easily distracted." He gave her another grin. "See you at noon."

Luke started to walk away but didn't escape the room before Gabby wandered over to say hello to him, and then Grandma joined them. Emma cringed. She could only imagine what kind of inquisition her family was putting Luke through.

Emma refocused on the six kids at her table, but in the back of her mind, she wondered what he'd meant earlier about someone being easily distracted. And why. And how come she was feeling exactly the same way every time Luke was around. "Okay, guys, now that everyone has a rock, it's time to decide on a design." Emma pulled out a series of pictures she'd printed out—butterflies, flowers, trees, dogs—that could serve as inspiration.

"I want to make a butterfly," Ashlynn Raymond said. "My daddy likes butterflies."

"My dad likes dogs." Joey Delgado picked out a tube of brown paint. Emma leaned over, gently took the mess waiting to happen from Joey, and poured a puddle of paint onto a paper plate sitting beside his rock. "I'mma make a big brown dog."

"Okay," Emma said, but her attention was on Grandma and Luke. At some point, Gabby had gone back to her table, and now it was just Grandma talking to Luke. A few seconds later, Grandma gave him a smile and a pat on the shoulder and then headed for her seat again. Luke sent Emma a wink before heading out the door.

What did that mean? And what did Grandma just do?

She didn't have much time to wonder because Drew Cashman was insisting that Emma draw a barbecue on his rock, something that definitely extended beyond Emma's limited sketching skills. She set each of the kids up with some paint and brushes, and they all got to work. It took a minute before she noticed Scout just sitting there quietly. "What are you going to paint, Scout?"

She shrugged. "I dunno. I was gonna do a bird, but I don't know if Daddy likes birds."

"Well, what does your daddy like?"

"I dunno." Scout fiddled with her rock, flipping it over and over. "My daddy works a lot. But my mommy's in the hospital now, so my daddy has to watch me. He's not gonna work so much, he said. 'Cuz he's supposed to be my babysitter."

"Your mommy's in the hospital?"

Scout nodded several times. "'Cept it's a special hospital, and nobody can go see her."

"Oh." Emma didn't know what to say to that. Or the characterization of Luke as a babysitter, not a dad. She knew he spent a lot of time on construction sites, working for builders all over the country. But that was about all she knew.

Including the fact that Luke had a kid. And that kid had a mommy. A mommy who was also Luke's girlfriend? Fiancée? Or worse…wife? Was Emma caught up in some kind of bigamy mess? Wouldn't *that* just put a big fat bow on her Emma Move of marrying a stranger?

"Well, your daddy is outside a lot, so maybe he'd like a flower on his rock? Or a house because he builds houses?" Emma suggested.

Scout thought about that for a while, her little mouth twisting left and right as she pondered. "Can I make a blue flower? Because my daddy likes blue."

"Your flower can be any color you like." Emma uncapped the bottles of craft paint and poured little puddles of blue, green, and yellow onto Scout's plate. Then she handed Scout a brush.

Scout hesitated again, the brush hovering over her rock. "I'm not a very good drawer."

"That's okay. Your daddy's going to love whatever you make."

Scout's gaze dropped. "Maybe."

"Want me to help you?"

Scout's eyes lit up with such surprise that it nearly broke Emma's heart. What kind of childhood had this little girl had that a stranger offering to help her paint a flower could be such a monumental thing?

And what did all that say about the man that Emma was—maybe, depending on the "mommy" relationship—married to?

❧❧❧

The warm May sun beat down on Luke's neck, causing a thin bead of sweat to trickle along his spine. He'd missed breakfast, and his stomach was already grouchy, but Luke was happy for the first time in more than two months.

For now, the job site was silent, but come Monday morning, it would be controlled chaos, the exact kind of environment he thrived in and loved. He was back, damn it, and hadn't realized how much he'd missed being a project manager until just now.

Twenty houses in various stages of construction lined the road he stood on, with the foundations for another twenty waiting to be poured on the next street over. This development, with 110 houses, a clubhouse, pool, and gym, was one of several the developer was building all over the country.

A long black sedan pulled into the cul-de-sac, stopping in the middle of the empty road. A dark-haired man in a sports coat and pressed jeans stepped out of the car. Hassan Ali had moved from his native Somalia to the United States just over ten years ago and had already made a name for himself in the world of home construction. He'd built one of the HGTV dream houses, a move that had rocketed his company up several levels. He'd gone from a busy builder to the most in-demand builder in the country in the space of a year. If anything spelled opportunity, it was this job, and Luke would be a fool to blow it.

"Mr. Carter," Hassan said, extending his hand, "pleased to finally meet you in person."

"Thank you for trusting me with your project," Luke said. He already knew from Brandon that Hassan wasn't a fan of small talk, which was fine because neither was Luke. He turned and gestured toward the buildings before them. "You were right—Berry Circle is pretty far off schedule, but I have a plan for getting things back on track and making the deadlines for move-ins." The project was already halfway sold, and missing the move-in dates for the people who had already bought homes would bring bad publicity that Berry Circle didn't need, not to mention carrying costs Hassan didn't want. Luke withdrew a sheet of paper from the binder in his hands. "If we shift the schedule for the concrete guys on Blueberry Road and have the drywall guys work twenty hours of overtime, we can get Loganberry Circle done on time, then be ready to pour foundations on Huckleberry Lane in six weeks."

Hassan studied the spreadsheet Luke handed him. "This is a pretty tight plan, you know. Weather delays, a sub quitting unexpectedly, a permit not coming through— any of those things could throw your entire plan out the window." He glanced up, and a flicker of doubt seemed to show on his face. "I need to know I can count on you, Carter."

"I've done this before, sir. When I was with Stadler Homes, I had a hurricane blow through the town in the middle of construction. We still made our deadlines, and the homeowners were sitting in their living rooms with hot cocoa and Christmas presents that winter."

"I'd like to see a detailed report on how you're going to make this happen, what it's going to cost, and how it will affect Phase Two," Hassan said. "By Monday morning?"

The question wasn't really a question. Luke nodded, already mentally calculating the extra hours he'd need to draft a report and a budget for the potential overtime. "Count on me, sir."

Hassan gave him a long, serious look. Then he nodded. "If you say that's what's going to happen, I believe you. I heard about the North Carolina hurricane that hit that development. Anyone who could get that Wilmington project done on time, after that year of weather they had, is someone I'm interested in having work for me." Hassan handed back the sheet. "If you do well with the Berry Circle project, there's another one coming up in Georgia, and one in Tennessee that I could use you on. We might have to make this a permanent job."

Six months ago, Luke would have leaped at the chance to travel and do what he loved to do. He'd thrived on living out of a suitcase and being able to see the entire eastern seaboard. But now that he had Scout full time, picking up and moving every few months was impractical. He couldn't have her starting a new school every season or keep uprooting her over and over again.

But he couldn't say any of that right now, not with the opportunity of a lifetime standing before him. He needed this job. He'd worry about where that job was going to go after Berry Circle was done. "Sounds good, sir." No matter what happened, this beat crunching numbers in a cubicle any day of the week.

Hassan smiled. "I like a man who gets things done. This project is a month behind, and as I'm sure you know, that is costing my company a significant amount of money. If you can get Phase One done on time, or even better, early, there will be a bonus in it for you. How's twenty-five thousand dollars?"

"That's great, sir." That kind of money would come in handy for starting over and finding a home where he and Scout could settle down. Luke thanked his boss and then watched the other man leave. Like Hassan had said, Luke had made some big—maybe impossible—promises. But with Scout's future on the line, Luke intended to keep every last one.

He checked his watch. Damn. Almost noon. He still had to pick up Uncle Ray from the grocery store and then go get Scout before heading back to his uncle's house to work some more. Every single day since he'd arrived in Harbor Cove had been rushed, with too few hours and too little sleep.

Uncle Ray was sitting on a bench outside the Save-Lots with his cart full of bagged groceries beside him. In the years since Luke had been away from Massachusetts, his uncle had aged considerably. He'd always been a bit of a loner ever since his return from the First Gulf War and his divorce, but it seemed as if those years of solitude were beginning to take their toll. Uncle Ray's shoulders were a little sunken, his hair thinner and grayer, and the smile Luke remembered from his childhood rarely made appearances. Luke made a mental note to take Ray with him more often, or at least engage him more when they were at home. Ray's tendency to hunker down and cut himself off from other people was clearly affecting his health in more ways than one.

"Hey, Uncle Ray. Looks like you bought out half the store." Luke grinned to cover his concern at how down his uncle seemed and how slow he was moving. Luke took the cart with one hand and helped Ray to his feet with the other.

The hated cane Uncle Ray had been given after his injuries and surgeries was out today, a clear sign Ray was hurting and had likely done too much while Luke was gone. Maybe it had been a mistake to send Uncle Ray to the grocery store. Maybe Luke should have done it himself.

"I see you looking at me like some damned porcelain doll that's about to fall to pieces. I'm made of stronger stuff than that." His shaky steps belied the sternness of his tone, as did the tight lines of pain in his face. "The army doesn't breed wimps, you know."

"I think the term you're looking for is *stubborn old goats*," Luke said.

"They do breed plenty of those." A faint smile appeared on Ray's face. He waved off Luke's assistance and settled himself into the passenger's seat.

Luke waited, watching, at the ready to help, until his uncle sent him another glare. Once Luke had the groceries loaded, he put the car in gear and started heading for the hotel. It was a beautiful sunny day in Harbor Cove, warm but with a hint of a breeze. A perfect day for a picnic on the water or a lunch outdoors. "Great weather today, huh?"

Ray harrumphed. "Same day as any day. Better above the ground than below it."

"I don't mean to overstep my bounds here, Uncle Ray, but it doesn't seem to me like you're doing too much living above the ground these days. You used to play baseball and run the youth ball camps and—"

"I know what I used to do. In case you haven't noticed"—he tapped his artificial leg with the cane—"I'm not exactly shortstop material anymore."

"You used to tell me a man can be anything he puts his mind to." Uncle Ray had been Luke's inspiration to go into homebuilding. He'd been the one who always welcomed Luke into his home without a single judgment or criticism. He'd been the unconditional love that Luke's parents had never managed to master.

"Well, I was wrong. Okay? Dead wrong." Ray muttered a couple of curses under his breath. "Just drop me at home. I don't want the ice cream to melt."

Luke sighed. There was no sense having an argument that would only lead to a long, tense day in a house that had enough chaos with Scout's mercurial moods. His uncle didn't say another word on the ride back to his little ranch house on the outskirts of Harbor Cove. For the first time, Luke realized that the house, seated by itself in a wooded area off a rarely used road, was as remote and distant as his uncle. Probably not a coincidence.

By the time Luke pulled up to the hotel, it was twelve thirty. The detour to Ray's house, compounded by taking the time to bring in the groceries, had added on time that Luke didn't have. He parked and hurried inside. Everyone else had gone, including Emma's family. He'd enjoyed chatting with her grandmother, who seemed like the kind of grandma every kid should have. She'd been friendly but nosy, clearly looking out for her youngest granddaughter. Whatever he'd said must have been the right answer because, by the end of the conversation, Eleanor Whitmore had invited Luke to family dinner.

He'd politely turned her down. Showing up for a

Sunday roast was a tad too intrusive with a woman he'd barely known when he married her. If he ever sat at Emma's grandmother's dinner table, he wanted it to be because Emma wanted him there, not because her family was trying to keep them together.

Emma and Scout were seated at one of the tables, surrounded by craft supplies and baskets of smooth rocks. All of the other children were gone, and the rest of the tables were clean, the floors swept. Clearly, Emma had already done the cleanup he'd promised to help with. Damn. He felt like a heel for letting her down.

As he crossed the room, he caught snippets of their conversation as Scout created something and Emma handed her supplies, an assistant to the surgeon who was concentrating very hard on the placement of her glitter. "My mommy doesn't live with me anymore," Scout was saying. "She had to go live with a doctor."

"Oh, is she sick?"

"I dunno. Sometimes she got sick when I was there. Mommy got lots of headaches, and I had to be quiet like a mouse all the time. And I couldn't turn on lights, 'cuz that hurt Mommy's head. And I had to get to bed early like a good girl because Mommy could only have her friends come over when it was late 'cuz they were animals, she said, and they were super loud, and I couldn't sleep so I had my bear, and he's a really soft bear, and he made me feel good 'cuz he's my best friend."

Luke's step faltered. His heart broke, and the guilt inside him became a tidal wave. No kid should grow up like that. The fact that his daughter had endured the very same childhood Luke had made him wish he could unwind the past and do it right the second time. He had no idea how to do things differently, though. There was no blueprint, no YouTube video that could tell him when to be stern, when to be fun, and most of all how to connect to a daughter who wasn't really connected to him.

"I know what it's like to not have a mommy there," Emma said as she helped Scout drizzle glue on her project. Luke stayed where he was, unabashedly eavesdropping as the conversation shifted into the category of Things He Didn't Know About Emma.

"Your mommy had to live with a doctor, too?" Scout asked.

"No, Scout. My mommy went to heaven when I was just a year older than you. I lived with my grandma, but I missed my mommy every day." Emma colored something on one corner of the paper. "Sometimes, I would tie a note to a balloon and send it to her."

Scout's gaze met Emma's, her face so full of earnest hope that it broke Luke's heart. "Can I tie this to a balloon and it will go to my mommy at the doctor's house?"

Emma smiled. "I'm pretty sure your daddy has a way to mail it. That's a bit more reliable than the balloon. And you know what?"

"What?"

"Your mommy is gonna love your picture." Emma covered Scout's little hand with her own. "It's going to make her so happy because it's so beautiful."

Scout beamed, her smile wide enough to take over her entire face. In that smile, Luke could see a craving he knew far too well. One that said, *Notice me, praise me, let me know I'm loved because I feel so invisible.*

Luke didn't know how to fill that need for his daughter, other than to show up every day and be far more reliable than he had been in the past. Except he was already messing that up today, and the longer he stood here like an idiot, the worse he made it. He hustled the rest of the way across the room. Emma looked up, and something that might have been happiness lit in her eyes as he approached. Maybe she was glad to see him or maybe she was glad to be free of preschooler duty. Or maybe he was reading far too much into one smile. "I'm so sorry I'm late."

"It's okay." Emma tucked a lock of her hair behind her ear, exposing the long, graceful lines of her neck. She had on a bright-pink T-shirt with the hotel's logo and a pair of faded jeans that made her look as carefree as a day at the beach. "Scout was a great helper, and we got it all cleaned up."

Scout popped to her feet. A shower of glitter tumbled from her lap to the floor. "And I made a present for you, Daddy, and it's supposed to be a secret so you can't see. And don't guess what it is, 'cuz it's a rock, and I want you to be surprised."

"I'll be so surprised, Scout." He bit back a laugh. "Thank you."

Scout thrust a multicolored sheet of paper at him. "I made Mommy a picture, too. Can we mail it to her? Or can I go see her and bring her the picture? Miss Emma says that Mommy will be very happy when she sees my picture 'cuz it's beautiful."

"Uh, we can't go see Mommy for a few weeks, but we can mail it to her. How about we take a picture of it and I can text it to her?" He pulled out his phone and framed Scout and the glitterpalooza she'd created before snapping the pic. He glanced at his watch. If he got back to Ray's now, he'd have an hour or so that he could work while Scout watched *Paw Patrol*.

"Wait, Daddy. Take a picture with Miss Emma, too.

She was my helper." Before Luke could say no, Scout was tugging Emma over to sit beside her.

Luke raised his camera again. Emma smiled, and the gesture hit him square in the chest. Stunning. Heart-stopping. Amazing. He clicked the picture with a little bit of regret, because Emma stopped smiling at him as soon as he was done.

"Hey, Scout, pack up your stuff."

"Do we hafta go now, Daddy?"

"Yes, we do." He could literally feel the minutes ticking away. Then his stomach rumbled and reminded him that he'd made a lunch date with Emma. Well, not really a date so much as a thank-you. After not showing up on time to do cleanup, there was no way he could bail on lunch, too. *I need to know I can count on you, Carter.* The two hours it would take to go out for lunch were two hours he didn't really have, not if he wanted to keep his promise to his boss.

"Daddy, did you see my picture?" Scout shook the paper, sending another shower of glitter onto the ball-room carpet. She jabbed at different blobs of color. "This is a horse, and this is a bird, and this is a butterfly because Mommy likes all those things."

To him, it all looked like glue and glitter, but he nodded and made appreciative noises. "It's awesome, Scout. But you're getting glitter all over the floor. Maybe we should put your picture away for now."

She pouted. "You didn't look."

The need to eke more time out of his day pounded in his head. He had a to-do list a mile long, and standing here looking at glitter wasn't going to get him there. Did he have all the information he needed to do an accurate budget? It had been a few months since he'd been in the

game, and in construction, costs could be mercurial, especially when it came to lumber and other supplies affected
by weather and demand. Then there was the schedule
he needed to create and be positive he could execute.
"Scout, I will look at it later. Let's pack it up. It's time to
eat lunch."

Scout turned away, her little face filled with disappointment. She started to slide the picture into her backpack
when Emma got up to help her. "Here, let's put it in this
folder so it doesn't get crinkled in your bag. We'll keep it
all pretty for your mommy."

"T'ank you, Miss Emma." Scout let out an enormous
sigh. "I gots to go eat now."

"I know. I'm coming with you." She glanced up at
Luke, a question in her eyes. "Unless your daddy is too
busy for lunch? Or changed his mind?"

Emma was going to be his ex-wife soon, and maybe
hanging out with her, even as friends or a thank-you or
whatever this was going to be, was a bad idea. Especially
after he'd thrown a monkey wrench into the equation by
kissing her. A moment that had been especially wonderful, he had to admit, and something he had thought about
repeating. But not now. Right now, he had work and Scout
and too much on his plate to try to balance resurrecting
a relationship with the woman who was divorcing him.
"I have to reschedule that. Work is crazy right now so
I was going to make it a working lunch at Uncle Ray's
house."

Scout had her backpack slung over one shoulder, the
cartoon dog face of Chase in his police uniform peeking
around her arm. She still had a downcast look about
her, shoulders heavy with disappointment. "Daddy, do
we hafta go to Uncle Ray's for lunch? Can we go with

Miss Emma? Miss Emma's tummy is rumbling like Pooh Bear's. She needs a sammich, too."

"I'm sorry, Scout, but I really need to work this afternoon. I'll make it up to you."

"You always say that," Scout muttered.

And Luke felt like a heel all over again. How did other single parents do it? How did they juggle all the balls of work, home, and kids, and not feel like they were letting people down every five seconds?

Scout was four. He told himself that he had plenty of time to make this up to her. She wouldn't remember one missed lunch. His boss, however, would remember one missed deadline. And with a job this new, Luke couldn't afford to screw up.

This was better, he told himself. Less complications. Less chance of making another foolish choice. "Rain check, Emma?"

"That's not really necessary, Luke." She turned away and began storing the supplies in containers. "I was, after all, just doing my job."

CHAPTER 7

E very time I go out of town, everything changes
  around here," Emma said to Gabby as she handed her
sister a store-bought pie. The vegan apple crumb pie was
No-Cooking-Skills Emma's contribution to Wednesday-
night family dinner, a long-held tradition at Grandma's
house after the girls all grew up and moved into their own
places. And also a means of buttering up her family before
she broke the news about leaving in July.

They knew she had a vague plan for quitting her job
and leaving town, but no one knew that her actual exit was
just around the corner because that information would
unleash a tornado of questions. Emma could hear the
long-range plans in Grandma's oh-so-innocent questions
about Luke, and in Gabby asking about the next kids'
craft day. They all expected her to stay when all Emma
wanted to do was leave.

Gabby grinned. "You call me setting a wedding date
and Grandma getting a boyfriend—"

"He's not my boyfriend!" Grandma called out from the other room, where she was sitting with Harry—her non-boyfriend who had brought her a dozen white roses when he came over—while a meat loaf finished cooking in the oven.

"Everything changing?" Gabby grinned. "I think it's just a usual day in the life of the Monroe girls."

Emma sighed as she walked in and out of the dining room with silverware and napkins. She loved these family dinners but tonight she wanted to just go home, open a bottle of wine, and binge Netflix so she didn't think about a little girl without a mother and how Emma was starting to feel an odd sort of kinship with Scout, and with Scout's father. And to avoid all the complicated feelings she was having for Luke. She could still feel his kiss on her lips— the man definitely knew how to do that and do it well— and that was a distraction she didn't need, not now, not when she was so close to her goal of leaving this town once and for all.

"Like when we'd play Monopoly instead of doing our homework," Gabby said with a wink.

"You always did your homework. I was the one who skipped it as much as possible," Emma said. Gabby and Emma had done lots of things together because Margaret had always been busy with *something*. Whether it was choir or Girl Scouts, Gabby had been Emma's de facto babysitter and escort to and from school. She'd always been closer to Gabby anyway, maybe because they were only three years apart. Margaret was just a year older than Gabby, but her driven, stoic personality had made her seem ten years older.

"Or how we'd stop to pet the frogs in the brook and some-times be late getting home from school," Gabby said.

"You never wanted to touch them," Emma said, and in her mind she could see one of those spring afternoons when Emma would splash in the water and Gabby would sit on a rock and sketch. "I wanted to take them home with me."

"I know. Eww. So gross." Gabby carried a dish of mashed potatoes out to the table then went back to check the meat loaf, talking as she went. "You always were way more outdoorsy than the rest of us and way more adventurous. You'd climb the trees or jump in the water or do anything anyone dared you to do."

"Maybe because I had that in common with Dad." Emma pulled five water glasses out of the cabinet and began filling them from the pitcher in the fridge. Davis Monroe had spent the most time with Emma after their mother died—which wasn't saying much, because their father had been so overcome by grief that he'd checked out for a long, long time. But as the years passed and Dad climbed out of his dark despair, it had been Emma that he took to the circus and the summer fair, maybe because the other girls were older and busy with their own things or maybe because Emma and Dad had always seemed to click. Unlike everyone else, Dad didn't criticize her wild side. He'd been the one to take her to apply for her first passport and give her the money to fly to Puerto Rico when she graduated from high school. He'd also been the first to say *go for it* when she told him about Karl Jensen's foundation, although that was without knowing how much money Emma had invested in something that was still in its infancy stages. Her banker father would undoubtedly not approve of that decision.

"Momma loved the outdoors, too." Gabby slipped on

two pot holders and picked up the meat loaf. "She was always doing something in the yard."

"I don't really remember that." As Emma placed the water glasses at each place setting, her gaze landed on a portrait of their mother that had sat on the dining room sideboard for as long as she could remember. It was a side view that showed the graceful lines of Penny's neck, the curve of her cheekbones, and the sweet, welcoming smile that her girls had inherited. To Gabby and Margaret, Momma was some amazing person who had brought light and magic into the world. To Emma, she was a distant memory that was more shadow than light. "I don't really remember her at all."

"Then maybe, my dear granddaughter," Grandma said as she came into the dining room, trailed by Harry, "you should spend some time going through the old family albums or the boxes up in the attic. There are so many pictures in there of your beautiful mother and you three girls. Then there's the movies—"

"The movies!" Gabby exclaimed. The four of them settled in at the table, leaving a space for Jake, who was running late after a photo shoot. "I forgot about those. We should watch those tonight."

Watching the family films *again* was not on Emma's agenda. It was like watching a play she'd seen a hundred times, where she only knew some of the actors and had memorized the story line but didn't have an emotional tie to the outcome. There were far more family movies of Margaret and Gabby, maybe because having three girls under ten took up too much time for Penny to remember to drag out the camera or maybe there hadn't been that many memories with Emma that she'd wanted to record. Either way, Emma told herself, it didn't matter. Momma had been gone for more than two decades, and Emma had outgrown the need for a mother a long time ago. Yet even as she thought that, it made her think of Scout and wonder if anyone ever really outgrew the need for a mother who loved them unconditionally.

Big questions to ponder some other time, like when she was in Machu Picchu, climbing some ancient ruins with a group of schoolchildren, far, far away from Harbor Cove.

Besides, this was a good time, with the family quiet and getting ready to eat, to tell them about the Atlas Foundation. But as Emma tried to screw up the courage to drop the news, what came out instead was, "Can you pass the potatoes?"

Gabby handed her the dish. "Em, do you want to do that tonight? I think Grandma still has the player so we can watch those old DVDs on the television."

"I'm not the sentimental type, Gabs. I don't need to watch those movies." She skipped the meat loaf and scooped up a hearty portion of green beans along with a few spoonfuls of the warm quinoa salad Grandma had made especially for Emma.

"It's been a long time since we've seen them," Gabby said. "Like, what, ten years? Remember the night when we all stayed up late, drinking hot cocoa and popping popcorn and watching all the old movies?"

"That was you and Meggy. I fell asleep early." Because watching all those happy memories of her sisters with a woman she didn't even remember had been oddly hurtful. As if Gabby and Margaret had another family all their own, one that Emma had never been a part of. Every time her older sisters trotted out their memories, Emma wished she could remember their mother like they did, but Momma still remained a wisp of a memory. An ideal that Emma wished she could aspire to, if only she knew how. "Grandma, these potatoes are delish."

"I made them with that vegan butter you like."

Harry took another scoop of mashed potatoes and plopped it on his plate. He was a tall man with gray hair and had that distinguished look about him. He'd moved in next door to Grandma about a year ago, and for the past couple of months he'd been doing his best to date her, even if Grandma remained stubborn—or played hard to get, Emma wasn't sure which. "They're delicious, Eleanor," he said. "Might even convince me to become a vegetarian."

"If you do, I won't ever serve you my roast beef again." Grandma raised her chin, all defiant, as if she really would do such a thing. The grandmother that Emma knew couldn't hold a hard line if it was glued to her hand. She was, in the best of ways, a pushover.

"And that is my favorite meal every Sunday." Harry thought a moment. He was sitting to Grandma's right, while she sat at one end of the table. "Yes, I don't think I could live without it, Eleanor."

Grandma blushed. Actually blushed. "Well, Harry, I'm glad you like it."

"Almost as much as I like you." He winked.

There was a pause in the conversation, and Emma straightened her spine, let out a breath, and started to speak. "So, I wanted to tell you guys some—"

The front door opened, and Jake came striding in. He dropped his backpack with all his camera gear in the foyer. "Sorry I'm late, Grandma El. Hope you saved me some mashed potatoes." He came into the dining room, bent down, and gave Gabby a giant kiss. "And my favorite girl."

Gabby laughed. "You're a dork."

"And yet you"—he slid into the seat beside her—"love me regardless."

"Thank you, Eleanor, for another wonderful meal, with the best company a man could ask for." Harry's hand covered hers, and he gave it a little squeeze.

Grandma gasped. "Harry Erlich, what are you doing?"

"If you don't recognize flirting at our age, then I don't know what to tell you."

"Exactly. We are far too old for such foolishness."

Emma bit back a laugh. Watching the two of them was like watching a couple of middle schoolers pretend they didn't like each other. Between Grandma and Harry, and Gabby and Jake, Emma felt decidedly like the odd man out. A true fifth wheel.

"Well, not everyone at this table is too old for a little flirting," Grandma said, turning her attention to Emma.

Oh crap. Emma wanted to shrink down in her chair. She knew what was coming next.

"I met that Luke of yours, and he seems like such a nice young man," Grandma said. "As handsome as the night is young, and as charming as can be."

"He's not my Luke," Emma said.

Gabby waved a fork at her. "Technically, Em, he is. At least legally."

Emma groaned. Why had she ever told her family about what happened back in Nevada? "The annulment will be final in a couple of weeks, so don't go inviting him to family dinners or anything, Grandma. He is not part of the family."

Gabby with the fork again. "Technically—"

Emma grabbed her sister's fork out of her hand. "You are not helping things."

"I already told him he would be welcome at a family dinner, should you two stay together," Grandma said. "That's for when you come around, my dear Emma, and see what a catch he is."

Emma rolled her eyes. "Grandma, I'm not going to do that."

"Yet," Grandma said. "Either way, there is always room at this table for more family."

That was one of the things Emma loved best about her grandmother. Anyone who came into their circle was welcomed with open arms. Over the years, there'd been dozens of people who had sat at this table, from folks she'd met at church to the editor of the newspaper to a new neighbor. Coming to Grandma's was like coming home—and having really good food.

"I can see these two aren't too old for a little flirting." Harry nodded toward Gabby and Jake, who were sitting so close together that their shoulders touched. Every once in a while, Jake would glance over at Gabby with a look of total adoration, and she would sneak looks at him in return. "Perhaps we should take a cue from the youngsters, Ella Bella."

"Harry Erlich, I have no idea where you get such cockamamie ideas." Grandma plucked a roll out of the basket. But there was a hint of a smile on her face.

If Emma was the settling-down kind, she'd want someone whose face softened the way Jake's did when he looked at Gabby and Harry's did when he glanced at Grandma. For a fleeting second, Emma wondered if Luke would ever look at her like that, if she stuck it out and gave their marriage a try. Canceled the annulment, stuck with the impulsive commitment she'd made back at the resort, and saw if she actually liked being Mrs. Luke Carter.

"What do you think about a September wedding, Grandma El?" Jake asked. "Gabby and I are thinking we might want to start a family soon and—"

Grandma let out a squeal of joy. "A great-grandchild? Oh my! I can't wait!"

Thank God someone had changed the subject away from Emma's nonexistent love life. Maybe Grandma would forget all about Luke and her family dinner invitation and put all her attention on Gabby's nuptials.

"Whoa, whoa, not yet, Grandma," Gabby said, putting up her hands. "We're going to get married first, buy a house, take some time to settle in..."

Grandma buttered the roll and then passed the basket to Jake, who took two for himself. "Whenever you want to start having babies is a good time for me. I always wished Margaret and Mike would have had some but it seems not. And Emma—"

Emma waved off that idea before it could even get off the ground. "Don't look at me. I am not mom material."

"That is not true." Grandma wagged a finger at her. "I saw you with those children at the hotel. You were as patient as a nun and just as sweet as can be. You'd make a wonderful mother, Emma Jean. You'd be just like Penny. She was like that with you three."

"Momma was awesome," Gabby said. "I remember her reading me books before bedtime. She'd do all the voices and everything."

"You girls might not know this," Grandma said as she ate a bite of meat loaf, "but your mother was just like Emma when she was young. She swore up and down that she'd never have kids. Then she met your father and fell in love. The second Margaret was born, Penny was head over heels. I think she would have had ten kids if she could have."

"I can't imagine more Monroe girls." Jake laughed and gave Gabby a teasing jab. "That might be more than any of the men in Harbor Cove could handle."

She poked him in the ribs. "Watch it, mister. You're still on probation."

"And when does this probation end, my wife-to-be?" Jake brought his face close to Gabby's, the two of them caught in a moment all their own.

"Maybe right now." She planted a quick kiss on his cheek and then spun back to her sister. "I agree with Grandma, Em. You're so great with kids. Maybe you should expand the hotel program this fall."

Here was her opportunity, and if she let it slip by again, there might never be a right time to tell them. "I'm leaving Harbor Cove in July."

The entire conversation ground to a halt, and four pairs of eyes stared at her. "You're what?" Grandma said. "But…but…that's only a month away. I thought you didn't have a definite date for leaving."

"I'll come back for Gabby's wedding, of course, and Diana's…maybe." Already, Emma could see the airfare adding up to an impossible amount of money. She had some savings, but it would disappear quickly if she had to keep flying back home. "I have a really great opportunity with this foundation that's helping children around the world."

"The Red Cross? UNICEF?" Grandma asked.

"No, not them. This is a foundation that was created by the father of one of the brides I met." Emma put up her hands, warding off the arguments she already knew were coming. "I know that probably sounds risky because I don't know the founder all that well, but the Atlas Foundation has a great business plan, and I think they're going to do amazing things."

"I've never heard of them," Gabby said.

"That's because they're pretty new." Really new, as in hadn't even started their first project yet. But Emma didn't say that. If she did, her family would lose it. "But like I said, they have a great business plan."

"So you've seen it?" Gabby said. "What are they concentrating on? How are they doing the fundraising? I know that can be a tough road to climb for a new charity."

"Well, I haven't really seen the actual plan. Karl Jensen, he's the founder, he just gave me the broad strokes. But he's got a lot of money and is funding a good portion of it himself." Emma could hear the apology in her voice. Mistake Number 502. She should have asked for more details instead of getting excited and going all in before she knew for sure if the ground was stable. "They're going to be setting up learning opportunities for children in underserved countries, run by volunteers like me. Schools, art academies, dance lessons, all kinds of things that will help fill in the learning gaps and give these children stability."

"What country are you going to?" Grandma asked.

"Well, I don't really know that yet. Karl is working out some kinks in the travel plans. He said he'll announce a destination soon."

Silence again. Gabby was the first to speak. "Em, no offense, but did you thoroughly check this organization out? I mean, it sounds kind of flimsy right now."

"Of course I checked them out." Not entirely the truth, Emma realized. She'd talked to Karl a couple times, exchanged some emails with the director Karl had hired, and had been anxiously awaiting the details, along with a dozen other volunteers who had signed on in the early days. Yes, there had been some nervous chatter on social media about being a little over a month out and not having a firm destination, but Emma was sure that would all get sorted out.

It had to. This was her escape plan, and she didn't have a backup.

"Some of those countries can be pretty dangerous," Jake said. "Do they have plans for security and safe housing for the volunteers? You see stuff on the news all the time."

"They've got it all under control." Emma's gaze landed on her sister and then her grandmother. "Will you all just trust me on this?"

Gabby shifted in her chair. "Em, you've made some... questionable choices in the past. There was that last-minute trip to Puerto Rico with that college group that forgot to book a place to stay and the hiking trip where the guide got you all lost because he'd never been there before, and then there's the...marriage thing."

Emma bristled. Okay, maybe those had been hasty, foolish choices, but she wasn't that person anymore. For the most part. "I hate how you all look at me like I'm some kind of idiot. Everyone makes mistakes, Gabby, even you. This is not a mistake. It's going to change lives, and I'm going to be a part of it."

A tiny voice in the back of Emma's head was asking all the same questions as Gabby. Had she researched it enough? Could she trust someone she'd met only a couple of times? Was she being foolish in giving up everything to make this happen?

"We are your family, and that means we will support you no matter what," Grandma said. "I think it's wonderful that you're continuing your work with children, although I hate that you're going to be so far away."

"Thank you, Grandma," Emma said. At least one

person at this table didn't think she was being stupid. Then she saw Gabby start to speak, undoubtedly to voice another criticism, and Emma popped to her feet. "Who wants some vegan apple crumb pie?" She pushed away from the table and tossed her napkin into her seat. "I do. I want pie. No, I *need* pie."

She hurried into the kitchen, her chest tight, her breathing rushed. She placed her hands on either side of the sink and drew in a deep breath. Another.

"Are you okay?"

Emma felt the light touch of Grandma's hand on her back. She nodded because she didn't trust herself to turn around and not lose her cool. "I'm fine. I...I...I just need a glass of water." She sprang to the side and fumbled in the cabinet for a glass then flicked on the water.

"You have a full glass in the dining room. What is going on, Emma? Was it everyone asking you questions back there? We're not trying to be mean. We just worry about you. I'm sorry if it upset you."

"It's okay, Grandma. I'm just a little stressed. And although I don't want to admit it to Gabby, because she'll just tell me how right she was—again—I am..." Emma blinked back the tears in her eyes. Her cheeks burned, and her stomach twisted. "I am worried that I'm making a mistake, like I did with that whole marriage thing."

Grandma took both of Emma's hands in her own. Her kind eyes held no judgment, only love and understanding. "Those aren't mistakes. They're you having the guts to go after what you want. You don't want to have a life full of regrets because you didn't chase after your wishes and dreams."

"I don't know about that." Emma sighed. "How do I know if I'm making the right decision?"

Grandma thought for a moment. The clock on the kitchen wall ticked softly in the background. "When a bird builds a nest, it knows exactly what materials to gather, what place to choose, and how to construct a pretty complicated home, given that it's only working with a beak. Birds are born with those instincts, and that's how they can create new life and keep moving forward. We're all born with instincts that tell us when we're taking the right path, or heading down the wrong road. The key is to learn to listen to what your gut is saying."

Emma thought of the feather she had given Scout. If only she had a magic feather to show her which path to take, which place to go.

Grandma brushed a tendril of hair off Emma's forehead. "What is your gut saying right now?"

Emma couldn't hear her gut, not above the hundreds of questions and doubts and fears rolling around inside her. "That I really need a piece of pie."

❧☙

"Miss Emma can draw flowers real good. She made some pink ones and some yellow ones and some blue ones. I liked the yellow ones a lot. They were really pretty. Miss Emma is really pretty, too. Don't you think so, Daddy?"

Scout had been going on for at least thirty minutes straight about her morning at the hotel with Emma. Without a doubt, Emma Monroe's number-one fan was sitting right here at Uncle Ray's kitchen table, chattering along while Luke tried to figure out a budget for getting Phase One of the Berry Circle project back on track. So far, he knew what Emma's favorite color was—pink, just like Scout—what her favorite toy was when she was a little girl—a stuffed dog named Peanut—and what her favorite pizza was—vegetable, which Scout pronounced yucky. It was more than he'd learned about his wife ever since he had met her.

And that was when Luke was only half listening because he was busy crunching numbers and typing up a report.

"Daddy, are you listening to me?"

"Uh-huh." The overtime figures were a little too high. He flipped to a new sheet of paper and started figuring out the cost of hiring one more drywall team, comparing that against the cost of overtime with the crew he already had. That might be a better option, and if he had a second trained crew, he could bring them in if either of the other projects fell behind.

"I wish Miss Emma lived here. Then she could draw with me and talk to me." Scout sighed and dropped her head onto her arms. "You're always working, Daddy."

"I know, Bean. I'm sorry." He gave her an absentminded head rub and then went back to adding and multiplying. The report was only a third of the way done, and the numbers were still too rough. So many details to manage, but Luke wouldn't have it any other way. This was where he thrived—in the pressure and the chaos of the job.

Unless there was a four-year-old tugging on his arm. "Daddy, can we go to the park? I wanna go outside."

He glanced at his watch. Already past six. More than an hour until bedtime. One very long hour at this rate. "It's going to be dark soon, Scout."

"Then let's watch a movie. Come on, Daddy. I'm bored."

He could hear the familiar whine in Scout's voice, like an air raid siren warning him that a tantrum was on its way. He looked at the pile of papers in front of him and knew it was going to be another late night. What he needed was to clone himself so that there was someone to deal with Scout while he got some work done. "Where's Uncle Ray? See if he wants to watch a movie."

"He went to see his friends." Scout sighed. "Daddy, I'm *bored*."

That meant Ray had walked down to the VFW for a cigar and a little trading of some war stories. Well, at least Ray was out, which was better than him staying cooped up at home and drinking alone.

"I wanna go see Mommy. Can we go see Mommy?"

"Scout, I have very important work to do. Can you just watch *Paw Patrol* for a few minutes and let me finish up?" Yes, he was letting the television be his babysitter, and he knew that wasn't the best option, but it was the only one he had. He'd already lost track twice of what he was calculating. Luke bit back his annoyance at having to do the math all over again. The constant interruptions were making him forget what he'd added and what he hadn't.

Scout didn't budge. She sighed even louder and flopped onto the table like a dramatic rag doll. "Daddy, play with me. *Please*."

Frustration bubbled up inside of Luke. Why did she have to pick now, of all times, to need his attention? "Scout, I can't. I have to do this. Let me think, please."

"But, Daddy, I'm so bored." She drew out the last word on a long whine. "I need you to come play with me. Why won't you—"

"I said not now, Scout!" His voice raised, and the words were out before he could stop them. Scout scrambled off her chair and darted down the hall. Her bedroom door slammed behind her.

Luke let out a long breath. Every time he turned around, he was screwing up the most important job in his life. Even from the kitchen, he could hear Scout crying in her room. Guilt flooded him. He put down the pen and pushed away from the table.

He found her on her bed, crying into her pillow, with Bear-Bear clutched to her chest. The threadbare brown bear had seen better days, but he had been the one constant in Scout's little life. More constant than either of her parents. Luke needed to find a way to do a better job of balancing work, life, and parenting. Or he was going to seriously screw up his kid. "Scout, I'm sorry I yelled at you."

"I want Mommy."

That was the one thing he couldn't give her. He hadn't heard from Kim in a few days, which meant she either had checked out against medical advice or was deep in the program and didn't want to talk to family yet. He hoped for the latter. He kept leaving Kim voicemails and sending her photos and videos of Scout. He could only pray that Kim was doing the necessary hard work and staying on track.

Luke put a hand on his daughter's back, but she shrank away from him. "I said I'm sorry, Scout. Come on, let's go watch a movie."

She shook her head. "I don't wanna. I want Mommy."

"Mommy isn't here. You're stuck with me, kiddo." He tried to add a joke to his voice but it fell flat. "So how about we—"

"I don't want you! You're mean!" Scout scrambled off the bed, ran into the bathroom, and slammed the door. At the same time, the front door opened, and Luke's uncle came inside.

"Sounds like you're having a great night." Uncle Ray appeared in the hall outside of Scout's room. "Have you resorted to the ice cream bribery yet?"

Luke dropped onto the couch and put his head in his hands. "I'm pretty sure I'm doing parenting wrong."

Ray clapped his nephew on the shoulder. "If there's one thing I learned in the army, it's when to call in reinforcements. My bathroom is being held hostage by a four-year-old, and here are two grown men, sitting in the living room with no idea what to do. I think we need to hire a professional."

Luke glanced back at the bathroom door, still shut, with a very angry four-year-old on the other side. "I think you're right. The problem is finding someone that Scout likes."

Ray tipped his head toward the glittery picture that was hanging on the fridge. "You already know who that is, Luke. The question is—are you willing to pay the price of having the current and soon-to-be-former Mrs. Carter spending time here?"

CHAPTER 8

Sharon was back.

She didn't bring her color swatches this time. Instead, she had a pile of Martha Stewart cookbooks and a grocery bag full of pricey ingredients she'd bought at one of those little boutique markets. Marshmallow trotted alongside her with a giant purple bow taking over half of the top of her head. The bow kept flopping down, blocking Marshmallow's eyes. The dog would stop, shake, and then start trotting again. Emma was surprised poor Marshmallow didn't accidentally run into a wall.

"I want to know which recipe the chef is using for the Chilean sea bass," Sharon said as she dumped her stuff on Emma's desk. "It can be easily overcooked, especially when prepared for a crowd. I'd also like to see the chef's cordon bleu recipe. It's my favorite dish, you know, and I want it to be perfect."

Oh. My. God. Emma counted to ten in her head before she let out a breath. *What would Grandma tell me to do?*

she asked herself. Nowhere on her grandmother's list of advice was *scream in frustration*, Emma was sure. "Chef Tyler doesn't share his recipes, Sharon. But I assure you he trained at the best school, and even interned in Paris for—"

"I am very particular about my meals, and so are my guests. Now, if you see this recipe"—she opened one of the cookbooks to a page she had marked with a bright purple sticky note—"Martha Stewart adds…"

The rest of whatever Sharon said turned into a muddled blur in Emma's head because she saw Luke Carter get out of his truck and come striding into the hotel with a bag in his hand. Five minutes ago, all she'd wanted was for this endless workday to come to a close, and now a flurry of butterflies filled her abdomen. She shouldn't get this excited about seeing someone who was going to be her ex-husband very soon. Even if that soon-to-be-ex could kiss like no one she had ever met before. "Uh, Sharon, I have another appointment. I'm so sorry."

"What? But I'm a paying customer."

A paying customer who'd waltzed in here for the second time in a week without an appointment, completely hijacking Emma's day. "I know that, I assure you. But I do have other appointments, so…"

Sharon's lips pursed. She stacked up the cookbooks and pushed them into the center of Emma's desk. "Have Chef Tyler look at these recipes, and then let me know which one is the closest to his. And tell him he is more than welcome to use Martha's recipe because it's my favorite."

"I will do just that." Emma could imagine the chef's reaction to that. The hotel would be lucky if Tyler didn't quit after this wedding from hell.

Sharon got to her feet and flicked the leash. "Come

along, baby. Mommy's got things to do with people who have the time to talk to her." She clicked her tongue, and Marshmallow scrambled to her paws. At the door, the little white dog turned back and gave Emma a look that she swore was part wistful.

Emma crossed to her office door in time to see Luke heading down the hallway in her direction. Her pulse did a little skip, and she automatically pressed a hand to her hair to smooth any flyaway strands. Sharon could have grown five heads in that moment and Emma wouldn't have noticed. All of her attention was riveted on the man heading toward her. "Have a nice day, Sharon."

Sharon harrumphed and brushed past Emma, storming down the hallway and nearly colliding with Luke, as if it were Luke's fault for being there in the first place. Marshmallow jumped and yipped behind her, pausing only to notice the stranger going past them, until the two of them turned the corner.

"Uh, who was that human hurricane?" Luke asked when he stepped inside Emma's office.

She swung the door shut because Sharon was known to come storming back, demanding another answer to her endless list of questions. As Emma did that, she noticed Luke's cologne, something spicy and warm and completely enticing. She also noticed that shutting the door made them alone. Very alone. Which meant he could kiss her again, if she wanted him to. Did she?

"Sharon is just my favorite bridezilla," Emma said because it was a lot easier to fill the space between them with words rather than whatever neither of them was talking about. "She's marrying a senator's son, and she's all freaked out that the eggplant dresses won't match the aubergine tablecloths."

"I didn't understand half of what you just said. And I think I'd have to give up my man card if I knew what auber-whatever was." He chuckled. "Maybe she should do what we did and just go to a mass elopement."

"What we did was wrong." Impetuous, spontaneous, an Emma Move, which sounded so derogatory, even if her siblings were right. Seeing Luke again—and again—was also wrong, yet every inch of her body was drawn to him, to finding out more about what would coax a smile to his face. She'd already been completely charmed by Scout and found Luke's struggle to deal with a four-year-old Tasmanian devil sort of endearing. He was growing on her, lingering in her thoughts, and if someone pressed her, she'd have to admit that she'd missed seeing him over the last few days.

"Well, I'm here to apologize for bailing on lunch last weekend." Luke put the bag in his hand on top of the mountain of cookbooks on her desk. "I hope I got what you like. If not, I can go back, because an apology is no good if I give you something you dislike."

She'd brought a salad to work today. She didn't need to have lunch with Luke. Plus she had a long to-do list and should be having a working lunch, not a whatever-this-was lunch with this undefined man in her office.

Still, Emma peeked in the bag because…food. A deliciously warm and earthy smell wafted up to greet her. Her stomach rumbled. "Is that a portobello burger?"

"It is indeed."

"Those are my favorite. How did you…" Then she remembered. That first day they were in Nevada, she'd ordered a similar vegetarian sandwich at the lunch they'd had during check-in and registration. Luke had been sitting at her table, the two of them completely unaware they would be married a few hours later. Apparently, he'd been paying attention to her even then. That warmed her in a way she didn't expect and made her realize how very, very close her body was to his right now.

Emma hurried around her desk and sat down, putting three feet of wood between them. She gestured to one of the teal visitor chairs. That was better than standing so close to a man who smelled so good and whom she wanted to kiss ten times more badly after the thoughtfulness of the sandwich thing. She took her burger out of the bag and then handed him the other paper-wrapped sandwich. "What'd you get?"

"No vegetables here." He opened the parchment paper. "Ham and cheese."

"This is why we would never work," she quipped. "I'm all about vegetables, and you're all meat and potatoes. I need a man who loves green beans."

"I am sure we could find a compromise, Mrs. Carter."

She ignored the title because it stirred up all kinds of memories of the hotel room and kissing Luke and the little whisper in the back of her mind wondering what it would be like to play Mister and Missus for real. She took a bite of the sandwich, which was as amazing as it smelled. "God, this is good."

He'd already taken two man-size bites of his sandwich, which was thick with ham and slices of Swiss cheese. "I got them from that diner around the corner. Uh . . ."

"Earl's. I eat there all the time." She took another bite and then leaned back in her chair. Her stomach gave a soft rumble of joy. "I'm surprised to see you here in the middle of the day. I thought you were working on a big project."

"I am. And I should be there right now. But I have

eaten every lunch there since I started and worked later than anyone else. I think I can spare a few minutes to have lunch with my—"

"Don't say it." She put up a finger of warning.

He grinned. "Wife."

"You just like teasing me, don't you?" Despite that, Emma found herself enjoying the banter between them. She couldn't remember being with someone who was so easy to talk to and be with.

"Of course I do. Because..." He leaned across her desk, so close that she could catch the scent of his cologne, and a desire for something that had nothing to do with lunch stirred deep inside her. She forgot all about the sandwich, her vow to keep her distance, and all the reasons this thing between them would never work. She waited, almost breathless, for what he would say next. "Because your cheeks get all pink, and your eyes get all fiery."

"Fiery?" And even as she said it, she felt her cheeks heat even more. "I don't think that's a word to describe eyes."

"It is for your eyes, Emma." He cupped her jaw, his palm warm against her face. She leaned into the touch, just a bit. "You look like you want to kill me and run off to Mexico with me at the same time."

"Or I might just want to kiss you," she said. The words were out before she could stop them. "Well, I mean, I don't—"

"Emma, it's okay. Because every time I see you, I want to kiss you, too. I haven't stopped thinking about that kiss on the diner steps. It was... You know what? Let's just have a quick recap and then decide if what we remembered was as incredible as we thought." He rose up, slid his hand to cradle the back of her neck, and then skated his lips across hers.

Damn him, because he had that scruff of beard that she couldn't resist. She shifted closer, cupping his face, feeling the rough-soft surface against her palms. Their kiss deepened, becoming hot and sweet and everything Emma had ever wanted.

A hard edge pressed against her thighs, and Emma realized the realities of kissing across a desk meant it got uncomfortable pretty quickly. She drew back. "We...uh...I don't know what that was."

Luke grinned. "That was a clear sign I need to bring you sandwiches more often."

I'd like that, she thought but didn't say. Emma smoothed the paper wrapper and avoided his gaze because she knew, if she looked at him right now when she was feeling all weak and vulnerable, she'd climb right over this desk and into his lap. "You know, I've dated a lot of people, and no one has ever paid attention to what I eat. I know I'm picky because I'm vegetarian—"

"That's not picky. It's personal. And probably smarter than my fat bomb here." He hoisted his sandwich. "And Emma, if you haven't met a man who pays attention to your needs, I think that's very sad."

"It's fine. I was just surprised that you got this so right." She waved off the moment and drew the mental shades over that little chink in her armor. She didn't need anyone to remember her favorite sandwich or to bring her lunch. Yet, it was a nice and thoughtful gesture that had opened a tiny window into the parts of Emma she kept sealed off from everyone else. "Never mind, it was silly to mention it at all."

Luke set his half-eaten sandwich on the wrapper and

leaned back in his chair. "Someone much smarter than me gave me some great advice the other day. She said that the most important thing I can do is pay attention to what someone needs to hear or see or feel. Because when the other person feels heard, they stop feeling hurt."

The air in the room was charged, heated with an unspoken, deep-seated need that Emma didn't know what to do with. She could feel her body leaning in Luke's direction, every cell inside her wanting another kiss, another touch, another kind word, while her brain was throwing up caution flags. Who was this man who paid such close attention to her and had a way of making her feel like the only woman in the world? Who could silence the normally talkative Emma with a single sentence that spoke volumes about the kind of man he was? "Well, that...that...uh, sounds like good advice."

"It was. And it works when I remember it, especially when Scout is fighting bedtime." He chuckled, and the tension between them dissolved. He picked up his sandwich and took another bite. "You should move in with me so you can remind me all the time to not lose my cool."

She blinked. "Uh...did you just ask me to move in with you? Are you joking?"

"Sorta kinda." He sighed, and she could see the weight of his responsibilities heavy on his shoulders and in his tired eyes. "Scout and I argued last night, and we both went to bed unhappy. I'm pretty sure one of us—maybe both of us—was crying. I am man enough to admit that I don't know what the hell I'm doing. And that I need help."

Damn it. Was there anything more irresistible than a man being vulnerable and honest? Emma's heart softened another degree.

"I, uh, can give you the names of a couple of girls I know who do babysitting." She started to scroll through her phone but he put his hand over the screen and stopped her.

"I don't want some other girl and neither does Scout. You are pretty much the only topic of conversation in our house. Ever since that rock painting event at the hotel, Scout has talked nonstop about you. You seem to have some kind of magic touch with her, and God knows I need some help."

It both touched and terrified Emma to hear that Luke and Scout were talking about her. That he thought about her outside of their hasty marriage and saw her as someone who could work magic with a meltdown. But that wasn't who Emma was. She was the girl who screwed up, the one who drifted around, trying to find where she fit. "I'm not a professional, Luke. There are plenty of people I can recommend who have the training to take care of a child like Scout."

"I don't want them. I want *you* in our lives, Emma. You're the only person I've ever met who makes everything all right again."

Their gazes met and for a hot second, she allowed herself to indulge in the fantasy that he meant that he wanted her in another way. That this wasn't about kids and temper tantrums, but about them, and all those unspoken words that had been between them ever since the wedding. That it was about finishing whatever it was they had started just a moment ago.

"Anyway, it's a silly idea," he said. "Forget I mentioned it."

"I'm leaving town on July first anyway," she said. "It's probably better for you to find a more…permanent solution."

She'd be leaving this town, this marriage, and this man, in her past. Moving forward into the unknown all by herself. That was just the way she liked it. Alone, unencumbered, free to do what she wanted.

No one to kiss. No one to cuddle with at night.

"But...I could help you with Scout in my spare time." Apparently letting go of all that wasn't as easy as Emma told herself it was. "Because...she's adorable and I'm happy to help. As long as we have an understanding that whatever that was a moment ago wasn't about anything and won't be something more in the future." As she said the words, she realized she was telling herself that as much as him. "Because we have an appointment with a judge and an annulment in three weeks."

He nodded, and she swore she saw a flicker of disappointment in his eyes. "Understood."

She took another bite and spent a moment enjoying the taste-agasm party of the portobello mushroom seasoned to taste like a regular burger. As good as the sandwich was, and as tempting as the idea of living with him was— even if he had been joking—there was one other pesky little factor that she couldn't overlook.

That being around Luke Carter made her make foolish decisions. Like get married. Like open up to him. And worst of all, allow him and his daughter to stake a tiny claim in her heart.

❧❧❧

His daughter came rushing up the stairs, sweaty and dirty from playing in the yard. Scout's hair was a mess of tangles and leaves, and she left a trail of dirt with every step she took. Luke had been back at Ray's house for exactly three minutes and had just sat down when Scout bounded onto the porch.

"Daddy! I found a secret hiding place! Come see! Come see!"

"Kiddo, your energy could power a small country." Ray leaned back in his chair. He propped his good leg up on an overturned bucket. He drained the beer in his hands and then grabbed a new one from the cooler at his feet. "Want a cold one?"

"No. I need to work on the budget some more tonight." Since Luke had moved in, he'd noticed that Ray sat on the porch either smoking or having a beer, stuck in his depression and regrets.

In his mind, Luke imagined Emma here on this porch beside him, bringing her bright, happy spirit to all of their lives. She was lightness and joy with a smile that could rival the stars. All three of the people living in the house on Dandelion Lane could use a little more of that.

He'd spent less than an hour with her at lunch yesterday, and aside from Scout, those minutes had been some of the best he'd ever had. How could any man not see how beautiful and smart Emma Monroe was? All he'd done was buy her a sandwich, and the smile she'd gifted him with had lingered in his mind all day. Then there was that kiss...

Even the memory of touching her stirred a craving in the recesses of his soul. He'd wanted women before, slept with them, dated them, but never before had he needed someone so much. It wasn't about sex; it was about a desire for the comfort of her presence. He couldn't get enough of Emma, which left him distracted pretty much all the time.

"Daddy, you gotta come see," Scout said. "It's so cool and so dark and maybe some elves are in there!"

He loved seeing Scout excited, not throwing a tantrum, but maybe not five seconds after he'd come home from work. "Scout, I just sat down. I was going to say hi to Uncle Ray and—"

"No! Come see! Now!" She grabbed his hand and tugged. "Daddyyyyyyy!" The last was a drawn-out scream of a word that could have woken the dead. Luke made a mental note to buy earplugs.

Scout was adorable and charming...until she didn't get her way. Luke sighed.

He'd only been half kidding about wanting to hire Emma to watch Scout. Emma had been the one to do the thing Luke couldn't—bring Scout back down to earth when she was frustrated. He had to admit that he and Ray had no idea what the hell they were doing over here on Dandelion Lane, and that they were being regularly bested by someone half their size. Like Uncle Ray had said, they needed reinforcements—and soon.

It wasn't just the frustration of dealing with a pre-schooler who wanted her own way. The need for peace in this house—and in Scout's life—went much deeper. His little girl had had more than enough chaos for four years of life, robbing Scout of the easy, simple childhood she deserved.

He'd lived through eighteen years of slammed doors and holes punched in walls, and ridden the insecure roller coaster of moods and affection. He'd never known if his father would be the loving dad who took him to his first T-ball practice or the angry man who threw a beer bottle at Luke's head for not turning the TV volume down fast enough.

Scout deserved better.

Luke worked a couple of the kinks out of his neck.

Being on his feet all day instead of behind a desk had left him sorer than he'd expected. All he wanted was a minute to rest his legs and give his back a break and then he'd gladly explore the yard with Scout. "I just got home, Bean. I'm pooped. Give me a minute."

She dropped his hand, wrapped her arms around her chest, and gave him the angry pout he had come to know too well. "You are a mean daddy."

For some reason, that hurt him more than he had expected. Every parent wanted their child to love them, and he knew Scout's words were more about impatience than actual dislike, but still... "I'm sorry, Scout."

"Come *on*, Daddy. Please?" She dashed down the stairs and stopped halfway through the yard to look over her shoulder. When she didn't see Luke behind her, she gave him the angry pout again. "You gotta see before it gets dark."

The most important thing you can do is pay attention to what someone needs to hear or see or feel. Because when the other person feels heard, they stop feeling hurt.

It was good advice, good enough that he'd said the same thing to Emma at lunch and vowed to be better at doing that with his own daughter. In Scout's eyes, he could see the need for connection, the very thing Luke had wanted from his own parents. He could relax later, maybe after Scout was all grown up. Right now, his little girl needed him to pay attention.

"Okay, let's go see it." He got to his feet, ignoring the protest from his back. "But first, what do we say?"

She mumbled something that could have been *please* and was punctuated by another angry face. Scout had a thousand and one looks for angry. But for some reason, Luke was a total marshmallow when it came to his little girl. Her pouts were almost as adorable as her smiles, and he couldn't stay frustrated with her for long.

"Good enough for today." Luke trundled down the stairs. Scout grabbed his hand and then dragged him across the small yard to a partially wooded area beside the shed.

"See? Secret hiding place." She pointed into a shadowy section that Luke knew very well. "I told you so."

Weeds had nearly engulfed the space, burying everything in a tangle of thick, ivy-like greenery. Luke could see one cracked headlight, a flat tire, and a flash of bright yellow peeking out from under the weed canopy. "You still have that old bus, Uncle Ray?" he called over his shoulder.

"It's more rust bucket than bus now, but yeah," Ray said. "Once upon a time, I thought about fixing it up, but... yeah, that's not gonna happen."

Fifteen, no, twenty years ago, Uncle Ray had bought a used school bus at an auction. He and his wife had talked about turning it into a mini home that they could travel the country in, seeing all those small towns and offbeat tourist traps that Ray loved. Ray had more of a wanderlust than his wife, who'd only tolerated the bus idea. Then he'd gone off to war, come home injured, and their marriage had dissolved. The bus had sat in the yard, decaying alongside Ray's enthusiasm for the project.

"Why don't we finish it up? I could help you. We could get Old Faithful back up and running again, maybe take a trip out to see the world's largest ball of twine or whatever it was you had a hankering to go see."

The Ray that Luke had idolized had spent more time outdoors than in. He'd taught Luke how to hang drywall, run electrical, and fix an engine. He'd been part wizard and part mentor, and just a hell of a guy all around. That wasn't the Ray that Luke saw in the opposite chair. Not at all.

Scout started to clamber inside, and Luke pulled her back. "It's not safe, kid. Maybe we can get Uncle Ray to help us clean it up, and then you can play here."

"But I wanna play now, Daddy." Scout gave him her best disappointed face.

"We need to clean it first. Then you won't get your new shoes all dirty."

She gave the light-up shoes a dubious look. They'd been her must-have purchase when he took Scout to the mall this week and the only pair of shoes he could get her to wear without a protracted battle. "Okay." She sighed, as if the decision was the worst part of her day. "But can we paint it pink? I like pink. Uncle Ray likes pink."

Luke chuckled. "If you can talk your Uncle Ray into that color, I'll gladly paint this thing pink."

Scout skipped ahead, on a new mission now, distracted from the more dangerous one of climbing all over an abandoned bus. "Uncle Ray! We can make it pink! Can we do that now? Can we? Can we?"

"I'm not painting anything pink." Ray snorted. "Besides, what am I going to do with it after that?"

Luke settled into the chair beside his uncle. There'd been a spark of interest in Ray's face when Scout asked him about the bus. Maybe this was a good project to get Ray moving forward again and stop spending all his afternoons working his way through a case of Miller Lite. "You could sell it, drive it around, heck, set it up as a party bus for bachelorette parties. Doesn't matter. Scout would love it if you fixed that thing up."

"Damn it. No fair, Luke. You know I'm a softie when

it comes to that kid." He leaned toward Scout. "I'll think about fixing it up."

"Yay! Thank you, Uncle Ray!" And then she was off again.

He watched Scout, a bundle of energy and joy now chasing after a butterfly, and wondered if he had ever been like that as a kid. It didn't seem as if he had. All he remembered about his childhood were rules and anger. It was only when he came here, to Uncle Ray's, that he'd been able to be a kid. Get dirty, take things apart, climb trees. He had a lot of good memories here, and maybe it was time to build some more. "I think a project might be good for you, Ray. Get you out of the house and out of that chair."

He grunted. "Maybe."

"Then let's work on it a little tonight. We have about an hour of daylight left, and Scout and I can—"

Ray jerked to his feet, knocking the half-empty bottle to the floor as he did. "I said maybe. That doesn't mean yes. That doesn't mean anything. Just let it go, Luke."

He stormed into the house, the screen door slamming like a punctuation mark. Luke sighed. He pulled up an app, ordered yet another pizza for dinner, and then called Scout to come inside.

CHAPTER 9

Emma loaded the last box, which seemed like the heaviest of them all, into Margaret's garage with an oomph. She stepped back and stretched. She'd packaged up pretty much everything in her apartment that wasn't critical for day-to-day living and stored it in Margaret's garage until she came back to Harbor Cove or settled somewhere else. She had two weeks, more or less, before July first, the day she'd marked for departure from Harbor Cove to . . . wherever.

As the vague but promised start date neared, the chatter on the Atlas Foundation page was becoming more frantic. This morning, Karl had posted, *We're negotiating with two possible sites, one in Morocco, one in Haiti. I know it's all last minute, but hang with us. Getting a brand-new foundation off the ground takes some doing. We're going to change the world together—soon!*

Emma had sent Karl a couple of texts and left him a voicemail yesterday, asking about the status of the project. Her family was probably right—she'd rushed headlong into this commitment without knowing if the Atlas Foundation even knew what they were doing. Not to mention giving Karl nearly all of her savings, too caught up in the excitement of being part of *something* to think about the rashness of wiping out her backup plan.

What if it all turned out to be a scam? Or the foundation crumbled before it could get off the ground? What if Emma had to go crawling back to her family and admit she had made another huge mistake?

No. No matter what happened with the foundation's plans, Emma was leaving town July 1. She would make her own purpose if this one fell through. Somehow, she would figure it out.

Her phone rang, and as if she'd conjured him up simply by thinking about the future—or maybe as a result of all her texts and voicemails—Karl Jensen's number and name lit the screen. "Hey, Karl. What's up?" She kept her voice light and happy, covering for the growing stone of doubt in her gut.

"Just calling to give you an update about the group," he said. "We've got a lot of wheels in motion, Emma, so I hope you'll be patient with me a little longer."

"Of course." His daughter's wedding had been a full-out affair, one of the biggest weddings Harbor Cove had ever seen (something that Sharon had said many times she intended to outdo). Karl's daughter Leigh, unlike Sharon, had been easy to work with and a fun bride.

A week before Leigh's wedding, Karl had come into Emma's office to pay the final balance for the reception. Emma had just returned from a three-day trip backpacking through Yosemite, where she'd worked as a chaperone for the youth group from Harbor Cove Baptist

Church. Karl had seen the brochure from the travel group on her desk, which had led to a conversation about travel and working with kids. A month later, Karl had returned, all fired up about starting a foundation and making a difference across the globe. Emma had signed on without hesitation.

In other words, she'd leaped without looking first. And now she was beginning to panic that she'd made the wrong decision. "So where are we at with a destination and a date? I gave my notice at work, and come July first, I'll be ready to go wherever you want to send me. Just tell me what flight to book."

"Well, there's still some negotiating to do but it looks like we'll start in Morocco." A pause. "Yeah, for sure Morocco."

"Okay, cool. I've never been there. Which program will we be launching first? Sports? Reading?"

"We're still working that out," he said. "All the details are mere days away, I promise."

"People are starting to get kind of nervous," she said. "There's a lot of chatter on social media."

"Everything is happening as planned." His voice sounded confident, sure, and Emma chided herself for her moment of doubt.

"Great. I can't wait to get started. Wherever that is." No matter where she was going, Emma figured it had to be better than here. They chatted for a couple more minutes about the details of the reading program Emma was hoping to head, then Karl said he had to go.

But as soon as the call ended, Emma's anxiety returned. Was the chatter right? Was this all going to crumble before it got off the ground?

Had Emma made yet another foolish mistake?

Margaret opened the side door and stepped into the garage. "Are you done already?"

Emma tucked her phone in her back pocket and tried to wipe the worry from her face. "That's it." What did it say about her life that ten boxes were enough to pack up pretty much everything she owned?

Margaret's lips pinched, and her nose wrinkled. It was a look of judgment that Margaret had perfected as the bossy older sister. "Remind me again why you are doing this?"

"Because I won't have anywhere to keep my stuff after I move out of my apartment. I'm going to be flat-out at work for the next two weeks, taking care of Sharon's wedding to the senator's son, so I wanted to get ahead of the packing while I could. I really appreciate you offering to store my stuff." Already, Emma was regretting the decision because a lecture on irresponsibility came as part of any conversation with Margaret, especially since she'd agreed to rent an apartment in a building her sister owned. Being five minutes late with the rent became a whole therapy session about stepping up to the plate and being a grown-up. She'd been hoping to avoid Margaret this afternoon, but the second Emma punched in the garage door code, she had seen her eldest sister's Mercedes. Odd that Margaret was home from work in the middle of the day.

"*Temporarily* store it," Margaret reminded her. "You won't be doing this forever, this foolish around-the-world thing."

Emma shrugged. "I might. I haven't decided yet."

"Good Lord, what is wrong with you? This whole thing is so irresponsible."

And her family wondered why Emma wanted to

escape this town so badly. All her life she'd been the one who was told she didn't do this right or at the right time. She was an adult, damn it, and the days when Margaret could boss her around—or criticize her decisions—were in the past. "Irresponsible to whom? Because one of the wonders of being single is that I don't have to answer to *anyone*, not even you, Meggy. I only have to answer to myself. And I happen to think traveling light for months on end while I support a great cause is a good idea."

"Why? You're abandoning your whole family—"

"Last I checked, you were all adults."

"And now you're leaving me with an apartment to rent. That's not a very adult thing to do."

Of course, it all came back to how this affected Margaret. It wasn't that she was worried about Emma's safety or how she was going to get from Morocco to Haiti or whatever country Atlas put them in. It was whether the *apartment* would be okay. Emma shook her head. "In this market, Margaret, the apartment will be gone in five minutes, so don't worry about your investment." And then, under her breath, "Or your little sister."

"Even if the apartment rents quickly, it's still work and effort for me, and I don't have the time or energy for this." Margaret paced the garage floor as she spoke, her heels clacking against the concrete like little jack-hammers. "You wouldn't even have that apartment if it wasn't for me."

"You bring that up all the time, Margaret." Emma shook her head. "Not everyone has perfect money management skills, you know. Yeah, I know I made some stupid choices with credit cards a few years ago and got behind and tanked my credit. It happens to all kinds of people. And yes, I'm grateful that you were there and offered me an apartment to rent and some time to get my feet back on a solid financial footing."

"And are you?" Margaret's brow arched.

"Of course I am. I'm not five years old, Margaret. I know how to open a savings account." She swallowed hard and hoped her sister didn't ferret out the truth about where all of those savings had gone.

Margaret crossed her arms over her chest. "But do you have enough saved in case this foundation thing goes under and you're stuck somewhere in Timbuktu? Because I'm not paying to fly you home, and neither should Grandma."

"I have savings." Emma glanced away as she said it and immediately regretted it. Doing that was akin to a deer wearing neon pink during hunting season.

Just as Emma expected, Margaret launched an attack question. "Let me guess. A hundred bucks?"

"I had ten thousand dollars saved." She mumbled the words and cursed herself for saying anything at all. There was something so...intimidating about Margaret that it made it impossible to lie. What was wrong with her that she felt so compelled to be honest?

"*Had*? That's the past tense. What happened to the money?" Margaret paused. "Wait, did you spend your inheritance from Momma's life insurance?"

Oh crap. Here it was. The one thing she had vowed never to tell her family because they would never understand her driving need to be part of something that mattered. Something that made Emma's work matter much more than coaxing a bride through plated dessert selections. The Atlas Foundation was doing the kind of work that gave Emma a sense of purpose, and that had been worth every penny she put into the mission. "I didn't spend it.

I invested it in the foundation. Karl is doing great things with Atlas, and I'm part of that."

"You gave those strangers your money? *Momma's* money?" Margaret threw up her hands. "Why do you have to be so damned irresponsible, Emma? That life insurance was for you to save. Buy a house or bail you out in an emergency. It wasn't for flushing down the toilet of some supposed foundation. That is not what Momma would have wanted."

"Who made you judge and jury on Momma's life insurance, Margaret? It was my money. I get to decide how to spend it or invest it."

"Or waste it."

Emma let out a growl of frustration. Being with Margaret sometimes made her want to rip her hair out. "Why is me living my own life bothering you so much? I'm not jetting off to the moon or spending my fortune on Beanie Babies. I invested in something I believe in, something that's going to work and do good in the world."

"The whole thing is such an Emma Move," Margaret muttered.

"I hate it when you say Emma Move! That makes me sound like some kind of stupid TikTok challenge or something."

Margaret shrugged. "When the actions fit…"

God, she was so sick of Margaret's snippy comments and her "my way or failure" attitude. All her life, Emma had failed to measure up to some impossible invisible standard in her oldest sister's head. "Did you just call me out because I'm not following your script in life, Margaret? Because last I looked, your life wasn't so happy."

The words were out there, harsh and cold in the warm

garage. One of the neighbors walked by, and Margaret gave them a halfhearted wave. "You don't get to decide what my life is or isn't, Emma," Margaret said, her voice low and quiet. "You don't know what's going on inside my head, or my heart, for that matter."

Emma reached for her sister. "I'm sorry. I shouldn't have said that."

Margaret brushed invisible dirt off her pants, shrugging off Emma's touch as she did. "All my life I've been taking care of you and making sure your messes were all cleaned up. I'm the one who bails you out when you do something stupid and rash. I'm the one who rented you the apartment when you didn't have first and last, who loaned you furniture when you didn't have any. For God's sake, Emma, you're twenty-eight, and you don't even own a dresser."

"Because there was already one in the apartment. And I don't need a dresser if I'm traveling for months on end."

"Exactly my point! You have one reason after another why you can't be like the rest of us. When are you going to grow up? And stop making me take care of you?"

Emma bristled at the implication that she couldn't take care of herself. Maybe that had been the case when she was younger and a budget seemed like a four-letter word, but for the last few years, Emma had managed to not just pay her bills, but also set aside a nice chunk of savings. Yet in Margaret's mind, Emma was still that same irresponsible girl who got expelled from college and made stupid financial decisions. That moment of praise back in the diner about the kids' program at the hotel had been just that—a moment. In Margaret's mind, Emma was the family screwup and always would be. "You don't pay my rent, Margaret. I do. You just happen to own the building."

"And I charge you five hundred dollars a month less because you're my sister and because I know you can barely string together your rent, never mind an increase."

"What is this, Criticize Emma Day? Because I don't need this from the Queen Bee, not right now." Emma could feel her temper simmering and brewing, rising in her chest. She was tired of being Margaret's punching bag, of her sister thinking that, just because she was the one who owned the roof over Emma's head, it was okay to make her feel like a moron who couldn't balance a checkbook.

"Apparently you do because you're giving thousands of dollars to someone you barely know and planning a trip to God only knows where, without even saving enough money to come back home. You're in such a hurry to get out of this town you don't take a second to think things through, Emma."

There were kernels of truth in those words, but Emma ignored them. A fire was boiling inside her, fueled by the argument and the scary reality that her sister had a point that Emma didn't want to accept. "I am tired of not living up to your impossible standards, Margaret. I am done. Done with this argument, done with you, and done with your screwed-up-little-sister-bargain apartment."

"What are you talking about?"

Emma waved at the shelves and the neatly stowed boxes that contained pretty much everything she owned. "You want that apartment and that extra five hundred dollars a month so badly, you can have it. I'll be out by tomorrow night."

"And back by Friday, I'm sure." Margaret rolled her

eyes. "Yet another impulsive Emma Move that you'll end up regretting. Why am I even surprised?"

"For the last time, stop calling it an Emma Move," Emma said, even as she knew that what she was doing was all the things Margaret had called her. Impetuous, rash, impulsive. "I'm not a child. You need to stop treating me like one."

"Then stop acting like one." Margaret shook her head. Her dark hair stayed in its tight chignon, as if not a strand dared to move. "I have to get to work, and you, apparently, have to hurry up and screw up your life. Again."

❦❦❦

Luke was on the job site before the sun even rose. Scout was with Uncle Ray, who had promised to get up in time to take her to daycare. Luke had called Ray twice, getting a very grumpy *I'm up already* the second time. In the background, Luke could hear a very awake and very cranky Scout demanding marshmallows in her oatmeal and telling Uncle Ray she had no intention of wearing shoes to daycare. Luke hung up the phone, secretly relieved he didn't have to have that battle this morning.

On the dash of his truck, Luke had an envelope addressed to the rehab center where Kim was, ready to be dropped at the post office on his lunch break. She'd finally FaceTimed with their daughter last night and spent over an hour talking to Scout, which had been exactly what their daughter needed. Kim had looked good, healthier, and it seemed like she was doing well in the program.

When Kim was done talking to Scout, he took the phone and had a few minutes of awkward conversation with his ex. They weren't acrimonious exactly, more like strangers who were bound together for life in order to co-parent. For Scout's sake, Luke vowed to find a way to become more connected with Kim and build a friendly relationship. Down the road, there would be first communions and soccer games and a hundred other times when he and Kim would have to set aside their differences for Scout's sake. It would be nice if his daughter's childhood contained two parents who got along, even if they weren't together as a couple.

Then maybe Scout would stop acting out. He'd read somewhere that kids who went through chaos in their home life reacted by misbehaving. He had a pretty extensive Google history on "ways to help your kid get through major life upheavals." The overall message? Consistency and calm, two things that were hard to find in the house on Dandelion Lane right now.

Last night had been another bath-to-bedtime battle with Scout that lasted until after ten. He finally allowed her to climb into bed with him, and within five minutes, she was out like a light while Luke stayed awake until one in the morning, running numbers, making lists, and worrying about making the deadlines he'd set. There were a lot of people depending on him—his daughter included—to make this job work out. Failure was not on the table.

But no matter how hard he tried, he couldn't seem to make anything work right now. His relationship with his daughter, getting enough work done, getting Ray to climb out of his depression, or figuring out what this thing with Emma was or should be. One thing at a time, Luke reminded himself. Tackle one thing and then the next. At least work was going well, and it looked like they'd be on time and under budget.

"Boss?" Jerry, a lanky kid in his early twenties, poked

his head up the staircase. His hard hat was askew, and his safety goggles were in his pocket. Soon as he saw Luke, he scrambled to put on the glasses and set the hat on his head correctly. Luke made a mental note to have another safety briefing with the crew. "Foundation guys say the pour is going to be late today. Truck died on the way over here, so they're sending another one."

Yet another setback that Luke hadn't anticipated. So much for being on time. He thought for a second, running schedules and costs through his mind, sorting and re-sorting options like assembling a jigsaw puzzle. "Switch the crew that was going to help the masonry guys over to house twenty-four. They can start framing that while we wait on the pour. Then have the masonry guys set the frames for the driveways in the new section that we're pouring next week."

"Sounds good." Jerry nodded and started to walk away. Then he pivoted back. "Oh, and there's a woman here to see you."

Probably one of the subs. Berry Circle had two female-run crews on the project, one for the foundation work and another for drywall. He'd only been on the job for a couple weeks, barely enough time to get settled and meet everyone, but the crews that had been hired all seemed to do good, quality work. There'd been some grumbling about the accelerated schedule, which Luke had expected. A few more days and they should be back to normal working hours—if there were no weather or other delays.

Luke picked his way through the half-constructed, two-story Dutch Colonial, across floors crisscrossed with electrical wires and tools. The men were starting to filter in for the day as the sun began to rise, and soon the sounds of power tools and the scent of fresh-cut wood would fill the air. Those sounds and scents were like music to Luke's ears. He loved this work, the tactility of it, the way an empty lot could go from dirt to home in a matter of weeks. He missed being hands-on and seeing all that take shape because of his own hard work. Maybe someday he'd buy a house and fix it up, like the old days when he'd worked for Stadler Homes doing renovation work.

On the front lawn that was still more mud than grass, he saw a familiar figure clad in a pair of black running tights, a bright pink Dri-Fit tank top, and running shoes. Emma had her hair in a ponytail and headphones dangling from one ear. She was fiddling with her phone, and he took a moment to drink in her beauty. He hadn't seen her in a week, but it felt like a year since that conversation in her office.

It was like a clichéd scene from a movie with the sun rising behind her, casting her in a little glow. She was breathtaking and completely unaware of the power she had over men. Luke wasn't the only man to be dumbfounded by the simplicity of Emma's beauty because several of the guys on the site had also paused to check her out.

She had no idea how she affected him, how much he wanted to kiss her again, or how often she invaded his thoughts. Maybe that was for the best, considering their annulment was coming up in a couple of weeks. After that, the two of them could walk away, leaving what could have been a huge mistake in their past. Either way, he was definitely going to miss running into this woman who only intrigued him more the longer he knew her. "Hey, Emma. What brings you by so early in the morning?"

"I was out for my run, and I saw the signs for the sub-division." She worried her bottom lip. "Well...that's not entirely true, Luke. I came by here on purpose because

I kind of created a major problem in my life yesterday. Can we talk?"

"Sure." He came down the porch stairs and led her away from the rising crescendo of workers getting settled in for the day. Luke and Emma stopped beside his pickup truck and stood on a small patch of stubborn weeds that kept their shoes out of the mud. "What's up?"

She squinted up at him. "Does that offer still stand?"

It took him a second to remember his hasty joke of an idea, blurted out when he brought her lunch. He'd been overwhelmed and scared that he was going to fail as a father, and all he could see was how tenderly and easily Emma got through to his daughter and how happy Emma's presence had made Scout. All day after the craft event, Scout had talked about Emma this and Emma that, so much so that it sounded like Emma had become her instant best friend. There was a part of Luke that was envious of that insta-connection and a part that wanted to know how the hell to do the same. Until then, he was a single dad who was drowning more by the day. "To move in and help with Scout?" He scoffed as if it was a joke. "Lord knows I need help there, if you know anyone."

There was a part of him that had missed waking up with her ever since they left Nevada. And another part that even here, in the bright sunshine with his entire crew as an audience, was dying to kiss her again but he didn't add either thought to the conversation.

"Oh. Okay." She worried her bottom lip and he swore she looked like she was about to cry.

"Why? What's wrong?"

"Yesterday, I had a huge fight with my older sister who also happens to be my landlord. I may or may not have told her I didn't need her stupid apartment and now I kinda…"

"Don't have a place to live?"

"I mean, I could stay with Gabby or Grandma, but that would mean telling them all that I screwed up. Yet again." She rolled her eyes. "In case you haven't noticed, I have a tendency to jump first and ask questions later."

"In case you forgot, I jumped with you the last time you did that." He grinned. The sun had moved higher in the sky, casting a bright beam straight into Luke's eyes. He shifted right, shading his eyes with his hand. "You go with your instincts, Emma. Not many people do that. I really admire that about you."

She blushed. "Well, thank you. My sister Margaret would call it acting irresponsibly and foolishly, but I like your interpretation better."

"It's not an interpretation. It's the truth. You did that with Scout with the feather and the whole thing about the birdhouse. You're smart as hell, and you take the risks most of us are too terrified to take."

"One of those risks might just backfire on me." She let out a long breath, and instead of telling him more, she returned to her original question. "Anyway, did you really mean it? Do you want me to move in and help with Scout?"

"I really mean it, not just because I need someone, but because I need *you*. You're the best choice all around, Emma." Both on a personal and parental level. Last week at lunch, Emma had made it clear that she had no interest in dating him. Maybe that meant she wasn't as attracted to him as he was to her, and all she wanted was a job. He should be glad because he was juggling enough plates right now, without adding on a relationship one.

"I was thinking I could move in, say"—she paused and toed at the ground—"um, tonight?"

Tonight? He shouldn't be surprised. They had, after all, gotten married after a five-minute conversation. It seemed almost glacially slow to move in together after being in the same town for two weeks. Either way, he needed the help with Scout, like, yesterday. "Of course. We have a spare bedroom, and I can come by after work to pick up your things—"

"I don't have much for things. I travel light, Luke." She started to turn away but then pivoted back. "And don't get any ideas that this is some kind of forever thing."

"Despite the fact that we did pledge forever just a month or so ago." Why did he feel compelled to keep mentioning that? They both knew it had been an impetuous decision that would be untangled soon.

Maybe there was a part of him that wanted the forever to last. To have her in his arms again and feel her stir when the morning sun began to rise. To kiss her before his first cup of coffee and at the end of every day. Maybe he wanted that fantasy he'd bought into that day at the resort, thinking that, with Emma, he could have everything he'd always wanted and never dared imagine existed.

"That... that was a mistake," she said, and any romantic thoughts he was having were good and doused as she spoke the truth he'd been hoping she still didn't feel. "This thing we're doing, this is a job for me. I'm not doing it to get a boyfriend or a husband or to make you fall in love with me. I'm here to earn some money before I set out on my trip, and if I earn enough, I can leave even earlier than I planned. Deal?"

She couldn't have been clearer if she'd written her

intentions on his arm in permanent ink. The disappointment that she would be gone soon lingered, stubborn and
solid. "Why do you want to leave earlier? Did something
happen?"

"My family happened." Her gaze went to the job site
for a second but then she shook her head and returned her
attention to him. "So do we have a deal or not?"

He'd be a fool to turn down the help with Scout,
regardless of where this was going to go later, if it went
anywhere at all. Having Emma in his house, though, in
the bedroom right next door, was going to be a temptation,
no matter how he looked at it. He hadn't married her just
for the free seminar. There'd been a whole lot of interest
and infatuation mixed into that equation, feelings that had
only grown since he'd come to Harbor Cove. "I'd love to
have your help as soon as you can be there."

"Great. Text me the address. I'll see you after work."
She stuffed the other headphone back in her ear and
then set off down the road. She jogged a couple of steps
and then turned back. Her face, all serious and tough a
second ago, softened into a grateful smile, and the spark
that had drawn him to her from the very first yoga class
lit her eyes. "Thanks, Luke. I appreciate it."

"Me too, Emma. More than you know." Behind him,
he could hear the workers pause, clearly eavesdropping
on the boss's conversation with a very pretty girl. He
took a step closer to her and lowered his voice. "I'm also
looking forward to spending time with you again."

"This isn't anything like…that. It's business. That's
all."

"Of course it is," he said, knowing full well that every
inch of his brain and body disagreed. His gaze dropped to
the curve of her lips and a craving rose inside him. This

idea was either going to be the worst one Luke had ever had, or the one that completely changed his life.

Before he could think about how much he was complicating everything, Luke kissed Emma. She responded in an instant, rising on her toes, pressing into him. He wrapped one arm around her waist and cupped the back of her head with his other hand, bringing her as close as he could. She tasted like honey and sunshine, and Luke knew he was already a goner.

He heard a wolf whistle behind him, and he drew back, ending the kiss. "I'm sorry, Emma. That was..."

"The last time we do that. It has to be, Luke, or this will never work. Understood?"

He nodded. "Understood."

She started to put her headphones back in her ear. Then she paused and put a hand on his arm. "For the record, you are a very good kisser." She gave him a quick smile and then went back to her run.

As soon as Emma rounded the corner, Luke turned back to the job site. "Guys, let's get a move on today." Because he now had one more reason to hurry home.

CHAPTER 10

Eleanor Whitmore hated to admit she'd been beaten by anything, especially a hulking silver piece of technology. She glared at the computer in the office she'd carved out of a corner of a guest room. Time was ticking away, and she was going to miss her deadline if she didn't get this newfangled portal thingy to work.

She picked up the phone but realized all her granddaughters were at work, so they couldn't come help until after five, when it would be too late. She could call Leroy, but at this time of day, he was undoubtedly in a production meeting. Not to mention, Eleanor didn't want to tell the much younger editor that she couldn't keep up with the newspaper's technological advances. Even if that was partly—maybe mostly—true. That left only one option.

Harry Erlich.

What do you know about computers? she texted him.

That if you get a virus, it's a "terminal" illness. He added a winky emoji.

Eleanor rolled her eyes and, against her will, laughed at his dumb joke. *I'm having trouble logging into the newspaper's new system. If it's not too much to ask, can you help me?*

Be there before you can get a byte to eat.

Good Lord, if that was what she was going to hear all day, she'd be better off missing the deadline. Still, a smile lingered on her face, and a little bit of anticipation filled her as she watched Harry cross the lawn dividing their properties. She let him in, poured them each a cup of coffee, and then led him up the stairs to her office.

"This feels a little sinful," he whispered in her ear. "You bringing me to your bedroom."

"First of all, it's not my bedroom, it's just a bedroom in my house." For years after Russell first died, she'd been unable to imagine another man in the master bedroom she'd shared for so long with her husband. As time passed and she changed the striped bedding for a light floral, bought white nightstands instead of the antique oak, and added a chaise by the window just for reading, the room had become less theirs and more hers, allowing the germ of a thought of a different future from the past she had clung to so stubbornly. "And I'm just getting help with the computer, so don't get any ideas, Mr. Erlich."

"It's *mister* again, huh? What did I do to fall from your good graces, Ella Bella?"

No one called her Ella, never mind Ella Bella. At some point over the last month, Harry had given her a nickname. She'd told him it grated on her nerves, but he had ignored her. "You mangled my first name, that's what."

He had chuckled. "I think Ella Bella suits you better because you are a beautiful woman, Eleanor Whitmore."

She had looked at him askance. "Do you have a cataract in your eye? I am way past the age of beautiful."

"You're just getting started." He'd smiled.

Her stomach had fluttered, and she could swear her entire body had turned red. It had been a long time since a man had flirted with her so...blatantly. What on earth did Harry see in a grandma in her sixties? Whatever it was, she would be a liar if she didn't admit she was enjoying the flattery and teasing. Just a little. "Well, enough of that. If you could just show me how to set up my profile on this website, you can get back to whatever I interrupted today."

"You didn't interrupt anything except a nap in front of the Golf Channel." He slid into the leather office chair and wiggled the mouse to wake up the screen. "Okay, it looks like you have your profile set up. All you need to do is log back in and go to the dashboard."

She arched a brow. "In English, please?"

He chuckled. "Here, sit next to me." Harry grabbed a chair from the corner and dragged it over beside the office seat. He slipped on a pair of reading glasses, and Eleanor couldn't help but think how distinguished and smart the eyewear made him look. "I'll walk you through it."

She sat down and was suddenly aware of how close Harry was. A couple of inches separated their bodies. The warm notes of his cologne drifted in the air. He had a rather nice profile with a strong chin and dark eyes that were pretty much always lit by amusement. His hair had gone white a long time ago, but on him the color looked distinguished. Maybe even a little...sexy.

"Are you paying attention or just drooling over my incomparable good looks?"

She snapped her attention to the screen. "I am not drooling over you!"

"Too bad." He shot her a wink and then shifted the keyboard and mouse in front of her. "Click the upper right corner, where the little outline of a face is. That's your login." He waited while she did that, and a form field opened up. "Type in your user name and password, because that gets you into the system."

She did as he said. "And it goes right back to the same page. What am I doing wrong?"

Harry covered her hand on the mouse and wiggled it over the face image. "See? It has your name there for the account so you're all logged in now."

"Oh, uh, that's good." She could barely think with his hand touching hers. It felt so warm, so comfortable, and so right. Foolish thinking. She had had her one true love. Dreaming of a second just seemed...selfish and silly. "How do I get to the page with my column?"

"Column? You write for the *Gazette*?"

She hesitated. How could she have let that information slip out? It was all because Harry was distracting her. That's what she got for inviting that man over today.

"You don't have to tell me," Harry said. "I like thinking you're a woman of mystery."

"My granddaughters would say it's time I opened up." Not just the truth about her identity but also her heart. For now, Eleanor would start with the first one. "It's a secret, but yes, I do write for the paper. I'm Dear Amelia."

"The advice columnist?" His gaze narrowed as he put the pieces together. "Wait. I wrote to you a couple of months ago. You told me that I had given my gay grandson the greatest gift simply by loving him as he was, and that all I could do was be an example of unconditional love to my son and pray that he came around. It was wonderful advice and ultimately mended my broken family. In fact, the three of us have plans to go fishing next month. That wouldn't have happened without your help. Thank you, Eleanor."

His gratitude warmed her. Most of the time, she had no idea how the advice she gave turned out. There'd been the few endings her granddaughters had machinated, but to hear straight from Harry that her words had helped him rebuild his family...that was exactly the reason she had written the column for so long. "Chad is a wonderful person, and Roger is a stubborn goat, but I'm glad to hear they've both come around. As for you, Harry, you are..."

"I'm what?" he prodded. "If you say a frog instead of a prince, you might just break my heart."

He was definitely not a frog. As for whether he was a prince, that remained to be seen. Harry Erlich was a man who frustrated and intrigued her, a man who had decided, for some unknown reason, that Eleanor was the woman he wanted when there were plenty of other single women in their group who might be better suited. He distracted her and made her heart flutter and forced her to question that empty spot she had kept reserved at the table for far too long. But she couldn't say all that, so she settled on, "Rather unique."

"I'm going to take that as a compliment." His hand covered hers again, and her pulse tripped. How long had it been since she'd been touched by a man like that? Far too long, clearly.

"Your advice was brilliant, Ella," he said. "I was really

struggling with how to mend the fences between my son and my grandson. You made me realize it wasn't my fence to fix."

"It's hard not to meddle in the lives of our kids and grandkids. Trust me, I know." She sighed, thinking of Emma and Margaret. Both were struggling with their own journeys. If only she could make their days brighter with a cookie and a hug, like when they were little. Everything was far more complicated now that they were grown up. "I probably shouldn't have, but I wrote my own letter to Dear Amelia hoping it would nudge Emma to give Luke a chance. It comes out tonight, and I'm hoping I didn't make things worse by interfering. My granddaughter is determined to divorce that man and hightail it out of town as soon as possible."

That was two highly personal secrets she'd shared with Harry in the space of five minutes. Either she was losing her mind or things were shifting between them. Was that a good idea?

"It'll work out as it's meant to," Harry said. "That's a little nugget I got from Dear Amelia, too."

She was oddly flattered that he read her column and liked the advice she doled out each week. "Well, thank you." The silence between them felt heavy with some kind of meaning that Eleanor didn't want to unearth. "So my, uh, dashboard, as you call it, is where on this screen?"

"Right under the word DASHBOARD. Click there, and you should be into the system."

She clicked, and a new page opened up that looked very similar to a social media site. Leroy had set the whole page up for her and pinned that week's letter to the top. It looked fairly straightforward, and only a little intimidating. "Now I just answer the letter, and we let the general public comment? That sounds like a disaster waiting to happen."

"Maybe, or maybe more people will see your sensible advice and make better decisions."

She blushed. This man had such a way with words. "If you're sucking up for a Christmas present, you're about six months too early."

"You've already made plans for us to be together at Christmas?" Harry asked with a twinkle in his eye.

"Of course not. I just..." She threw up her hands. Harry made everything so convoluted. She hadn't thought about him being here at Christmas. Well, that wasn't exactly true. She had thought about it, but only in terms of whether he would like her annual prime rib dinner.

He leaned in and smiled at her. He had a nice smile, she had to admit. "Is it that hard to believe that I'm interested in you, Ella? That I like you, find you attractive, and want to date you?"

"Yes. No." The man made her so rattled that she could barely think straight. At the same time, anticipation trilled inside her. A date? What would that be like? Was she too old to do such a thing? "It's just been a long time since I dated anyone."

"But you've been a widow for many years."

"And for most of those years, I couldn't imagine anyone filling Russell's seat at the table or in my heart." But now she had the strangest urge to lean closer to Harry. She wished he would touch her again, say something else that made her pulse skitter. At the same time, she wished he would leave so she wouldn't have to deal with the flutter of emotions running through her.

"Maybe it's time you made some room, Eleanor. Life is too short to live it on the sidelines."

She looked into his deep, dark eyes and saw only kindness and honesty there. "I'm afraid, Harry," she said softly.

"Then we'll take it easy. And I'll be right here every step of the way." He brushed a lock of hair off her forehead, his gaze lingering on hers. Her heart began to race, and she shifted in her chair, ever so slightly closer to him.

He smiled the smile she had come to know and secretly treasure. He was so close now, close enough for her to see the flecks of gold in his blue eyes. "I would like to kiss you, Eleanor."

"Kiss me?" She blinked. "Here? Now?"

"What better time than the present?"

Her face flushed. "It's just…I haven't kissed anyone besides my late husband in a very, very long time."

"I hear it's just like riding a bicycle." He grinned. The combination of his smile and the joke eased her nerves. "Let's see if both of us remember how." Then Harry leaned in and kissed Eleanor. The kiss was short, sweet, yet wonderful, and left her thoughts in a dizzy mess.

Before she could react or process what just happened, he pushed the office chair back and got to his feet, putting some distance between them. True to his word, he'd only taken a baby step in the direction of dating.

"I am glad for one thing, Ella Bella," he said.

Her pulse was still racing, and she could swear her lips tingled in the aftermath of that kiss. "What's that?"

"That you're a PC girl. If you were a Mac kind of girl, I'm not so sure we'd be compatible." He shot her a wink and then headed out of the office.

❧❧❧

"You are my favorite sister." Emma scooped up another bite of cake, the second they'd tasted thus far this afternoon. The salted caramel frosting smoothed across her palate in a concert of sugar. "Chef Tyler makes amazing cakes." Being able to taste many of the chef's creations was one of the perks of working at the Harbor Cove Hotel. Today Gabby had come in for a cake tasting, starting, as she'd said, with the biggest priority of her wedding—dessert. Emma might not be in town to help her older sister plan the wedding, but she was definitely on board to give a second opinion on cake.

"I can't believe I'm cake tasting for my wedding to Jake," Gabby said. "The whole thing still seems like a dream."

Joy radiated from Gabby's pores, as bright as the diamond on her left hand. It was impossible not to be overjoyed for her sister and Jake, two of her very favorite people. Would Emma have been like this with Luke, if they'd met and dated and done it the old-fashioned way?

No, no, no. That was a train of thought that could easily derail every plan she had. Best not to even wonder.

"I think it's amazing that you're marrying your best friend and one of the hottest guys in Harbor Cove," Emma said. Jake and Gabby had been friends since childhood, with the family kind of adopting Jake over the years until it seemed as if he'd always been there. Emma had often wondered if there was something more simmering under their friendship, and when they'd fallen in love, it had seemed like the most perfect happy ending ever.

"One of the hottest guys in Harbor Cove, huh?" Gabby grinned. "Would the other one be Luke Carter?"

Emma sighed. Just thinking about him made her pulse

race. "Not gonna lie, Gabs. He is hot and also very distracting." There was no doubt Luke was handsome, with all that height, dark hair, and the muscles from working in construction. The last time she'd seen him, he had a slight tan going from being outside so much. And then there was that scruff of beard that always made her a weak woman.

Gabby laughed. "Well then, why aren't you doing something about it, Mrs. Carter? Isn't the fun of being married consummating the union?"

"So what do you think of the chocolate mousse cake? I love the raspberry filling. It has just the right amount of tartness to offset the chocolate." Changing the subject was a lot better than admitting that she had thought about consummating a lot of things with Luke Carter ever since she'd woken up in a bed with him. Doing that would be the exact opposite of breaking it off with him and going her own way. *And what would you call kissing him?*

"I see what you're doing," Gabby said, waving toward herself, "and since today is all about me being the bride, I'll let it go. So back to me. And my cake."

Emma laughed. "Don't you dare turn into one of those nightmare brides."

"What, you don't want me in your office every other day demanding to see your fabric samples?" Gabby said.

Emma rolled her eyes. "Lord, no. Sharon is bad enough. Thank God her wedding is less than two weeks away. Although I'm sure she'll have ten thousand details she'll want to address between now and then. She's driving me crazy."

Sharon had been blowing up Emma's phone and email over the last few days with constant questions and concerns. Apparently the Chilean sea bass and cordon bleu answers weren't good enough for her, so she wanted a one-on-one with Chef Tyler. That would probably make the mercurial and high-strung chef walk out, and frankly, Emma wouldn't blame him if he did. So she nixed that idea from Sharon, instead promising to give him the five pages of notes Sharon had written about the menu.

Sharon's wedding would be the last one Emma did for the Harbor Cove Hotel, which kind of seemed fitting, considering what a dumpster fire the whole thing had been. Not every bride was as big of a pain in the ass as Sharon, thankfully, or Emma would have quit long ago.

She checked her phone, and although there were five texts from Sharon, there were none from Karl, nor any emails from the foundation or new messages on the social media page. Still no departure details. The knot of worry in her stomach began to tighten. Had she made another massive mistake in trusting a near-stranger with her future?

Which, come to think of it, seemed to be a pattern lately.

Gabby slid the salted caramel cake to the side and hesitated over choosing the next of the five samples on the table. "These all look so good. I don't know which one I'm going to pick. And Em, you have no worries about me as a bride. You know me. I'm not picky about anything, except my dress, and since I'm wearing Momma's, I already have the prettiest dress in the world."

Emma thought of that day in the attic a couple of months ago, when all three sisters were together amid the memories of their mother and a shared mission to bring some joy into Grandma's life. Those days seemed a million years ago, and as much as Emma was anxious to leave Harbor Cove, a part of her was always going to be back in that attic with the women she loved most in the world. "You're going to look gorgeous in it. She would be so proud of you."

"And of you, Em. I think it's brave of you to quit everything and go work in another country."

"I thought the whole family thinks I'm being foolish. Margaret sure made herself clear on that front."

Gabby waved that off. "Margaret is a grumpy goat who loves telling everyone else what to do."

Emma laughed at the truth of that statement and then sobered. "We had a big fight yesterday and I told her I was moving out of the apartment today."

"Wait, what? You're not leaving for a couple weeks though, right? Where are you going to live?" Gabby slid the strawberry-filled yellow cake aside and chose a lemon cake with raspberries. "You could come live with me if you want. Jake's there pretty much all the time, so if you don't mind tripping over his stuff, you're more than welcome."

"And interrupt the engaged lovebirds? Thanks for the offer, but I'm good. I found a part-time job that also gives me room and board." Which was a completely cowardly way to tell her sister that she was moving in with Luke and possibly opening a whole new can of worms. It was only a couple of weeks, though. Surely she could resist entangling herself with that man any more than she already had.

"I want to hear all about the job, Em. And as for Margaret, just ignore her. She has her own crap going on, and I think she takes that frustration out on us instead of dealing with her issues."

"She says they're going on a couples' retreat in the fall," Emma said. "Frankly, I'm not sure their marriage will last that long. Things have been rocky with them for quite a while. Meggy and I had lunch a couple of weeks ago, and she opened up a little about what's going on. I got the feeling that she was downplaying how bad it is."

Gabby sighed. "I wish they would talk and work it out. Mike's such a great guy."

"Me too." Emma tried the lemon and raspberry cake. Not as good as the salted caramel one but still better than anything she'd ever tasted in a restaurant.

"As for you leaving, Em, it's not about us thinking you're making a dumb move. We all know you're smart and strong. We're just selfishly trying to get you to stay here." Gabby forked up a bite of cake. "And plan my wedding from hell."

Emma laughed. "Your wedding is going to be amazing. Especially if you pick one of these cakes. They're all so delicious."

"I know." Gabby sat back and surveyed the cake samples they'd made serious dents in eating. "I wonder if it would be too over-the-top to have five cakes instead of one."

"As a fellow dessert lover, I say go for it." Emma pushed a crumb around her plate. As much as she loved supporting her sister, there was always this emptiness whenever the girls went through a major life event. Even though Emma couldn't remember her mother, there'd been many times when she'd wondered how things would be different if Momma had lived. "I bet you wish Momma were here."

"Every single day. She's been gone for more than two decades, and I still find myself thinking, *I should tell Momma about that.*"

"I wish I had memories of her like you and Margaret do, but it's like all those years before she died are a blank wall."

"She was incredible."

"Everyone says that, and I'm sure she was, but it's just so weird. It's like I have this hole in my life where a mother should go. I'm grateful we had Grandma, of course, but I wish I had at least one memory of Momma to hold on to."

"Maybe you should spend some time in the attic. Grandma kept a lot of her things."

Maybe it would be a good idea to go through Momma's things on her own. Emma had avoided the attic most of her life, afraid that holding mementos from someone she didn't know would only make the emptiness worse. "Do you know anything about Momma starting a kids' thing? It never happened because she died before she could get it up and running."

Gabby thought for a second. "No, but I was pretty young when she died, too. It doesn't surprise me, though. It sounds exactly like something Momma would do. And look at you, following in her footsteps without even realizing it."

"I guess I am." She shrugged. "Maybe it's in my DNA or maybe it's because I know what it's like to have your childhood interrupted and suddenly turned in a new direction, but I've always wanted to help kids who are going through crap."

"Well, I think it's great." Gabby speared another bite of cake, chewed, and smiled at the taste. "I had a lot of fun volunteering at that rock painting event. If you ever need another volunteer, let me know."

"Thanks, but I only have one more event left before I leave this job." Once the Father-Daughter Dance was over, there would be no more events at the Harbor Cove Hotel that Emma was involved with. She glanced at her phone again, cringing at the six new Sharon texts. Nothing from Karl. Every hour that passed without a plan from him raised Emma's anxiety levels. It seemed like everything she touched was either falling apart or being self-sabotaged. Maybe it was being among all the cake samples in the empty ballroom or maybe it was a little bit of envy for her glowing sister's joy, but that weird feeling of missing out that she'd felt back in Nevada kept returning. "Can I ask you something?"

Gabby picked a bite off a slice of a fourth cake, a white cake layered with a lemon-and-lavender curd, and ate it. "This lemon filling is awesome. Sorry, got distracted by cake again. What'd you want to ask me?"

"How did you know Jake was the one? And how did you know you wanted to do forever with him?"

"Whoa. Are you thinking of settling down? Canceling the annulment?" Gabby looked nearly as excited at that thought as she was about her own wedding.

Emma put up her hands to stop that idea in its tracks. "No, no, of course not. I was just curious. I mean, you've known Jake practically your entire life, and then one day you decided you were in love with him. How did that happen?"

Gabby thought about it for a second. Her features softened, and a dreamy smile took over her face, and that nagging feeling of missing out tugged at Emma again. "I think I've always been in love with him, to be honest. And then one day, I just noticed him in a different way. I kept telling myself he was just a friend because I was so scared of being hurt again, of being wrong about another man. It would have broken my heart to lose Jake from my life, and I think both of us were terrified to mess up that friendship. But when he kissed me, it was like launching fireworks inside. Fireworks I've never felt with anyone else."

Emma had definitely felt fireworks with Luke, and if the number of times she replayed their handful of kisses in her head was any indication, she was still feeling them. Emma shook off the thoughts. None of this mattered. In a couple weeks, she would be in another country, living another life. There was no room in her heart, or her suitcase for that matter, for a relationship with Luke. "Well, I'm glad you two found each other. You look so happy."

"We are. Life is good, Em." Gabby's smile widened. She forked up another bite of the lemon-and-lavender cake. "Almost as good as this cake."

CHAPTER 11

Emma tucked the keys to her apartment into an envelope and slipped them through the mail slot of Margaret's downtown jewelry store after the shop had already closed for the day. They landed with a soft clunk on the carpeted floor. Okay, so maybe that was a coward's way of handling the whole thing, but frankly she didn't care.

That week's copy of the *Harbor Cove Gazette* was sitting on the stoop of the shop, folded into threes and bound with an elastic band. Emma saw the hand-drawn image of "Dear Amelia," really just a generic middle-aged woman who looked kindly and wise. The real Dear Amelia was Emma's grandmother, and she wasn't just kindly and wise but also generous. She'd been such an instrumental part of the girls' childhoods after Momma died and Dad had checked out for so long. Grandma had filled their younger years with the kind of hugs and cookies and memories only a grandma could create.

She could easily pull up to Grandma's house tonight and explain the whole mess. Grandma would open her arms and her home and take Emma in, like a wayward puppy. A part of Emma wanted to lean on Grandma's shoulders and let her family carry half the weight of her worries and rash decisions, as she'd done so many times before.

As much as Emma hated admitting it, Margaret was right. For too many years, Emma had taken the easy way out, relying on her sisters and her grandmother to get her through all the impulsive decisions she'd made. They'd been there, every time, to pick up the pieces. Heck, now she had cousin George taking care of annulling a marriage she'd given less thought to than her burrito toppings at Chipotle.

So no, she wouldn't be calling her sisters or her grandmother to bail her out this time. She'd been the one to overreact and tell Margaret she was moving out, and she was the one who had to solve her own problem of housing. Hence the decision to take Luke up on his offer, even if it hadn't been a serious one on his end.

And yes, a teeny-tiny part of her, the part that tossed and turned at night, wondered what it would be like to get to know Luke better. To find out the story behind Scout and her mom, and how a man she barely knew could kiss her like he'd been with her for a lifetime.

A distraction. That was all that would be.

As she stepped off the stoop, Emma caught just a few words of the headline under DEAR AMELIA, but the words were enough to make her sit down on the cement step and unfurl the paper. IS HE LOOKING FOR A SECOND CHANCE OR A WAY OUT?

Dear Amelia, the letter began, *I've been married a*

short time to a wonderful guy. We got married very quickly and didn't really take the time to get to know each other first. I got a little panicky after the wedding and went back home to my family. My husband has arrived in town, and I think he wants to give it another go. I'm afraid to ask him if he wants a second chance or if he's just here to tell me it's over. What should I do?

Signed, *Nervous New Bride*

"Grandma, I can't believe you did this," Emma muttered. There in black and white was Emma's life, pretty much word for word, instead of the misappropriated garden gnome letter. Was Grandma desperate for an interesting letter or was she trying to send Emma and Luke some not-so-subtle advice?

Either way, Emma hoped no one in Harbor Cove put it all together because that would only add up to a whole lot of well-intentioned advice that would only make the situation worse. The masochistic side of Emma kept reading, skipping to the short but direct reply from Dear Amelia.

Dear Nervous New Bride,

Although you rushed into marriage (which Dear Amelia does not recommend, but she has seen work out more than once), that doesn't mean your feelings aren't real. If seeing your husband again has you wondering about second chances, I say you quit waiting on him to make a move and just take that chance yourself. Many a squirrel has been run over by indecision. Don't be a squirrel. Hurry over to him and see where this new love ends up. A life without risks is a life without adventure.

Emma folded the paper, rewrapped it with the rubber band, and put it back on the stoop. The stuff about taking a chance with Luke was obvious but that last line— *A life without risks is a life without adventure*—sure sounded like Grandma was telling Emma to fly off to parts unknown with the Atlas Foundation. Except doing one negated the other—she couldn't be working on her marriage to Luke and be wandering solo to far-flung locales at the same time.

Emma sighed. Who knew what Grandma meant? Either way, she would undoubtedly find out at the next family dinner. Which should be super fun—not—if Margaret showed up. Emma was undoubtedly going to have to explain her new living arrangement, and she would...after she was settled in at Luke's.

She climbed back into her car, acutely aware that she was doing exactly what Grandma advised *Nervous New Bride* to do—driving to her husband. Only this wasn't for a second chance. It was for a Margaret-free living arrangement and a little extra income. That was all.

Deep down inside, she knew she was doing what she did best—running away from anything permanent. That tendency to bolt was what had kept her from having a relationship that lasted longer than a few months. It was what bounced her from job to job, place to place, searching for...

What, she frankly didn't know.

The only thing that had driven a desire to anchor down somewhere was working with the kids. She'd seen so much of herself in them and knew what it did to a kid to lose someone important or to be suddenly uprooted and then keep going through losses. She looked at kids like Gregory, Macy, and Scout and knew she didn't want them to grow up and be like herself, as skittish as a wild mustang in a corral.

Terrified, she supposed, of being hurt. Of someone letting her down. Or worse, leaving. So she left them before they could run out on her. *Great philosophy there, Emma. Just avoid and run, like some life-size game of dodgeball.*

She took out her phone and dialed her father's number. "Hey, Dad."

"Hey, kiddo. You sound down. Everything okay?"

"I'm fine. I just..." How could she explain her impetuous decision with the apartment? How everything seemed to be falling apart with the foundation? "Just stressed."

"You're completely upending your life. That's bound to be stressful." Her father paused, and when he spoke again, his voice was softer. "You've got this, Emma."

"Thanks, Dad. I think that's all I needed to hear." She told him she loved him before she said goodbye and tucked her phone away as she climbed into her car. Maybe things would work out, and all of this was just a hiccup along the way. Maybe.

The ride to where Luke lived took fifteen minutes from the main part of Harbor Cove, which meant it was a short commute to work but also a quiet enough area to make living here a huge change from her downtown apartment. Luke's uncle lived in a remote area Emma knew well from late-night high school parties in the woods. There was a lake back here, too, where she remembered camping with her friends once or twice. For the most part, the area was quiet, almost another planet from the cutesy, tourist-focused downtown.

A small ranch-style house sat at the end of a long, cracked driveway. Weeds thrust their scraggly bodies through the narrow slits in the tar, determined to reclaim the dirt. The lawn was half overgrown, as if someone had given up on mowing before finishing. Thick trees lined the backyard and shaded some kind of hulking metal shape in the back. The remains of a firepit sat beside a couple of metal lawn chairs and a metal trash can. The whole place screamed *bachelor pad* and had a bit of a serial killer vibe.

She had stayed in worse, that was for sure. That hostel in Puerto Rico, a last-minute accommodation when her trip went sideways, had been a halfway house for prisoners and barely habitable because the landlord only cared about the government check, not the safety of the people who lived there. Emma had slept with her back against the wall and the dresser against the door every night for a week. If she could do that, she could sleep just about anywhere.

Even in a room near Luke's.

She slung her backpack over her shoulder and grabbed the rolling suitcase she had packed with clothes and toiletries. Everything else could stay in the car, not that she had that much after storing the boxes at Margaret's. The door opened before she started up the walkway, and Scout came barreling down the porch. "Miss Emma! My daddy said you were coming. Can we make pictures? Want to see the frog in the yard? Let me show you my bear!"

Emma laughed. "Okay, okay. One thing at a time. Let me put my bags away, and then we can go exploring, okay?"

"Daddy says we gots to have dinner first, and I have to eat all my peas." Scout made a face. "I don't like peas."

And then Luke came out onto the porch. He was still in his work clothes—a pair of dark-wash jeans and a polo shirt with the name of the developer in the center of a small logo—which gave him a rugged, broad-shoulders-kind-of-guy aura. He looked tired but handsome as hell, and Emma questioned all over again the wisdom of yet another impetuous decision.

"We all have to eat our peas, Scout." He came down the stairs, slid the backpack off Emma's shoulders, and took the suitcase from her hands. "Isn't that right, Miss Emma?"

Damn him for being a gentleman. That kind of behavior was downright irresistible. Pair it with the scruff of his beard and she could barely concentrate. She looked away from him before she did another stupid thing like kiss her husband.

"Your dad is right, Scout, but..." Emma bent down to Scout's level. "That doesn't mean we can't play Peas and Straws first."

Scout jumped up and down. "That sounds fun! I wanna play!"

"Me too," Luke said with a laugh. "I have no idea what that is, but if it gets Scout that excited about vegetables, I'm in."

"It's just something I did when I was a kid. Drove my grandmother crazy, to be honest, but it made my sisters laugh." Many times when she was with a troubled kid at one of the hotel events or on that chaperoning trip she'd taken, Emma had relied on her childhood with Grandma and her sisters for a way to connect. When they were younger, the three of them had had a bond so tight that no one could come between them. Maybe it was because the Monroe girls had closed ranks after Momma died or maybe they all knew instinctively that they had to keep what was left of their family together. Her sisters and her grandmother had been a lifeline for so long, and Emma could only hope she could do the same for any of the dozens of kids she'd met who needed someone to support them.

Someone like Scout. The little girl had two parents who clearly loved her and an uncle who was wrapped around her finger, but she had also gone through a lot in her childhood already. Much of the acting out that Emma saw with Scout had to be because of that trauma—because it was pretty much a carbon copy of how Emma had behaved most of her life.

She trailed along behind Luke and Scout as they went into the house. The interior was dim with older furniture that kept with the bachelor theme. A threadbare couch, a beat-up recliner, and a coffee table that had been scarred almost beyond recognition. The kitchen was 1970s yellow, full of linoleum and vinyl chairs with chrome accents.

"It's a little dated," Luke said as if he'd read her mind, "but Uncle Ray loves it."

"Dated is the new retro, Luke," she said, putting on a brave face. Now that she was here, right beside him and all his tempting height and strength, she was beginning to wonder if she'd made the right choice.

And whether her hand could fit back into the mail slot to grab her keys so she could run out the door and leave Luke behind one more time, avoiding all the questions and possibilities that moving in created. Running away, just as she had so many times before. *One of these days you're going to have to grow up*, Margaret had said.

Did that day really have to be today?

❧❦❧

"I'm going to beat you, Scout!" Uncle Ray stuck his straw back into the plastic cup just as Scout did the same with her own. Luke watched the two of them inhale at the same time, but when Uncle Ray drew back, he lost suction and the pea he had just sucked onto the end of the straw landed back in the cup with a plop.

Scout grabbed her pea and popped it in her mouth. "I won!"

Luke and Emma laughed. It turned out that Peas and Straws was an excellent way to convince Scout to eat her vegetables. She was a competitive little thing—probably a lot like her father—and the goal of sucking up as many peas as possible from her cup and getting them in her mouth before her great-uncle had been irresistible. Luke hadn't had this much fun at dinner in a long, long time, if ever.

Uncle Ray wiped his eyes. "I haven't laughed that hard in years. Good job, Scout." They high-fived. Scout sat back in her chair with a satisfied grin on her face, her plate empty and every single pea in her belly.

"Another miracle brought about by the wizard Emma Monroe," Luke said. "Thank you." Emma's idea had been so simple and effective that Luke was mad at himself for not thinking of it months ago. But then again, if he had, he wouldn't have needed Emma to move in here.

"Gabby and I used to do that whenever Grandma served peas. It drove her crazy, but it got us to eat them." Emma dished up some more peas onto her plate. "And now I happen to love peas, maybe because I have so many great memories with them."

"Daddy, I finished all my dinner," Scout said. "Can I go play?"

Scout had, indeed, cleaned her plate without a single

argument. The whole evening, in fact, had been wonder-ful and…utterly normal. Like how he imagined other families did dinner everywhere else in the world.

He nodded, and Scout scrambled out of her chair. "Uncle Ray, come play Barbies with me!"

Uncle Ray tossed his napkin on his plate and got to his feet with a little groan and a back stretch. "Seems I'm being summoned."

"Dolls, Uncle Ray?" Luke arched a brow. "I might have to take a picture of that."

"If you tell any of the guys down at the VFW," Ray said, "I'll have to kill you."

Luke chuckled. He was happy to see Ray engaged and enjoying himself. The darkness that had hung so heavy on his uncle when Luke first arrived was slowly beginning to lift. Scout's exuberance and smile were behind a lot of that, Luke was sure. "Your secret is safe with me."

Ray lumbered over to the living room and dropped into his recliner. He extended the base, and Scout spread a pile of dolls across the surface. She chatted nonstop about which one was which, although they all looked exactly the same to Luke. But Ray played along, taking the entire setup very seriously. Scout put him in charge of assembling boxes into some kind of house—that truly looked more like a trailer park—while she dug through the box of accessories, sending clothes and teeny-tiny shoes all over the living room.

"The whole house is happier and calmer," Luke said to Emma. "On top of that, I feel a lot happier and calmer, more than I ever have after a meditation or yoga. I owe so much of that to you."

"I've only been here for twenty minutes. That"—she

nodded at Ray and Scout—"was all you guys. You're doing a great job with her."

Luke shrugged. "I'm winging it ninety-nine percent of the time. I gotta admit, I was mad at myself for not coming up with the idea of turning dinner into a competition. That would have saved us a lot of meltdowns."

"You just have to think like a kid." Emma fiddled with her fork, pushing a lone pea around her plate. "Some of my siblings would say I still act like one."

"Don't we all? Being a grown-up sucks." At least most of the time. Right now, with Emma beside him and Scout and Ray laughing quietly in the living room, life was pretty damned good.

"If only adulthood didn't come with bills and bedtimes, life would be a lot more fun." She shot him a smile before getting to her feet and stacking the empty plates in a pile.

He put a hand on her arm. A zing went through him, as it did every time he touched his wife. "You don't have to do that, Emma. You're not here to be the maid."

"But I am staying here rent-free, and that means I should pull my weight. Not put more on your shoulders."

"I appreciate that. But you also have a full-time job and you're helping with Scout, which can be a second job in itself, so let's compromise and do it together." He gathered the rest of the dishes and followed Emma into the kitchen. As if they'd been working together for years, she set the plates in the sink, filled it with sudsy water, and began to wash while he slipped into place beside her and picked up the other half of the job. Luke grabbed the dish towel from the stove handle and dried each dish as she handed it to him, sliding the plates and glasses into their respective cabinets. They worked in silence for a couple of minutes with only the sound of the running water and Scout's nonstop doll narrative filling the space in the kitchen.

It was...nice. Like a Hollywood version of what his life could be like...if only. If only he had met her sooner. If only they had had a normal relationship that gradually progressed to marriage. If only she wasn't leaving town and he was settling down right here. And if only she wanted him half as much as he wanted her.

He had a bone-deep craving to know everything about her, every little detail, but most of all, why Emma Monroe was so determined to put some distance between them. "I heard you telling Scout you lost your mom when you were little," he said.

She nodded as she slid the sponge along a fork, then another and then a third, the silverware stacking up in her hand as she worked. "My mother died in a car accident when I was five. I don't remember much, but I do remember my dad sitting all of us girls down to tell us what happened. The next thing I remember is moving into my grandmother's house for her to raise us." Emma sighed. "The only thing I don't remember from that time is my mom."

"That must be tough."

Emma shrugged, as if it didn't matter. "My sisters remember her. And my grandmother, of course. They tell lots of stories about her, but for me, it's like they're talking about a stranger." Emma rinsed the silverware under the faucet. "I guess if I don't remember her, I don't know what I'm missing."

"And yet you're so good with children." He took the silverware from the strainer and dried each piece before slotting it into the plastic organizer in the drawer. "I'm not kidding. It's like you have some kind of magic touch."

She plunged the sponge into a glass, swished it around, rinsed it with clean water, then did the whole process all over again, as if the words were hard to come by. "I think it's just that I understand them, especially kids who are going through stuff. I'm not saying my childhood was tough, because it wasn't, not like some of the kids I've met. We were blessed to have Grandma there to step into my mom's shoes. But there was always this...hole in our lives, especially mine, because I don't remember ever having a mom. Whenever I had an event to go to, like a birthday or graduation or whatever, I would get this feeling like I was forgetting something. I'd make these little checklists—keys, present, coat—thinking that I was leaving something behind. But I wasn't leaving some*thing*— I was missing *someone*."

Luke's heart went out to a little Emma who had missed so much, and to his own daughter, who had spent more than two months without her mother. He could only pray that Kim stuck to her program and was back in Scout's life like the mother she used to be because he didn't want to see Scout's face as filled with regret and loss as Emma's was right now. "Scout's going to go through some of that. I don't know how to prepare her, especially if things don't go well with Kim. Scout's birthday is in October, and frankly, I have no idea if her mom will be here or not, or if her mother will be in any shape to be a parent."

"If you don't mind my asking, and feel free to tell me if it's none of my business, but what happened with Scout's mom?" Emma washed the last glass and then began wiping the countertops. "I mean, are you guys still together?"

"No. We were barely together when she got pregnant with Scout." Luke dried the glass and stored it in the cabinet. "I was young and dumb back then and made decisions that weren't the best."

Emma scoffed. "Welcome to the club."

He hadn't talked about what happened with Kim to anyone other than Uncle Ray. There was just something about Emma that made him want to open up to her, to discuss the things he'd done his level best to ignore for years. The mistakes he had made, the detours he'd taken, all of which had led him here, to this kitchen, where he was washing dishes with his wife while his daughter played in the other room.

Maybe not all of those decisions had been bad.

"Kim and I knew right away that we were like oil and water together," he said. "It was the old clichés of opposites attracting. Which turns out well in movies, but in real life, not so much. The day after we broke up, Kim found out she was pregnant. She decided to keep the baby, and I told her I would pay child support and pitch in as much as I could. But..."

His gaze went to Scout, happily playing with her uncle, completely unaware of the regrets that filled her father every day. All those what-ifs and if-onlys he allowed to plague his thoughts didn't change anything. "Work consumed my life back then, and I was gone more than I was home. I was lucky if I saw Scout twice a month, and even then it was only for a couple of hours." He thought of all those years he had missed, the milestones he'd been too busy to see. And for what? To finish another job, collect another paycheck? "I was basically a drive-by dad, which made it pretty tough to establish a relationship, hell, to be any kind of parent."

Emma turned off the water and pulled the drain. Soapy water circled the sink and then disappeared. "So how did Scout end up with you?"

He handed her the towel to dry her hands and then nodded toward the back door. "Let's grab a beer and enjoy the night for a little bit." Scout was still happily playing with her dolls, but she could dash into the kitchen at any second. He didn't want her to hear anything negative about her mother, even accidentally. Scout was too young to understand such adult concepts as alcoholism and rehab, so Luke had learned to keep it simple and light. The truth was Kim's conversation to someday have with her daughter, not Luke's.

Emma and Luke crossed to a pair of metal folding chairs that flanked an extinguished firepit. The weather was warm, just a slight breeze with a hint of summer in the air. June was warming up every single day with bright, clear beautiful days and warm, breezy nights. The clouds from a quick summer storm earlier this afternoon had parted, and the night sky sparkled above them. On an ordinary day, in an ordinary marriage, this could be their life. Dinner, dishes, a few minutes alone under a starlit sky. But none of this situation was ordinary. Or permanent.

"Honestly, it's a miracle Kim even thought of me to take Scout," Luke said. "I barely knew my kid and had dumped pretty much all the parenting on Kim's shoulders. I had no idea, frankly, how much work it is to be a parent. It was wrong of me, and selfish, and if I could do it all again I sure as hell would do better." He rested his elbows on his knees and let the beer dangle between his fingers. "I regret deeply that I wasn't there for Kim, or for Scout, like I should have been. Maybe if I had been... well, truth is, I don't know if it would have changed anything."

Emma put a hand on his shoulder, a touch that said she understood the regrets he carried on his shoulders and didn't judge him as harshly as he judged himself. "You did the best you could at the time. That's really all any of us can do, Luke."

"You're probably right, but it's going to be a long time before I forgive myself for missing all of the signs that Kim needed help and that Scout needed me." He took a long sip of beer, but the beverage tasted sour and wrong. A night bird called in the distance, its lonely song carrying alone on the night air.

"Scout said her mother is in a hospital?" Emma asked.

That was what he'd told their daughter. The last thing he wanted to do was darken Scout's world with words like *alcoholism* and *detox*. If the time came when he had to, he would, but hopefully Kim would stick with her program and stay on track after she got home.

As a kid, Luke had known way too much about the pain those bottles could bring, and he prayed Scout had been spared the dark days Luke had experienced. "She's in rehab. She's been there for more than two months now." Luke toed at a charred piece of wood, nudging it back into the stone-ringed pit. He could still see Kim getting into the cab and leaving, both her and Scout crying as the cab left. Luke had tried to pick Scout up, but she'd jerked away from him to cling stubbornly to Kim's mother instead, unfamiliar and unwilling to rely on the man who'd given her his DNA and not much else.

"It was that bad that she needed rehab?" Emma asked.

He nodded. "I went to pick up Scout one day and noticed the recycling bin was overflowing with vodka bottles. Kim brushed it off, saying she'd had a party over the weekend, and I believed her. I knew Kim drank a lot, but you know, we all did in our twenties. There were always bottles in the bin, but I just didn't pay that much attention until that day. Then I came back for Scout a couple of weeks later, and the bin was filled to the brim with liquor bottles again. I finally realized that Kim had a problem. So I called her mom, and we did an intervention kind of thing, and Kim thankfully agreed to go get help."

"Wow. That's pretty awesome that you did that and even better that she agreed to go to rehab."

"I should have seen the signs earlier," he said. "I can't tell you how many times I've beaten myself up about that. I *knew* what alcoholism looked like, and I *knew* what it could do to a kid's childhood, and yet I was too damned wrapped up in my own crap to notice it in my daughter's life." He cursed and kicked a burnt log into the firepit. The guilt in his gut was a sour stone, constantly churning and reminding him of how close he had come to completely failing his little girl. "My dad was a drinker. Get a couple of beers in him and he'd turn, like the Hulk, into someone mean and cold. He'd punch holes in the wall, throw bottles at us, scream at my mother."

"Oh God, Luke. How terrifying that had to be as a kid."

"Probably explains why I left home the second I had my diploma." He went to take another sip of beer but the drink had lost its appeal. He poured the remaining alcohol onto the ground and then set the bottle on top of one of the stones. "And also probably why I'm not so good at the relationship thing, either. Loss and trauma, you know? Screws us all up somehow."

"That it does. But most of us do a good job of pretending it doesn't."

He glanced at Emma and saw an echo of himself in

her eyes. All those fears and insecurities that their pasts had saddled over their hearts. "So true."

"I'm grateful I had a good childhood despite my mother dying so young. Even though I didn't remember her, it took me a long time to get past losing her, which makes no sense at all. When I was little, I blamed myself." She shrugged. "I probably still do."

"You were, what, five? What could you have possibly done?"

"I forgot my backpack at school." She put her hand up. "I know, I know. People forget stuff; I shouldn't blame myself...I've heard all that before. But the fact remains that I forgot it, and because it was dark, my mother went to go get it. I don't even remember now what was so damned important about that backpack that I couldn't wait until morning. We had a torrential rainstorm that night, and she skidded off the road and hit a tree." Emma's voice was choked and thick. He reached over and took her hand in his. She gave his fingers a gentle squeeze. "So I know what you mean about wishing you could have a do-over."

"Kids forget stuff all the time, Emma. That's not your fault."

"But if I'd remembered it that day, she wouldn't have been out in that storm." She pulled her hand out of his to brush invisible dirt off her skirt. "I think all of my sisters carry guilt in some way about our mother's death, maybe because it seemed so wrong that someone so young could die like that. Anyway, we're all a little screwed up, like you said."

"I like spending time with you," he said. "Even if what we're talking about is a hard subject."

"We could always talk about something else. There's

a new yoga studio opening in the town next door. I was thinking of checking it out. Maybe you'd want to, too. Or..." She gestured toward the house, and when she spoke again, the softness of her voice had shifted into something brighter. "Maybe we should go back in?"

"Let's stay awhile longer." He could see her ducking and avoiding anything that smacked of getting closer or opening her heart, just like he did. Two wounded people who were doing their level best not to get hurt again or be let down by the people they loved. "You know, it's a good thing you're leaving town because we'd probably be a mess together."

"A total train wreck." She let out a little laugh. "And you should be glad you're avoiding that because I'll be somewhere on the other side of the world."

"I don't know if I'd call us a train wreck. I mean, look at Scout and the dishes. If you ask me, Emma Monroe-Carter, we can make a pretty damned good team when we want to."

"You may be right about that." She tipped her beer in his direction and tapped it against the arm of his chair. The glass made a soft clink in the quiet night. "Do you and your dad get along now?"

"Not really. Not everyone changes, you know?" He shrugged. "My parents are the ones missing out on seeing their granddaughter. I won't let Scout be around that and my dad knows it. Maybe someday he'll change, but I'm not holding my breath. I send them pictures and videos of her, especially now that I have her full time. Keeps them in the loop but at arm's length."

"Probably smart."

"I have to do what's best for my daughter. I still love my dad, even more than I did when I was a kid. As I got older, I began to understand that he was battling some kind of mental demons of his own. People cope with mental health issues in all different ways. Some crawl in a cave, some talk it out, and some turn to a bottle."

"And some of us do our level best to avoid everything," Emma whispered.

She didn't elaborate, and he didn't ask. If Emma didn't want to share more, he wasn't the kind of guy to nudge her since he lived by that sentiment pretty damned all the time himself.

"Call me a foolish optimist, but I have hope that it'll all work out eventually," he said. "And it has to, for Scout's sake, especially with her mom. Kim's a good person, and she loves Scout to death. She's just got something going on inside her head that she needs help and time to straighten out."

Emma gave him a look of shock and, maybe, a tiny bit of admiration. A smile curved across her face. "Wow. You surprise me, Luke. Most people don't look at mental health with that kind of compassion."

Luke shrugged. "Maybe they should. The world would be a much better place if we all just gave each other a break."

"Amen to that." Crickets chirped in the shrubs behind them. The lonely night bird's call was answered by another. Beside him, Emma was biting her bottom lip, something that he found so damned endearing. "Can I tell you something that even my family doesn't know?"

"Sure."

She took a deep breath. "I've been taking courses for a degree in social work for the past two years. I've been going to school online so that I can still work full time and everything. I'm hoping I can continue to carry a few credits when I start working with the foundation. If I want to make a career out of this, I know that I need at least a bachelor's to work with kids. A master's if I want to go into therapy." She toed at the ground. "I don't know why I told you all that. It's just a pipe dream, and I am so not a career kind of girl. Anyway, it's probably a terrible idea."

It touched him that she'd told him something personal and sacred. Maybe they weren't as far apart as he'd thought, if Emma was opening up about things she hadn't told anyone else. "It sounds like the perfect career for you. You're amazing with kids, Emma."

She shrugged. "Kids these days go through a lot of really tough things, and I think it helps if they have someone in their corner, even if it's just the girl at the hotel with two years of college under her belt."

He shifted closer to her, his knees almost brushing against hers. "Why do you do that? Downgrade your achievements. Your smarts."

"Because I'm the one who graduated from high school on a wish and a prayer, as my grandma would say. Margaret is the one who accomplished all the things. Graduated at the top of her class, got the degree, the husband, the successful business." She peeled part of the label away, tossing the paper into the pile of ashes. "I've spent most of my life trying to figure out what I want to be when I grow up."

"I think you've already done that. You're in school, working on a degree. You have a plan with this foundation—"

"Trust me, it's not as together as it looks." She let out a harsh laugh and peeled off another strip. "*I'm* not as together as I look."

"Stop."

"Is me peeling the label annoying you?"

"No." He put a hand on hers and met her gaze. "Nothing you do annoys me, Emma, except when you don't see your own worth. You are incredible in every way, and one of the most intriguing, determined, and giving people in my life."

Even in the dim light from the moon, he could see her cheeks flush. "I've never met a man who says what you say to me."

"Then you've been dating the wrong men."

She laughed. "You're definitely right about that. And you're also right that I struggle with compliments. A lot of what I do doesn't exactly turn out like I envisioned."

"What, an elopement at a yoga retreat wasn't your dream wedding?" He grinned. "Some of the best inventions and companies in the world came from what others viewed as risky mistakes. And you're a risk taker, where most people aren't. You have a gift with children, Emma, that's a fact. If the route you take to get to that career is different from everyone else's . . . so what? It's your route. And if you ask me, that makes it pretty special."

She rolled her eyes, but a wide smile lingered on her face. "How much of that beer did you drink?"

"Almost none." He took both her hands in his, and that familiar spark ran through his veins. He wanted to hold her, kiss her, take her back to that hotel room in Nevada and begin all over again. "I know we haven't been together very long, but it doesn't take a genius to see that you're special. The man who finally wins your heart"— even inferring that another man could be with her someday pained him deep inside—"is going to be the luckiest man on this planet."

"Yeah, maybe." She pulled her hands out of his and rose. "It's getting late. I'll see you in the morning, Luke."

Some of us do our level best to avoid everything. The foolish optimist in Luke watched Emma walk away and hoped that, someday soon, Emma would stop avoiding what was so obvious he could practically feel the truth stamped on his forehead...

Luke Carter was falling in love with his wife more and more every single day.

CHAPTER 12

Luke leaned against the doorway and watched Emma tie a bow on Scout's new dress. Emma had her hair up in a messy bun, and she'd changed out of her usual maxi dress for a soft blue one that skimmed her knees. A row of gold bracelets dangled from one wrist, making a soft clank every time she moved. She was, for lack of a better word, breathtaking.

A week had gone by since their conversation by the firepit, and Luke had noticed a decided distance between himself and Emma. She'd been here every day, helping with Scout, helping with dinner, but as soon as Scout went to bed, Emma said she was tired or had extra work to do. She'd disappear into her bedroom for the night. More than once, he'd paused by her door, debating whether to knock and ask her to talk. He'd even invited her to the new yoga studio, and she'd said she might meet him there, but when he showed up for class, Emma wasn't there. Instead, she'd gone running or meditated in her room.

Their marriage was going to be undone in a week. Emma was leaving for anywhere but here the following day. Why was he trying so hard to hold on to something she was clearly ready to let go of?

Because, he thought, as he watched her with his daughter, he could see something beautiful and rare in Emma that he couldn't quite let go of.

"I bet you're pretty excited, Scout, because you're getting ready super early. The dance isn't for another hour or so." Emma helped Scout into her new white dress shoes. "Are you looking forward to your first dance?"

"I can't wait!" Scout did a spin that made her skirt bloom around her waist. "Daddy, do you like my dress?"

"I love it, Bean." Emma had taken his daughter shopping earlier today and bought Scout's choice of a bright-yellow dress because it made her look like some Disney character she loved. Flowers decorated the toes of her new shoes and matched with the plastic butterfly necklace around her neck. Emma had even curled Scout's hair so that her normally untamable locks were soft and bouncy. "You look so grown-up and so pretty."

Scout beamed. "Thank you. I'm a big girl today."

"You are indeed." Even in the space of two months, Scout had grown so much. Was this what the next thirteen years would be like? Done and over in a blur, his daughter suddenly an adult hurrying off to college?

"Miss Emma, are you coming to the dance, too?"

"I am." And Luke's heart did a little leap at her words because it meant he'd have another chance to see her. "But I'm working, not dancing."

Scout pouted at that. "But isn't your daddy coming? To dance with you?"

Emma smiled as she bent down to fix a runaway tendril

of Scout's hair and then give the bow a final straightening. "He said he might stop by, and if he does, he'll dance with me for sure. You're all set, Scout."

"T'ank you, Miss Emma." Scout leaned into Emma and wrapped her arms around her in a tight hug. "I love you."

Emma's eyes widened but then she recovered from the surprise and hugged Scout back, whispering, "Aww, I love you too, Scout."

He felt like telling Scout, *I know how you feel because I kinda love her, too*, but of course he didn't. In the weeks they had been together, his feelings for Emma had only grown. She was thoughtful and kind, sweet and smart, and he had no idea how the hell he was going to let her go in a week.

"Daddy, I'm gonna go show Uncle Ray my dress!" Scout bounded out of the living room and headed for the kitchen where Ray was heating up leftovers for dinner.

As soon as Scout left the room, Emma rocked back on her heels, a look of total shock on her face. She swiped at her eyes and then got to her feet. "Kids, you know?"

It touched him that she was just as overwhelmed by that moment as he had been. It was easy to see how much Emma loved Scout, from the way she talked to the little girl, to her patience with every single thing. The two had bonded from that very first moment with the feather on Main Street, and Luke knew he wasn't going to be the only one heartbroken to see Emma leave.

"She's an amazing kid, isn't she? One of these days, Kim will return, and I'll be sharing custody again," Luke said. "I think it's going to break my heart not to see Scout every single day."

Emma gave him a watery smile. "I'm going to miss

that little booger when I'm on the other side of the world."

"And she's going to miss you a hell of a lot," Luke said. He paused for a breath, afraid to scare her off, to damage this fragile thing that was happening between them. "We all will, Emma. More than you realize."

Emma shot Luke a look he couldn't read. Irritation? Affection? Or maybe a little of both? "Luke, I—"

Scout, with the timing only a four-year-old could have, came running back into the room, followed by her uncle. "He thinks I look pretty, too! And can we get pizza, Daddy? Uncle Ray said it's okay."

Luke arched a brow in his uncle's direction. "Didn't we have a conversation about making healthier eating choices with a certain someone?"

Ray shrugged. "I'm a sucker for those big blue eyes. What can I say? I promise to make her eat a celery stick before she goes to bed."

"And I think we should get two pizzas, 'cuz Miss Emma likes pizza and so do you, Daddy. We can get a big one for me and Uncle Ray, and then another big one for you and Emma 'cuz she likes yucky mushrooms on her pizza and I don't."

"You don't like mushrooms?" He bent down and pretended to study her. "Are you sure you're related to me, Scout?"

She stomped her foot and crossed her arms over her chest. "I am."

He lightly ruffled her hair and laughed at her indignation. "I know. You've got my stubbornness, that's for sure."

"There's going to be food at the dance, you know," Emma said. "Including macaroni and cheese, which I think you might like just as much as pizza."

"I do! I love macaroni and cheese. Miss Emma, my tummy is so rumbly, I can't wait to get macaroni and cheese." She rubbed her belly, making everyone in the room laugh. Luke wished he could bottle every one of these memories for the days when he didn't have Scout right beside him.

"I'll make sure to save extra for you then."

"Hey, if there are any leftovers, someone else in this house loves mac and cheese, too," Ray said. "And since you're coming straight back here afterward, Emma..."

She laughed. "If there's any leftovers, I'll bring them here." Emma took both of Scout's hands in her own and swayed with her. "So, Scout, are you ready to do your best dancing tonight?"

"Yes. I'm a very good dancer." Scout spun out of Emma's grasp, making the skirt of her dress float back and forth. "Daddy says he's a bad dancer."

Emma glanced at Luke. Her eyes lit with amusement. "Really? Is that true, Mr. Carter?"

"That's the rumor going around town that I may or may not have started myself." He grinned.

Scout tugged at his sleeve. "Daddy, we should practice before we go! So's we can dance good."

"I think that's a great idea, Scout. I'd love to see your daddy dance." Emma shot him a smile and then grabbed the remote, flipping the TV to an easy-listening music station. Michael Bublé crooned from the speakers.

"I'm out of here before I get recruited to be Fred Astaire," Ray said. He turned toward the kitchen. "Have fun, kiddo."

Scout jumped up and down, as full of energy as a meteorite. "Come on, Daddy, dance with me! Please?"

How could he resist that? Especially when he could

see the excitement and joy lighting Scout's eyes. Luke pushed off from the wall and took his daughter's hands. She was half his height, so after a few minutes of swaying back and forth that made his back ache from bending over, he scooped Scout into his arms and spun around the living room. She giggled and giggled, the sound filling the room like the soft patter of a spring rain. This—this was the moment he would treasure. His daughter in his arms, her face a literal balloon of joy, and the sweet sound of her calling him *Daddy*.

The song came to an end far too soon. Scout scrambled out of his arms but held on to his hand. "Now dance with Emma, Daddy. She's all pretty, too."

"Oh, I don't know if—" But Scout was already tugging Luke toward Emma, who looked as dubious as he felt. Scout stared at them with high expectations in her eyes. Truth be told, Luke was just as much of a sucker for those big blue eyes as his uncle was. It certainly wouldn't do to disappoint Scout, not tonight. He smiled at Emma. "Shall we?"

"I think we kind of have to or someone will be quite unhappy with us," Emma said under her breath.

"And we wouldn't want that," Luke said, leaning closer to whisper in Emma's ear. God, her perfume smelled so amazing he had trouble forming a coherent thought. "Because I don't have any ice cream in the house to tame the tantrum monster."

"That would be a disaster of epic proportions." Emma laughed as she stepped into his arms. "Okay. In the interests of world peace and quiet, I'll dance with you."

"Thank you for your sacrifice for our household." He grinned as he placed one hand on her back and then caught her opposite hand with his. She fit into that space as perfectly as the missing piece to a puzzle. She always had, he realized. She'd fit into his arms, into his life, and into his family from the minute he'd met her. "I have to say I'm a pretty lucky man."

"Why's that?" She followed his lead in a four-count move of four steps back and then four steps forward. There was no stepping on toes, no stumbles. They moved together in concert, as if they'd done this a million times before.

"Because I have the most beautiful date in the world"— he gave Scout a grin that she returned with an even bigger smile—"and right now, I'm dancing with the woman of my dreams."

She paused. "Luke..."

"Em, it's just a dance." He pressed lightly on the small of her back, nudging her into dancing again. "Not a legally binding lifetime commitment."

"And that's what we both want. Right?" Emma said.

If she'd asked him that question a month ago, heck, a week ago, he would have agreed. The marriage had been a means to an end, not a love match. But as he spun Emma out and then back into his chest, he wished Etta James would never stop singing and he and Emma could keep dancing. Every word of "At Last" rang bittersweet and true, as Luke realized this might be the only time he ever got to dance with his wife.

Scout, her mission clearly accomplished, said something about finding her bear. Luke barely noticed her leaving the room.

The floral notes of Emma's perfume teased at his senses. His hand, nestled just above the curve of her buttocks, ached to explore every inch of her body. He shifted closer, until his lips brushed against her temple, a whisper of a kiss. Her breath caught, and she stumbled.

Luke caught her in his arms, giving him an excuse to haul her even closer. He could feel her heart racing against his. "Careful you don't fall."

"I won't."

"Ever?" He couldn't be imagining this moment between them, the tension in the air, the heat charging the space. Or the way she had responded to his kisses, his touch, his words over the last few weeks.

Her big blue eyes met his and held for a long moment. "It's only practice, Luke."

"You keep saying that. What if it was the real thing?" There were a hundred other implications in his question about their marriage, whatever was brewing between them now, and a future he didn't dare imagine.

"I don't do the real thing. I told you that."

He reached up and brushed a tendril of hair off her cheek. Her lips parted, and her eyes widened. If Scout wasn't just down the hall, he would have kissed Emma, long and slow and forever. "That's a shame, Mrs. Carter," he whispered, "because I think we would have rocked the real thing."

"Uh, I think you have the hang of this dancing thing now." She stepped out of his arms, avoiding and escaping again. "I need to get to the hotel early and make sure everything is set up for tonight."

"Sure. Of course." He masked his disappointment with a smile. It was probably for the best that she cut off that train of thought. His only focus should be on providing the life his daughter deserved, not on a woman who was doing everything she could to undo their spontaneous entanglement.

Scout came back into the room holding Bear-Bear. "Are you leaving, Miss Emma?"

"Yes, but I'll see you soon, Scout." She grabbed her phone from the coffee table. "You look so pretty in your dress."

"T'anks, Miss Emma. You do, too. Isn't Miss Emma pretty, Daddy?"

"She's stunning."

Emma blushed. She spun away and grabbed a light jacket from the hook by the door. "See you guys at six."

Luke passed the next hour by burying his head in budgets and timelines while Scout forced Uncle Ray to sit through a stuffed animal tea party. The war vet looked about as comfortable as a cat on a boat, but he indulged the niece he adored. Luke laughed at the sight of gruff and manly Uncle Ray holding a plastic teacup no bigger than a mini muffin. "Pinkie out, Uncle Ray."

Ray scowled at him. "Why don't you come over here and show us how it's done?"

"Yeah, Daddy. Come have a tea party!"

"I have to work, Scout. Sorry." He turned his attention back to the computer screen, but his mind kept wandering to the sound of Scout and Ray laughing, which brought him back to thoughts of dancing with Emma. "Just give me a couple of minutes."

What seemed like a second later, Scout was tugging on his sleeve. "Daddy, Uncle Ray says we gots to go or we'll be late!"

His little girl was waiting for him, looking so pretty it nearly made him cry. The email he'd been composing could wait. He shut down the laptop and got to his feet. Then Luke bent down and crooked his elbow. "Will you do me the honor of accompanying me to the Father-Daughter Dance, Miss Scout Carter?"

"Yup." She slipped her arm into his as if she'd done

this a hundred times before. Luke could practically feel the years whizzing by as he watched his daughter grow up more every second.

❦❧❦❧

If her granddaughters could meddle in the Dear Amelia column's outcome, Eleanor had decided she could, too. Emma was too stubborn to admit the truth—that she had fallen for her husband. Eleanor had seen it all over her face every time she talked about Luke and his daughter.

And if someone didn't do something about those feelings soon, it would be too late. Emma would be halfway across the world, bound and determined to stay as far away from Harbor Cove as possible.

Desperate times called for desperate measures, and in this case very, very desperate measures. Eleanor pulled out her phone and texted Harry Erlich. *I need your help with something tonight. Are you available?*

Have you lost Control...or Escape? Or just need me to find your mouse?

She rolled her eyes. This man and his terrible jokes. *If you promise not to tell any more computer jokes, I'll buy you dinner tonight.*

Is this a date? Harry texted back.

Eleanor stared at the screen. Of course this wasn't a date. Even if it involved dinner and dancing. Wait...was it a date? *No. It's a mission. But you're driving. And you should wear a tie.*

Sounds intriguing. I'll be there soon. On the dot of five thirty, Harry pulled into Eleanor's driveway in his sleek Chrysler sedan. She was waiting in the foyer and headed outside as soon as he parked in case he got any foolish notions about this being a conventional date where he needed to come to the door to fetch her. As she approached the car, Harry hopped out and came around to open the passenger's-side door. "Good evening, Ella."

"Good evening, Harry. Thank you for the ride." Goodness, he looked handsome. He'd worn gray slacks, a white button-down shirt, and a dark-blue tie with pale-gray and pink pinstripes. He'd just gotten a haircut, she noticed, and she wondered if he had done that because it was part of his routine or because he was seeing her.

He shut her door and then got back in on the driver's side. His hand hovered over the gearshift. "You have your own car and you can drive, so why are you asking me to be your chauffeur? Don't get me wrong, I am delighted to spend time with you, but I also don't want to be arrested for being an accessory to a crime, if that's what you have in mind."

"You have got to stop watching the Lifetime Movie Network. Not everyone who wants to keep something secret is plotting a murder."

He chuckled. "So what are you plotting, Eleanor Whitmore? Because you have told me very little about the plan tonight. And you look beautiful, by the way. Forgive me for not saying that the minute I saw you. You look lovely in emerald green."

She never knew what to do or say when Harry complimented her. Or whether to admit that his words warmed her and made her long for things she had thought she was long past wanting. "We are going to Bella Vita for some dinner. I think we need to have some chicken parmesan in our bellies before we do a little...meddling."

He put the car in reverse and backed out of the driveway. He was a patient driver, taking his time to look in all directions before making a move. "What kind of meddling do you have in mind?"

"My stubborn granddaughter is divorcing the man she is in love with, and I think someone should bring them together before she pulls the plug. So we are going to create a little in-person…magic tonight." There, she'd said it. Both in print and in person.

"Like grandmother, like granddaughters. It wasn't that long ago that you and your girls plotted another coup like this to shake up my family."

"And it worked out, didn't it?" She settled her purse on her lap and stared straight ahead because she'd get distracted if she looked at the strong lines of Harry's jaw. Tonight was not a night for distraction. "Sometimes people just need a little nudge in the right direction."

He chuckled as he stopped at a red light. "Sounds more like a shove in this case."

"Are you saying you don't want chicken parmesan in exchange for being my accomplice?"

He grinned and leaned over, his breath warm on her cheek. "Sweetheart, I'll be your accomplice any day, anytime. And you don't even have to feed me."

"Well…" She swallowed. "That would be easier on my wallet at least."

"Always the practical one," he said. "What is it going to take to get you to step outside your comfort zone?"

"I think involving you in my plans is a huge step outside my comfort zone." Asking a man to help her with something, relying on him, including him in something so personal—Eleanor never did that. Maybe she was getting soft as she aged.

"You may call it meddling, but I really like how important family is to you," Harry said. "The older I get, the more I realize that family is...well, everything."

"I couldn't agree with you more." A man who understood her and her fierce love for her girls was a rarity. Harry scored a few—just a handful—of brownie points.

He made a right and then turned into the parking lot for Bella Vita. There was only a handful of cars at this time of night, maybe because a good portion of the town was attending the Father's Day dance. "We're here."

The Bella Vita smelled heavenly. Frank Rossi, the owner, bustled between tables, making sure everyone's meals were perfectly cooked, their wine chilled, and their appetites sated. Over the last month, Frank had run an ad campaign in the *Gazette* that encouraged diners to splurge on the lovebirds' dinner for two because "Valentine's Day can be any day," an idea his new girlfriend Sandra had come up with. Eleanor had known Sandra for years and was delighted to see the two of them so happy with their second chance.

A little voice in her head whispered, *That could be you*, but she brushed it off as she waited for the hostess to return and seat them at a table. Harry stood just beside her, so close she could feel the warmth of his body.

Since the day Frank opened the restaurant, he'd kept it connected to his heritage. The Old World décor, with its dark wood and stuccoed walls, gave off an Italian vibe, accented by the wall-length mural depicting an Italian countryside. There were some things in Harbor Cove that stayed exactly as they were, and Eleanor liked that just fine. "I love this place," she said to Harry.

"Me too," he replied. "This was the first restaurant I visited when I moved to Harbor Cove, and I have

to say, I've never had a lasagna quite as good anywhere else."

"Well, you haven't tried mine. You might find you like
being at my dinner table much more than being here."

Harry cocked a grin in her direction. "Did you just flirt
with me, Ella Bella?"

"I would never." She started to explain when the
hostess gestured them toward a table in the back.

"For the record," Harry whispered in her ear as they
walked, "if that was flirting, I loved it. Don't stop."

She giggled like a schoolgirl, and when he put out
his hand to take hers, she let him, for balance, she told
herself, not because she was starting to like this man who
seemed so determined to court her. When Harry released
her hand to pull out the chair for Eleanor, a flicker of
disappointment stirred inside her.

Instead of choosing the seat opposite her, Harry sat in
the chair to her right, moving it a little so that they were
closer together. "First, some ground rules."

"Ground rules?"

"I know you haven't really dated since your husband
died." His face was serious but his eyes still held that
constant state of good humor she'd come to like about
Harry. "I've gone out on a couple of dates since my wife
died, but I haven't exactly been filling my dance card,
either. Since we're both a little out of practice, I think we
should establish how we want this to go."

How they wanted *what* to go? Them dating? Did she
want that? "It sounds like you're planning a merger and
acquisition."

"Only if I get lucky." He winked, and she laughed
harder than she had laughed in a long time. "Seriously,
Ella, I don't want you to feel uncomfortable for a split

second. So if me sitting this close is too much too soon, say the word, and I'll take my silverware over to the next table."

She laughed again. "I don't mind you sitting next to me. Besides, you've already kissed me. A little peck, but still, a kiss. Although...I will admit I am a little freaked out by the thought of dating."

"I get that. And that's why the ball will be in your court, today, tomorrow, and down the road. You call the shots here, Ella, and you always will."

She caught his hand in hers and held it tight. It was the first time she had purposely touched Harry, and even though the whole thing was terrifying, it felt good. Right. "Thank you, Harry. I appreciate that."

He gave her a warm smile that lit his dark-blue eyes. "Now let's get a lot of garlic bread so you have a reason to say no to my good-night kiss."

She laughed at his joke, but at the same time, a thrill chased down her spine. Harry Erlich wanted to kiss her good night?

That was the thought that lingered in her mind all throughout dinner. She had a single glass of wine while Harry opted for a snifter of Four Roses. The chicken parm was, as always, amazing, but the company was even better. The urge to rush through part two of her plan just so she could get to the end, where Harry dropped her off and walked her to her door and kissed her good night, had her eating her meal in record time.

As the waitress cleared their dinner plates, Eleanor looked down at her watch. "It's getting late. We have to hurry."

Before she could even offer to split the tab, Harry slipped a credit card into the waitress's hand. "You make me dinner at least twice a week, Eleanor. The least I can do is pay tonight."

"Well, just so you don't think this is a date."

At some point, Harry holding her hand had become the most natural thing in the world. "Would that be so bad?" he asked.

Would it? Was she ready to open her heart again? To risk another heartbreak? The irony of her plan to meddle in Emma's love life while avoiding her own was not lost on Eleanor. "I have other things on my mind tonight. You're not my date, Harry. You're my cover."

⚜⚜⚜

Emma pressed her back to the cold stone wall of the service hall that ran between the ballroom and the kitchen of the hotel. The Father-Daughter Dance had begun a little while ago. The music was muffled by the wall, which gave Emma a bit of privacy to take this call and have a conversation she'd been dreading. "Karl, people are getting worried that there's no plan."

"It's all good. We're working on some things on our end, just some details we need to finalize, and then I'll make an announcement to the group." Karl Jensen's robust voice filled the phone line. He'd always been so positive, so confident, and maybe that was part of why she'd gotten swept up in all his grand plans for the foundation.

"You said that last week. And the week before that." Emma ran a hand through her hair. She had quit her job, given up her apartment, told everyone she was leaving a week from Tuesday, and still, Karl had nothing set in stone. This was her escape from Harbor Cove. It couldn't fall apart. It just couldn't. "I invested all my savings into this foundation because I believed in you. We all did. And now...I'm not so sure."

Even as Karl scrambled to reassure her, Emma could hear the notes of dishonesty in his words. They'd probably always been there, but she, in her typical impetuous fashion, had barreled full-force into something that was turning out to be, at best, a flop. At worst, a scam.

What was she going to tell her family? She'd been so adamant that the Atlas Foundation was going to be a success. How could she admit she'd been wrong about all of it?

Failure hung over her like a cloud. She willed Karl to say that it was all a misunderstanding, that the foundation was on solid ground. That she was worried for no good reason. Instead he rambled about the same unforeseen delays and empty promises.

In the stark hallway, a world away from the elegant ballroom, a reality she could no longer ignore was staring her in the face. The job with the Atlas Foundation wasn't going to happen. Not now. Probably not ever. Emma had leaped without looking, and this time she was going to crash miserably, losing everything in the process. Maybe she could at least get her inheritance back and use that to start over.

"Karl, if you don't have a firm plan in place by Tuesday," she said, "I'm asking you to return my donation."

There was a pause. A long, uncomfortable silence. "Uh, Emma, those funds have already been poured into infrastructure."

Her heart sank. Momma's legacy, her gift to her daughter that was supposed to be used wisely, invested in something smart, was gone. Her future, gone. The career she'd barely begun, gone. All of her time and money wasted. "What infrastructure? Because as far as I can see, all you have is a website and a social media page."

He started sputtering about permits and plans, but Emma had already stopped listening. The Atlas Foundation was crumbling, and she was a fool if she believed in it for one more second.

"Just give me back my money," she said. "I have to go."

Then she hung up the phone and tucked it in her pocket and finally admitted to herself that she had been wrong.

Emma wanted to cry, but she was too depressed and depleted to muster up some tears. How could she have been so stupid? What was she going to do now? What would she tell her family?

Her phone buzzed with texts from Diana. *Be back in a minute*, Emma texted back. Except her feet were made of concrete and moving from this hallway seemed like a gargantuan task.

Her father found her there a few minutes later. Davis Monroe was in his forties, still as handsome as the day he'd married Momma. He worked as a manager at the Harbor Cove Bank & Trust, a job he'd had for many years. His dark hair and blue eyes were an echo of Emma's while his love of sports was something he shared with his sons with his second wife, Joanna. Her father's life had crumpled after Momma died, but he'd eventually found a new beginning with the woman who had been Momma and Dad's friend for a long time. Gabby and Margaret had struggled to embrace Joanna or even to accept that Dad would move on after he was widowed, while Emma had been much quicker to welcome her stepmother into the family. At least Gabby had repaired her relationship with Dad this past spring. Margaret, however, had yet to extend an olive branch.

"Hey, Diana is looking for you," Dad said.

"I know. Hi, Dad. Happy Father's Day." She crossed to him and hugged her father tight. Tears burned at the back of her eyes. All she wanted to do was go back to her apartment and hide under the covers until all of this was a distant memory. Except she no longer had an apartment of her own and nowhere to hide. And right now, she couldn't afford to hide out for more than an hour.

He patted her back. "Hey, kiddo, you don't sound all right, and you haven't the last couple of times we've texted. Is everything okay?"

"Nothing's okay." She drew back and swiped at her eyes before the tears had a chance to fall. Her throat was thick, and a heavy stone of dread had sandwiched itself in her stomach. "All I've ever wanted to do was leave this town and make something of myself. Become someone that you all would be proud of. And now I can't even do that."

Her father cocked his head and stared at her. "What are you talking about?"

"Never mind. It's fine, Dad." She attempted a smile and failed. "I'll be fine."

"That all sounds like the exact opposite of fine. Let's talk for a minute. You're no good to Diana or anyone else when you're this upset." He took her hand and led her to a pair of chairs. "So tell me what's going on."

She told him the rest of the story, dumping out all the details about giving her inheritance to the foundation, how she'd put in her notice at the hotel, and how she'd let her temper get the best of her with Margaret. "I've burned every bridge I have, Dad, and now I have nowhere to go."

"That's not true, Emma. As long as I'm alive, and I'm

sure your grandmother and your sisters feel the same, you have someplace to go."

"Thanks, Dad." She leaned into him and rested her head on his shoulder. If only she could go back to being the teenage girl who would run to her father when someone was mean to her at school or she'd suffered a broken heart.

"Help me understand why working with this foundation is so important to you?"

"I want to make a difference. I want my life to have a purpose." At eighteen, she hadn't cared about things like meaning. But as she'd gotten older and added more and more meditative practices to her life, a yawning cavern had opened inside Emma that no amount of adventure trips or mountain retreats could fill. She'd sat there in the lotus position with her mind empty, concentrating on breathing in and breathing out, with the nagging feeling that she was missing out on something deep and profound.

"You're already doing that in the job you have now," her father said. "Every person you help is changed in some way by you."

"I wouldn't call that a purpose." She scoffed. "All I do is help picky brides figure out whether they want a two-tier or three-tier cake, pick up the rose petals they drop in the bride's room, and run around behind them with safety pins and hairspray. That's not meaning. That's not anything."

"Maybe not to you. But to the bride whose day you made special and perfect, it has meaning."

Her father had a point. Not every bride she worked with was a Sharon, and there had been many who had thanked Emma for taking much of the stress off their shoulders, allowing them to enjoy their wedding and not worry about the details. "You're my dad. You're supposed to say those things." She sighed. "I want more. I want to be like Momma."

"There is not and never will be anyone like your mother." He chucked Emma under the chin. "Don't try to be like Penny, Em. Try to be Emma because there is no one like you, either."

Emma had wandered most of her life, trying to find that little niche that fit her best. On the surface, Dad's advice seemed so simple, but if it were that easy, Emma would already have the answers she needed. She would know where her own brand of uniqueness fit in the world. She would have a sense of direction. "The problem is that I don't know who Emma Monroe is other than a screwup and the butt of family jokes. 'Oooh, another Emma Move.'" She put air quotes around the words.

He chuckled. "That's just your sisters trying to get under your skin. You know they don't mean it. None of us think you're a screwup."

"Yeah, maybe." Emma doubted Margaret would agree with Dad. Emma and her father sat there for a moment in the quiet of the corridor with the muffled sound of music coming from the other side of the concrete blocks. "Tell me something about Momma. Anything you can think of."

"I used to love it when we played that game." Her dad grinned. Years after Momma died, when it became clear to Emma that she wasn't going to remember anything more, she would beg her father for details about Penny. Some nugget that would trigger a memory or bring back an image. They'd made it into a game where her father would start the sentence and Emma would try to finish it.

She'd guess and guess and never get it right but sometimes Dad would pretend she did.

He thought for a moment. "I remember everything, but then there are other days when I feel like I remember nothing."

"Just anything, Dad." She curled her arm around her father's and leaned her head on his shoulder again.

"She could take a handful of pasta and a piece of chicken and turn it into a gourmet meal. She was a great cook, like your grandmother," her father said. "She loved butterflies and bees and spiders, and if one got in the house, she'd catch it in a cup and release it in the yard. She couldn't whistle to save her life, but she could sing, oh how she could sing. Sometimes I'd come home from work and catch her singing in the kitchen. I'd just stand in the doorway and listen to her. She had a beautiful voice, so sweet and light, like listening to a harp."

Emma closed her eyes, willing some memory of a casserole or a butterfly or a song to come to mind. There was nothing but shadows in her memory. Maybe blocking those moments had been some kind of defense mechanism after Momma's death. Or maybe Emma just sucked at remembering.

"You're the most like her, you know," Dad went on. "Gabby has her energy, Margaret has her smarts, but you, Emma? You have her spirit. You're always doing for others, whether you're trying to help them through a hard time or help them achieve a dream."

"And losing all my savings in the process by getting sucked into a scam." That wasn't the kind of success her mother had been and surely wasn't what her mother would have wanted her youngest daughter to do.

"Well, we all make mistakes. That's the only way

you learn."

"I think I've learned enough for a lifetime." A short, maybe slightly hysterical laugh escaped her. "I can't believe I got caught up in something that's very likely a scam."

"Maybe it is. Maybe not. The point is you took the risk, Emma. I'm proud of you for doing that. Most people sit on the sidelines wishing they had the courage to get in the game."

She drew back and looked up at her father. There'd never been a moment when he hadn't been in her corner shouting *attagirl* in one way or another. "Why do you support me so much, Dad? Everyone else tells me to put on the brakes, but you're the one who got me my first passport and paid for that trip to Puerto Rico. You're sitting here now telling me you're proud of me when it's very likely that I blew my entire inheritance from Momma on a Ponzi scheme."

"Because no matter what you do, Emma, you have a way of making it all work out." He brushed a lock of hair off her forehead. "You're a smart girl. You'll find a way."

On the other side of the wall, she could hear the muffled sounds of people talking and the bass thumping. She really should go, but a part of her wanted to linger, for just a moment, in this space where her father made everything better. "Margaret told me that Momma wanted to open a community center."

He nodded. "That's right. I forgot all about that. Yes, she did. In fact, you were the reason she thought of it in the first place."

"Me? Why?"

He sat back and crossed one leg over his knee. "When

you were three or so, your mom used to take you to a playground around the corner from our house. Your sisters were older and already in school, so it was just you two every day. She met some moms there who were struggling, whether it was because they were single parents or they'd lost a job or whatever it might be. I remember your mother telling me that there were not enough programs to help moms like that, or their kids. She wanted to create a place where these kids could go to learn, create, and make friends while their moms received training or support."

"That sounds amazing." In her mind, Emma could see it. A building buzzing with children and talented instructors who helped them get through their tough times while their mothers built résumés and connections.

"It never really got off the ground, though. Your mother was still in the planning stages when she died. She was talking about finding some other people to organize it, but she never got a chance."

"Do you know anything more about her plans?"

He shook his head. "I'm sorry, I don't. It's been a long time, and most of the details are lost to me now. But…" He cocked his head and thought for a second. "I remember her having a notebook where she wrote down everything she was thinking. I have no idea what happened to it. I don't remember seeing it again after she died, but then again, I was a mess for a very long time after I lost Penny."

Emma covered her father's hand with her own. He'd checked out for so long after their mother died, and had told her how much he regretted not being there for his daughters. Grandma had been the strong one, the one who united them all and made sure their family stayed together. "We all were."

"Indeed. You are so wise, Emma." He gave her a smile. "And in case I haven't told you today, I'm proud of you."

She waved off his words. "You always say that."

He paused and spoke again when her gaze met his. "Because I always am, Emma. I am always proud of you."

"Thank you, Dad." She gave him a hug and then leaned against the wall. Another minute passed and still Emma couldn't move. She sighed. "I guess I have to tell everyone I screwed up. Again."

"Give it a minute. See what this Karl guy does. You believed in him for a reason. Let's see how that pans out."

"Dad, my money is gone. I was duped. I rushed into it without doing my research. Just like Margaret said." As she had with the apartment. And her marriage to Luke.

"You do have a tendency to jump without looking first, like your mom used to, but that's what makes you so special, my brave, fearless daughter." He gave her a smile. "You take the leaps and the rest of us think maybe, just maybe, we can do that, too."

"Dad, I—"

"You are inspiring, Emma. To me, to your sisters, to anyone who has ever met you. Trust your instincts, because they're very rarely wrong." He got to his feet and put out his hand. "Now, will you be my date to the Father-Daughter Dance?"

The walls seemed less suffocating, the music brighter. She took her father's hand and thought, for now at least, everything was going to be all right. "It would be my honor."

❧❧❧

Forty little girls and their fathers filled the ballroom along with a handful of staff members manning the non-alcoholic punch bowl and a table of snacks and bowls of macaroni and cheese. Luke watched the room hum at a fast but organized pace, which Emma kept running smoothly.

The dance was open to any little girl and whomever she considered a father figure. For the girls who didn't have one of those, there was Jake, who was wearing a shirt that said HONORARY DAD. In one corner sat a photo booth with a wide variety of silly props, while a three-piece band was set up on the opposite end of the ballroom, cycling through requests and a pattern of two fast songs, one slow song.

Each of the girls had received a little wrist corsage when she entered the room with a matching boutonniere for her father. Pretty much every girl was dancing, some in a small circle of other girls, some with their fathers. Most of the guys looked the same way Luke felt—happy to be with their daughters but pained by the dancing part. If there'd been a Father-Daughter Super Bowl Watch Party, Luke would bet a million dollars every single man in the room would gladly sign up.

When he and Scout had first arrived, Emma wasn't there, which had surprised him because he'd seen her leave a solid hour before they did. A woman he didn't know had done the check-in and handed them their flowers. Around ten after six, Emma walked into the room and he'd felt a jolt of happiness. He'd crossed over to greet her, but as soon as he saw her, that happiness morphed into concern. Emma's face was flushed, as if she'd been crying, but when he tried to ask her about it, she was called away by one of the servers. When she returned to the ballroom, she danced a couple times with a man who must have been her father, given the strong family resemblance.

Luke and Scout danced several times in between Scout running off to play with the girls she'd met at the rock painting event. Already, she had friends in Harbor Cove, and he could literally see his child putting down roots with every little girl she hugged. Staying in this town could be good for Scout. But would it be too painful for Luke to see Emma's shadow everywhere he turned after she was gone?

"Daddy, I'm gonna go make a picture with Hayley and Macy," Scout said. Two other girls about her age were standing beside her, looking like twins to Scout with their pink and pale-blue outfits. Apparently princess dresses were a thing. "They're my friends."

It filled him with joy to hear Scout talk about her friends, to live a normal life like so many of the other children in the room. Maybe she would come through this period of her life unscathed, and he and Kim could give her the childhood she deserved.

"Sure. Have fun." Luke wandered over to where Emma was standing. The older man she'd danced with earlier was over by the punch bowl. "Looks like this event is a success, too. You pulled it off, Emma."

"Well, not entirely perfect. We had one crisis in the kitchen when a server dropped the entire platter of mini PB and J's, but Chef Tyler was able to whip up some more. They should be out any second." Emma turned to the man coming up beside her with two glasses of punch in his hands. "Dad, this is Luke Carter. Luke, this is my father, Davis Monroe."

"*The* Luke Carter?" Davis said with a grin, and Luke

liked him instantly. "The one who managed to pin my daughter down for a minute?"

Emma's eyes widened. "You know I got married?"

"It might have come up when I saw Gabby for dinner the other night. I didn't mention it to you because she made it sound like it was a temporary thing." He glanced at Luke and then back at Emma. "*Is* this temporary?"

The part of Luke that was saddened by the mere thought of Emma leaving spoke before his rational half could stop the words. "I'd love to make it—"

"Yes, Dad, it is." Emma cut Luke off before he could say the word *permanent*. "Annulment hearing is a week from Monday. And then it'll be like it never happened."

Whatever moment Luke thought he'd read in that dance with Emma in the living room earlier tonight had been a figment of his imagination. Emma was no more interested in forever today than she had been back in Nevada. He was a glutton for punishment if he thought otherwise.

The woman who had done check-in came up to Emma. "I have a question for you."

"Sure. Guys, I'll be back in a second." Emma took a few steps away, leaving Luke and Davis alone.

"Listen, I didn't want to put you on the spot back there," Davis said. "I'm just surprised she agreed to settle down with someone she hadn't known that long."

"The whole thing was spontaneous for both of us."

"I do believe that's my daughter's middle name." Davis's gaze landed on Emma, who was crossing the room toward one of the little girls. "I've seen how she looks at you, and I think there's more between you two than just an accident at a retreat."

"There is for me, sir, but as for Emma..." Luke shrugged.

"She keeps her cards close to her chest, like I do. But underneath it all, Emma is just a marshmallow." Davis clapped Luke on the shoulder. "If you love her, don't give up too easily."

Given that Emma was moving across the world in a few days, Luke wasn't quite sure what Davis meant by that. Hop on the next jet and fly to wherever she was staying to pledge his undying love? Luke was pretty sure a stunt like that would make Emma run away from him, not toward him. "I'll keep that in mind. She's a pretty amazing person."

"You and I know that," Davis said. "Emma is still figuring it out."

"Heck, we all are." Luke watched Emma bend down and start talking to a little girl who was crying. Emma was calm and confident and within seconds, the little girl had stopped crying and was nodding along with whatever Emma was saying. Every time Luke saw her, he was more impressed by how much she could go with the flow and yet keep a roomful of little kids under control.

Davis leaned over his shoulder. "I think it's part of the Dad rules that I have to tell you that I'll hunt you down if you break her heart."

Luke chuckled. "I'm pretty sure she's going to break my heart first. In all seriousness, sir, I only have your daughter's best interests at heart."

Davis studied him for a long moment. "I can see that. She needs someone like you."

"Emma?" Luke shrugged. "She doesn't need anyone."

She was walking back toward them now. The little girl she had helped was back in the crowd, playing with her friends. Emma looked fierce and independent, just as she had the first time he met her.

"All marshmallow underneath," Davis whispered just as Emma rejoined them.

"Sorry about that. Kid crisis. Did I miss anything? You didn't tell Luke any stories about me as a little girl, did you?"

Her father grinned. "Only the embarrassing ones." His cell phone buzzed. "That's Joanna. Her car is in the shop so I promised to pick her up from her parents' house tonight. Do you mind if I go, Emma? Because if you need help, I can stay."

"No, Dad. You've already helped me more than you know." Emma rose on her toes and wrapped her arms around him. "Thank you."

"Anytime, kiddo." He pressed a kiss to her temple. "Always remember I'm proud of you. Every minute of every day."

"You might be a bit biased in that area, but..." She smiled. "Thank you. I will."

Luke watched their interaction, envious of their obvious closeness. Could he and Scout be like that in twenty years? A father and daughter who weren't just family but were also friends? He sure hoped so.

As Davis headed out, Eleanor Whitmore entered the room with an older gentleman on her arm. She stopped to talk to Davis for a couple minutes. Emma spied her grandmother at the door and muttered a curse. "She better be here because she wants to volunteer."

"Why else would your grandmother come?" He'd liked Eleanor when he met her at the rock painting event. He liked the entire family, in fact. How would his life have been different if he'd grown up amid such love and support? How would Scout's life turn out if he could give her such a precious gift as a warm and loving family?

"Grandma is most likely here to work her unofficial part-time job—meddling in her granddaughters' lives. She is determined to make sure every one of us gets a happily-ever-after."

"Sounds like a great grandmother to me."

Emma rolled her eyes. "You only say that because you haven't been on the receiving end of said meddling. But I think you're about to be right now."

Eleanor headed in their direction with her date on her arm. "What a wonderful evening, Emma," she said. "Looks like this has been a hit. Like everything you've done at this hotel."

"Hi, Grandma." She pressed a kiss to her grandmother's cheek. "And Harry. What a pleasant surprise. Are you two on a date?"

"No, no, of course not," Eleanor rushed to say. A flush filled her cheeks. Harry simply smiled and nodded, amusement in his eyes. "We just wanted to stop by and see if you needed any help with the dance. Harry has had lessons at Arthur Murray so I bet he's quite the dancer."

"Great." Relief flooded Emma's face, maybe because there'd been no hint of the dreaded meddling. "Thanks, Grandma. There are a couple of girls here who don't have a dad or father figure. Jake's been the de-facto date for them, but I'm sure he'd love some help in that department."

"It would be my pleasure," Harry said. "After I dance with my favorite girl first."

Eleanor swatted at his arm. "We're not here for ourselves, Harry."

"Then look at it as practice." Before she could protest again, Harry swooped Eleanor into his arms and began waltzing her around the dance floor. They moved easily together, stepping and twirling to a Norah Jones song.

"Looks like you were wrong," Luke said to Emma. "Your grandmother is only here to help."

"Oh, I don't believe that for a second. She's already told me how she wants us to stay together. I don't know what you said to her at the rock painting event, but she thinks you're the best thing next to brownies."

Well, well. Emma's father and her grandmother had both said something about their relationship. Emma's family rooting for them to stay together added an interesting twist to their unconventional marriage. "Just so you know, I *am* the best thing next to brownies."

"You're incorrigible." But a smile lingered on her face.

Luke opened his mouth to ask Emma to dance, but before he could get out a single word, Scout came running over. "Daddy, dance with me!"

"Okay, but only if you say the magic word." He lifted his daughter into his arms.

She snuggled against his chest. "Pretty please."

Luke caught one of Scout's tiny hands in his and wrapped his arm around her back. They did several turns around the floor, moving among the rest of the father-daughter pairings. They waved to Harry and Jake and to all of Scout's newfound friends. Then as they passed a long white table filled with craft supplies, Scout scrambled out of his arms. "I'm gonna make Mommy a picture!"

"Be careful not to get any glue on your dress," Luke said, but Scout was already gone, pairing up with another little girl and debating glitter choices.

The Norah Jones song came to an end. Harry wandered over to where Jake was standing while Eleanor made a beeline for Luke. Uh-oh. Maybe it wasn't going to be a meddling-free night after all.

"So nice to see you again, Luke," Eleanor said.

"You too, Mrs. Whitmore."

She waved a hand at the title. "You're part of the family now. Please call me Eleanor. Or Grandma."

For a second, he allowed himself to imagine he *was* part of their close-knit group. Going to family dinners with Emma, decorating the Christmas tree, trading inside jokes and long-term memories. "I'm only part of the family for one more week."

"About that." Eleanor's features became more serious as she shifted from pleasantries to the meddling Emma had warned him would happen. "Since this is your last week, and apparently also the last week my headstrong granddaughter will be in town, I'd like to invite you and your darling daughter to family dinner on Wednesday night. You turned me down the last time I invited you, but I hope you'll say yes this time. Six o'clock sharp. I hope you like lasagna."

"I love lasagna." He glanced over at Emma, who had been roped into dancing with Harry. The two of them seemed to be engaged in a very serious conversation. "Are you sure Emma will be okay with that?" It was why he had refused the first time but now . . . with Emma living with him and the time ticking away, he was reconsidering Eleanor's invitation.

Eleanor paused a second, her lips pursed. "Sometimes, you have to show people what they want before they realize how much they need it."

He chuckled. "Emma warned me about this."

"About what?"

"She said you have a part-time job meddling in your granddaughters' lives."

"Well, what grandmother doesn't?" A smile that looked decidedly crafty curved across Eleanor's face. She glanced at Harry, who gave her a nod, before returning her attention to Luke. "Care to take an old woman for a turn on the dance floor?"

❧❦❧

Harry was, as Grandma had promised, a very good dancer. He led with light presses to Emma's shoulder or palm, graciously ignoring when she stepped left instead of right and ended up on his foot. "This is such a great event, Emma. I'm impressed."

She blushed at the praise. "Thank you."

"Will you be doing similar work when you leave to work with the foundation?"

Out of the corner of her eye, Emma could see Grandma chatting with Luke as they joined the other pairs on the dance floor. Undoubtedly she was giving him some Dear Amelia advice about wooing his wife. There was nothing Emma could do to stop Grandma's well-meaning interference so she focused on Harry—and trying not to step on his feet. "I really enjoy working with kids, especially ones who have been through difficult circumstances."

"Like you and your sisters," Harry said, then spun her gently to the right, past the crafts table. "And like little Scout over there."

"I never thought of it that way, Harry. But you're right. Scout lost her mother, too, in a way. Hopefully only temporarily." Losing a parent, even if it was only for a few months, was a difficult trauma for someone so young to comprehend. Emma and her sisters had known that jarring pain in a much deeper and more permanent way.

"I daresay that's why the two of you have bonded." Harry was quiet for a moment as they danced, his face almost wistful as he watched the little girls and their fathers. "You know, when I was a young boy, my father died. He had a brain tumor and went very fast. Much faster than any of us expected."

"Oh, Harry, I'm so sorry. That must have been very difficult."

The normally jovial lines of his face settled into a map of grief and sadness. "I won't lie, it was tough. I was the oldest and had two little brothers who needed a dad, too, and I think my mom expected me to fill that role. I was only twelve, far too young to be any kind of parental role model. And my poor mother...she had lost the love of her life and it took a long, long time before she could be there for us."

"Sort of like what my sisters and I went through. Our dad just sort of checked out, which was why we were raised by Grandma."

Harry nodded in sympathy. "The death of a parent is like having an earthquake split apart your life. I was so close to my father that when he was gone, there was this...hole. I didn't know how to fill it or what to do with all the emotions I had rambling around inside me, so I started getting into trouble. Acting up at school, picking fights at lunch, hanging out with the wrong crowd, that kind of thing."

Emma chuckled at the idea of Grandma's mild-mannered, sweet neighbor ever being in trouble. "You? I can't see you picking a fight, Harry."

"I'll have you know I used to have a mean right hook."

He grinned and then sobered again. "I was on the cusp of making some lifelong bad decisions and I needed someone to rein me in, provide some boundaries and rules, but my mother was just so distraught, I don't think she even knew what day it was. My brothers were starting to act like me and I knew I was letting them down, but I didn't know how to deal with all the pain I was feeling."

Emma thought of her sisters and how each had gone through their own painful years. If Grandma hadn't been their steady, loving rock, all three of them could have ended up in very different places.

"That summer, school let out and us boys were on our own a lot, which is never a good combination. There was this neighbor, a guy I'd seen a hundred times, who was working on renovating his house on the weekends. One afternoon, the neighbor asked if I could help him. I had a long empty day ahead of me with nothing but trouble on the menu, but for some reason, I said yes." Harry stepped to the right, avoiding two little girls chatting and dancing together. "He and I spent that entire afternoon tearing out cabinets and ripping up the old vinyl flooring. Then the next weekend, we worked on laying a new tile floor. The weekend after that, I helped him install new kitchen cabinets. He taught me everything he knew about remodeling, but more importantly, those weekends filled the empty hours and taught me that I could do pretty much anything I put my mind to, even if I was afraid to screw it up."

"That's so sweet."

Harry pressed her back and shifted to the right. Emma easily followed his lead. "In between painting walls and installing a dishwasher, the neighbor became someone I could talk to. Confide in. Cry with. His own father had died a few years before, and he told me it's something that hurts no matter what age you are."

"He was a kindred spirit."

Harry smiled. "He was indeed. He was also very smart because he got me so interested in figuring out how to fix things and, later, how computers and radios worked, that I stopped hanging around with the wrong crowd, stopped getting into fights, and started behaving at school and at home. My brothers settled down, too, because I became a more positive influence. I grew up a lot that year, and I credit Anand Patal with helping that happen. He became a father figure when I needed one pretty badly."

"I'm so glad." Emma thought of everything Harry and his grandson had gone through a few months ago. "I think you kind of did the same with your grandson when he and his father had a falling out."

"I'd like to think I did." He sashayed them past the craft table again. Scout gave Emma a little wave and a beaming smile. "Scout has literally blossomed since she met you. You've changed that girl's life, Emma."

Emma was no substitute parent, not like Anand had been for Harry. Her own life was too much of a mess to be any kind of positive influence. "I don't know about that. I just got her enrolled in some activities."

"You did so much more than that. Your grandmother has told me how she's seen Scout change in the last couple of weeks. Anyone with two eyes can see that little girl is attached to you." Harry met Emma's gaze. "I think you're both going to be a little heartbroken when you leave."

She glanced over at Scout, who waved her glittered picture in Emma's direction, sending tiny sparkles to the floor. Emma couldn't imagine no longer seeing the little girl's winsome face every day or answering a thousand questions about butterflies or reading *Where the Wild Things Are* at night and doing all the roar-y monster sounds because that always made Scout giggle.

Emma had only known Scout for a short period of time, but was it enough time for such a young mind to hold onto? She was about the same age as Emma had been when her mother died, and Emma had only a whisper of memories of Momma. "I hope she remembers me."

"Of course she will. You've become her Anand Patal, Emma, and that's someone she'll remember even when she's collecting social security like me."

"I know for sure that I'll never forget her," Emma said softly. There was a catch in her throat and a rush of tears in her eyes. These days with Scout and Luke were swiftly coming to an end and Emma could already feel the cavern in her heart begin to grow.

"It's a shame, really," Harry said as they went past the craft table and Scout one more time. Three times in one dance, Emma realized. Almost like Harry was doing it on purpose.

"You dance so good, Emma!" Scout shouted, giving her a tiny thumbs-up. "And your dress is so pretty!"

"Thank you, Scout! You too, kiddo." A second later, a man and his daughter blocked Emma's view of Scout's giant smile. "What do you mean by *it's a shame*, Harry?"

"You have such an incredible gift with children. I've seen it in action when I've volunteered at events like this. I'm sure wherever you go, you will change some lives. But there are still so many lives right here in Harbor Cove who need your magic touch, too. You don't have to go so far from home, Emma. Sometimes you can change the world simply by being the neighbor who steps in at just the right time."

"I have a plan, Harry. A plane ticket. I can't stay."

"Can't is merely a word people say when they're scared to be vulnerable and trust other people," Harry said. "There's always a way that you can, if you want to badly enough. And that concludes the lecture from an old man who probably has no business giving you advice."

Emma laughed, but as her feet moved in time with Harry's tempo, a deep ache started to grow in her heart.

❦❧

"She really is amazing, isn't she?" Eleanor said to Luke as they waltzed along the perimeter of the ballroom. He could see Harry and Emma talking as they danced. Whatever Harry was saying seemed to make Emma a little upset. She had that furrowed brow that she got whenever she was troubled.

"She is the most remarkable woman I've ever met." Luke had never known a woman like Emma. Part adventurous spirit, part grounded being, and beautiful from the inside out.

"Our family is very close," Eleanor said, as they wove their way between the fathers with their daughters, "which means we look out for one another."

He grinned. Emma called it meddling, but Luke could see the protectiveness and love in Eleanor's eyes. "Of that I have no doubt."

"As you are doing for your own daughter."

"I sure hope so." In the last couple of months, Luke's relationship with Scout had taken on more depth and meaning. He wasn't the drive-by parent anymore; he was forming an honest bond with her that he hoped lasted the rest of her life. He wanted his relationship with Scout to be as close and loving as the ones he saw in Emma's family.

"This is a great town to raise your daughter. We have some of the very best schools in the state of Massachusetts right here in Harbor Cove. And housing is still rather affordable."

Luke chuckled. "Are you an ambassador for the town or trying to convince me to stay?"

She shrugged and gave him an innocent look. "I simply think you fit in nicely here."

"You mean with Emma."

"Well, if that's where your path leads you..."

"Emma does not want to take the same path as me." To be honest, he'd been thinking about a long-term life with Emma for a while now. A waste of thinking, as Emma had made abundantly clear.

"Let me tell you something about my youngest granddaughter. She's always been, without a doubt, the wildest of the three. Her sisters think she is brave but foolhardy, jetting off here, there, and everywhere, but that's not it. Underneath it all, my darling Emma is terrified of being hurt and so she runs from the slightest hint of heartbreak. Just like her mother and...frankly, just like her grandmother."

A marshmallow, like Davis had said. "Everyone's afraid of being hurt."

She nodded in agreement. "All I'm saying is that Emma is a lot of bluff and bluster. You might have to work harder to win her heart than you ever have at anything else. But she's definitely worth the effort, and you, my grandson-in-law, are up to the challenge." Eleanor gave him a quick but sincere hug just as Emma and Harry came within touching distance. "See you Wednesday night. Six sharp."

Then Eleanor and her date waltzed away, leaving Emma and Luke together on the dance floor. Emma's cheeks were red, her eyes cloudy. She crossed her arms over her chest. "Well, that was an interesting dance with Harry."

"Why? Did he say something? You look..." He wanted to say *heartbroken,* but instead he settled on "upset."

She waved off the question and shook her head. "Never mind. It's a long story."

"You'll have to tell me sometime." *Sometime* implied a future. Implied them staying together. Emma didn't argue that point, so Luke pressed his luck a bit more with the stubborn marshmallow he'd married. "Shall we?" he said as he put out his hand.

"You know we're only giving my grandmother what she wants if we dance together, right?" Emma said.

"And what is so wrong with a happy ending once in a while?"

The stubbornness lingered in her eyes before finally yielding to amusement. "Okay. Maybe just for tonight, just one more time, we can pretend we could have the fabled happily ever after."

"Someone believes we could," he whispered. He caught Eleanor's eye, and she gave him a thumbs-up, obviously a lot more certain about his relationship with Emma than he was.

❧❦❧

By eight thirty, most of the kids had gone home. The food had all been eaten and only a few sips of punch remained in the bowl. The staff began quietly cleaning the room while the band played a couple more requests. Harry and Eleanor had danced several times in between helping with the kids before they left.

Scout insisted she wanted to stay until the end, but that last hour past her bedtime had been too much and she'd fallen asleep on Luke's shoulder somewhere between "Somewhere Over the Rainbow" and "My Girl."

Emma wandered over to them. "She's all tuckered out."

"It's apparently very exhausting for Scout to watch Dad to do all the heavy lifting." He hoisted her higher on his shoulder. All that snoozing weight was heavy. "I think it's past my bedtime, too."

Emma laughed. "Why don't you go on home? I have to oversee the cleanup but it shouldn't take that long." Someone called her name. "I should go see what they want. I'll see you later, Luke."

For the last two and a half hours, Luke had danced with his daughter at least twenty times but had yet to dance with the woman who made his heart race. Every time he'd gone to ask Emma to dance, she'd had some emergency that pulled her away, an excuse that got her off the floor. Those few minutes in the living room with her in his arms had stayed in his mind, a bittersweet memory that he knew, one day, would just be part of someone he used to know.

Luke caught Emma's arm as she turned away. "Come home with me."

She blinked at him. "I'll be back at Ray's house tonight. Just like I have been for the last week or so."

"In a few days, our marriage will be dissolved, and you'll be gone. We never even really had a chance to be a couple. Aren't you curious what it would have been like?"

"If this"—she waved between them—"was real? Like, we were really married? That was a mistake, Luke. *We* were a mistake."

He refused to believe that. "If we were really married, Emma, you'd finish up here and come home to my world-famous pasta. You'd put your feet up and have a glass of wine while I cooked and cleaned up, and then we would sit up way too late talking about our day and making plans for a trip to Spain or Italy or hell, Idaho."

A smile teased at the edge of her lips. "Well...who goes to Idaho?"

"People who really like potatoes?" He brushed his thumb across her bottom lip and fought the urge to kiss her. "Just for tonight, Emma, let's pretend that you're not leaving and we're not getting divorced."

She considered him for a moment. In her eyes, he saw all those inner fears mingling with curiosity. "What'd you call it? World-famous pasta? How come I've never heard of this amazing pasta dish?"

"Because you didn't marry me earlier, Mrs. Carter." The more he saw her, the more he began to picture a forever with Emma. Waking up to her beautiful face in the morning and then whispering good night as she fell asleep in his arms. Lazy Sunday mornings with breakfast in bed, the two of them lingering under the covers for as long as possible.

"You've got to stop calling me that," she whispered.

"I will." His face was so close to hers that he could feel the warmth of her breath against his cheek. It was as intimate as two people could get in the middle of a hotel ballroom surrounded by busboys and a few stragglers. "Just not until it's official."

Then he said goodbye and headed out to his car before

he did something really foolish like ask her to call off the annulment.

Forty-five minutes later, Luke had tucked a sleepy Scout into bed, set the kitchen table, and started dinner. He was in the middle of chopping tomatoes when he heard Emma's car pull into the driveway. Anticipation rose in his chest, even though he'd just seen her. He had never had a chance to properly date and romance Emma, something Luke intended to remedy if he could somehow convince her to stay in Harbor Cove, but for now there was Uncle Ray's dated, crowded kitchen and a bowl of noodles.

She came inside and shut the door quietly before kicking off her heels. "Is Scout asleep?"

"Yup. Uncle Ray too. It's just you and me." He had connected a wireless speaker to his phone a moment ago. The soft sounds of an oldies station provided a quiet undertow for the tension between them. A tension filled with the questions neither of them dared to ask, the words they were afraid to say.

"Oh. Okay. That's fine." Without the distraction of other people, Emma seemed a little lost. She hesitated in the kitchen as if caught between wanting to stay and wanting to go.

"I'd offer you a glass of wine, but in case you didn't notice, this is a bachelor pad through and through. We have Miller Lite or . . . Miller Lite."

The joke was enough to make her laugh and ease the tightness in her shoulders. "Good thing I stopped on the way home." Emma pulled a bottle of chardonnay out of her tote bag. "I hope you like white wine."

"I'm not picky." He fished around in the junk drawer, came up with a dubious-looking corkscrew, and managed to wrestle the cork out of the bottle. "I don't think we have anything as fancy as wineglasses here."

"Juice glasses hold wine just as well." She rose on her tiptoes and reached past him to grab two glasses out of the cabinet. Her perfume teased at his senses, luring him closer.

Luke caught her around the waist, and she spun into him, still holding the glasses. Her eyes widened but she didn't move away. "You said earlier tonight that we were a mistake. None of this was a mistake, Emma. I don't believe in things like kismet or fate, but I do believe that we are drawn to the people we need in our lives. You and I have been drawn to each other several times over the last year. There's a reason we ended up in that ballroom together at the same exact time and got married."

She turned out of his arms and got busy pouring the wine and avoiding his gaze. A moment later, she handed him one of the glasses. "I believe it's because you convinced me it would be a good idea."

"Does that mean you've felt nothing since we met? No spark of attraction?"

"Well, that's not really relevant."

"Oh, really? You're my wife. I think it matters if you're attracted to me."

❧❧❧

Emma could see by Luke's grin that he was only half joking. Had he thought about kissing her even half as much as she'd thought about kissing him? Because right now, in the dim, small, quiet kitchen, all she could think about was how alone they were and how very tempting that was. "Wife in name only," she reminded him as much as herself. "And in a week, I won't even be that. So the point is moot."

"So you didn't feel anything when I kissed you?" He shifted closer, took her wine from her hands, and set their glasses on the counter. He rested his hands on her waist and her body betrayed her by swaying a little closer.

"Depends on how you define *anything*."

Luke chuckled. "Well, did this"—he cupped the back of her neck, tipped her head, and placed a soft kiss on her neck—"make you react at all?"

"Well, you've..." She swallowed hard. The scruff of his beard sent a delicious thrill through her. "You've never done that before."

"That's true. I should have started here." He pressed another kiss to the same tender spot.

Emma wanted him to kiss her again. Wanted him to walk away. Wanted this to end, wanted it to keep going. "What...what are you doing?"

His thumb rested against her cheek. His gaze met hers. A hundred emotions she didn't even want to acknowledge swam in her head and heart. "We're something," he said. "You know it, and I know it. I just want to figure out what that something is."

Then she heard a persistent sound and turned to look to the side. "Your, uh, pasta is boiling over."

"Crap!" He jerked away, yanked a wooden spoon out of the drawer, and laid it across the pot. The bubbling water calmed, and the rolling boil began to subside.

A perfect interruption, Emma decided, because it had made all that simmering desire between them ebb. She gestured toward the spoon and the now-calm pot of water. "I've never understood why that works."

"The wood is a natural insulator, which means it won't

conduct heat or electricity. It's also much cooler than the boiling water."

The science was clearly his comfort zone, a place where he could explain the inner workings behind something. "When the bubbles, which are filled with hot air, hit the spoon, they burst, releasing the steam and taking all the power out of them."

"That's hot," she said.

"Well, yeah, it's boiling water."

"No, I mean, the fact that you're so smart and good-looking is pretty hot." Had she just said that out loud after deciding that getting involved with Luke was a bad idea?

A big grin curved across his face. "So you think I'm hot, huh? Five seconds ago, you told me we were nothing."

"We might be, but you're..." She shook her head. "Different from anyone I've ever met. I don't know what to do with you."

"I'd say take me home and feed me supper, but I'm already doing that for you."

She laughed. "If that's so, then where is this world-famous pasta?"

Their conversations were a dance of getting close and then stepping it back with a joke. Emma was the wary one, circling and circling him with her words and her actions in this constant internal debate about trusting him. Luke was the one who took more risks with his heart, laying his feelings out on the table. That both terrified and fascinated her.

"Just watch the master chef create magic." Using tongs, he lifted the cooked pasta out of the pot and put it into a big stainless-steel bowl. Next he poured in some melted butter and olive oil and seasoned it with fresh-ground pepper. He tossed the pasta with the tongs in one hand and sprinkled handfuls of freshly grated Parmesan cheese into the bowl with the other. When the pasta and cheese were thoroughly mixed, he tossed in a handful of cut cherry tomatoes before adding a scoop of the hot pasta water and one more tablespoon of butter. A final swirl with the tongs and the dish was complete. He held it out to her, like a present. "I present Cacio e Pepe Pasta à la Luke."

"That looks really good, Luke." She glanced up at him. "What is Cacio e Pepe?"

"Pasta with cheese and pepper. It's a really simple Italian dish, made a little more special by the addition of the tomatoes. That's the à la Luke part, because I love tomatoes."

"So do I. And cheese. And pasta."

"Sounds like a match made in heaven." He twirled a pile of pasta onto her plate and did the same with his. They each took a seat at the table while the radio played love songs and the rest of the house went on sleeping.

Emma took the first bite and let out a little moan. "Oh my God, that is so good. You're going to have to teach me how to make this. It looks easy enough even for me to master."

"To do that, you'd have to stay in town. A masterpiece like this might take a few lessons." He winked.

In this kitchen and this moment, the idea of staying in town called like a siren to her. She could have a hundred more moments like this, if only she took the biggest risk of all and opened her heart. Her family had made it obvious they wanted her to stay with Luke, but Emma's pulse raced at the thought of anything more permanent than this. "I saw you talking to my grandmother earlier. Let me guess, she told you to be determined with me and not to let me get away?"

"She did say you were worth the effort. I have to agree." He took a bite of pasta and washed it down with a sip of chardonnay. "Answer me this, then. Why have you spent your life avoiding relationships?"

"We've had this conversation." Which meant she wanted to avoid this topic as much as she wanted to avoid being serious with anyone.

"We've had a version of this conversation but you've never really answered the question," Luke said. "Come on, Em. You're divorcing me anyway. The least you can do is give me a little closure."

She sipped her wine and considered him for a long moment. He had a point. What did it matter if she had one evening of being open and transparent? In a few days, she'd hopefully have some kind of plan and be somewhere else and this...this would be a memory in their rearview mirrors. Maybe it was the wine, maybe it was Luke's clear interest, or maybe it was just a need to be vulnerable, but she found the words spilling out of her in the quiet of the kitchen. "I told you my mom died when I was little. Some psychologist would probably say that an early-childhood trauma like that made it hard for me to trust that people would hang around. Maybe that's true or maybe I just haven't met anybody who makes me want to keep them in my life. Either way, I've always been the one who broke it off first. Get out before they get me, you know?"

"I do. I've never been one for sticking around, either. The people in my life have continually disappointed me. Then Scout came to live with me, and I realized it wasn't the other people disappointing me as much as it was *me* letting *them* down." He spun the glass between his fingers. The wine slid up and down the sides in glossy waves. "I let work and travel and pretty much everything else come before my daughter, my family, and my life."

"We'd be a mess together." She'd told him that before, but this time the words didn't have the same emphasis. It was like her heart was tiptoeing around the idea of more...of Luke.

"So you have thought about it."

She fiddled with her fork, swirling a bite of pasta but leaving it on the plate. "Okay, so I have. There was a moment in the ballroom back in Nevada where all those people were pairing up and I was jealous of them. Like they had some secret to happiness that I didn't. Except in reality they were all there because their relationships were in trouble so there was nothing to be jealous about."

"I don't know. If you find that special person, even if the two of you hit a rough patch, I think it's something that other people can sense. Like the two of you are soul mates or some greeting card crap."

She laughed. "Yeah, exactly. Maybe it was the rum punch or just wanting what they had, but I said yes to you, and when I woke up that morning, there was a moment when I was lying in the bed next to you and it felt like...like we really were married."

"And did you like that feeling?"

"It was nice, okay?"

"Just nice? Because it was a lot more to me. In fact, Emma—" He took her hands in his. "I think I love you."

And there were the words she had both dreaded and

wanted to hear all her life. This man, who'd been nothing more than someone she practiced Warrior Three beside, had become something more that night at the hotel in Nevada and something she hadn't quite defined in the weeks since he moved to Harbor Cove. Now he was complicating all of that by throwing in the one four-letter word that Emma hadn't expected him to say. *I think I love you.* "What? How? When?"

His dark eyes met hers, and his features softened. "I fell in love with you the minute you said, *Are we really doing this?* You had that giant smile on your face and that little flower thing on your head, and you looked so beautiful and adventurous and like everything I've always wanted."

"You sure it wasn't the rum punch talking?" She tried to deflect him with a joke, but Luke didn't take the bait.

"Actually, I didn't have any of that punch." He leaned toward her, his cologne teasing at her senses, urging her to winnow the distance between them. "Every single woman I've ever dated has needed me to rescue them. They were either down on their luck or freshly out of a toxic relationship or an addict like Kim. But you...you don't need anybody, Emma. Least of all me. You're fierce and independent and smart as hell. Being around you challenges me and brings out the best side of me."

"You're in love with me because I don't need you? That sounds crazy. And you have me all wrong. I don't have my crap together, not in any way, shape, or form." Everything in her life seemed to be spinning out of control, going in the wrong direction. The last thing she needed was Luke adding a layer of complication.

"I'm in love with you," he said again, slowly, confidently,

"because for the first time in my life, I've met someone who makes me want to be a better person."

She shook her head. "Luke, I'm as screwed-up as the next person. That whole thing with the foundation? I—" She cut off the sentence.

"What?"

"Nothing. Nothing." How could she tell him the truth about her mistake? This man was the first man she'd ever met who saw her as smart, responsible, capable.

"Do you find it that unbelievable that I would fall in love with the only woman who has ever made me want to settle down, have a couple more kids, buy a house with a fence, even get a damned dog?"

"But I'm not a settle-down girl. I'm leaving this town soon." And she was glad to be doing that. Right?

"As you keep telling me. What does the rest of the world have that this town lacks?"

"Opportunities. Everything here is the same as it has always been. Out there, I can be anything, do anything." But the words lacked the conviction she had felt when she made the plan with Atlas. Maybe she was just tired after the long week at work and the event tonight.

"I've traveled a lot, and I have to say, every other place is like this, just with different buildings," Luke said. "People have the same problems, the same challenges. The same hopes and dreams. They fall in love, they get married, and they make it work, here and everywhere else. We could do that, if you're willing to take a risk, Emma."

She got to her feet, grabbed the wine off the counter, and refilled her glass. "Thanks for dinner, Luke."

"You keep changing the subject."

"Because the end of the conversation is going to be the

same. I'm not staying here. I'm not starting something with you. I'm leaving." But a little part of her seemed to break inside when she said those words.

His features hardened, and his voice turned colder. "Running away, in other words."

"I prefer to call it running toward something. What that is, I just don't know yet." She walked out with the bottle because she had a feeling she was going to need that tonight. "Good night, Luke."

CHAPTER 13

The sun was warm and lazy with a slight breeze coming in from the Atlantic Ocean, just enough to take the edge off the heat. Birds chirped, bees buzzed, and a pair of yellow butterflies darted in and out of the plants edging the yard.

The lumber company had pushed out the latest delivery until tomorrow, which meant Luke got to send the subs home early and take the rest of the day off himself. Scout was overjoyed to leave daycare at two o'clock. He'd stopped by the market on the way home, with a bouncy, happy Scout, to pick up some burgers and hot dogs for the grill.

The day would have been completely perfect if Emma was here, but she'd already texted and said she was working late. Luke had a feeling she was avoiding him. He'd barely seen her since Sunday night when he'd gone and told her he was in love with her. Clearly not his smartest move.

"Daddy, can we have a picnic?" Scout asked.

"Why not? It's a picnic kind of day. Here, help me clean off Uncle Ray's table." Luke swept branches off the wooden table while Scout used a dust broom to clear the bench seats. After a deep-dive search in Ray's pantry, Luke found a plastic tablecloth and some clothespins. He and Scout smoothed it across the table. "We have to clip it underneath here so it won't blow away." Luke showed Scout how to pinch the corners of the tablecloth together and attach a clothespin.

"Daddy, I can't do that. I only gots two hands." Which she had used to clap the two corners together under the table and hold on for dear life.

He chuckled. "Points for creativity, Bean. Okay, you do that part, and I'll do the clipping part." They worked together, and when they were done, Luke put up his palm. "High five, Scout. We had some good teamwork there."

She stood on her tiptoes and did a little jump, slapping her palm against his. "We're a team, Daddy?"

If someone had asked him last month, heck, last week, if he thought he and his daughter could ever be anything resembling a team, he'd have said no way. He couldn't see a path through the tantrums and the crying jags— never mind Scout's attitude. But here they were, on a warm, early-summer day, and his daughter was grinning at him like he'd just given her the entire galaxy on a platter. "Yes, kiddo, we are a team."

"Forever?"

He scooped her up and held her to his chest before touching her nose with his own. Her bright-blue eyes stared into his, and Luke realized he loved his daughter more than he loved the air he breathed. Never again would he let work take the place of being a parent. And never again would he disappoint her. "Forever and ever."

She squealed and wrapped her arms around his neck. If there was a heaven on earth, it was right here, with her blond curls in his face and her little arms squeezing the air out of his throat. Best. Moment. Ever.

Just then, he heard the crunch of tires on the gravel driveway and turned, his heart hammering in his chest, thinking it was Emma, home early from work. Instead it was a familiar Camry that made him freeze.

"Mommy!" Scout scrambled out of his arms and was barreling toward the car just as Kim stepped out, bent down, opened her arms, and caught her daughter in a hug.

Last he'd talked to her, Kim had said she was probably going to stay another week in rehab. She'd completed the rehab program but had felt unsure about handling life on the outside so soon. Clearly, she'd changed her mind but hadn't given Luke a heads-up. For a second, Luke worried she'd checked out too early.

Kim was thinner than the last time he'd seen her, and she'd cut her long brown hair into a bob, but she looked sober and healthy, and more grounded. It seemed like the time at the rehab had agreed with her in more ways than one. Kim and Scout embraced for a long moment and then Kim took her daughter's hand and walked toward Luke. "Thanks for watching her."

He bristled. He hadn't been "watching" his daughter. He'd been her father. Period, end of story. And for his ex to just walk in here and think she could pick up where she left off...

Well, it wasn't going to work quite like that again. Luke wasn't going to give up his fragile relationship with

Scout. And he was never going to live without his daughter being an active part of his life. "It was more than that, Kim. I'm not a babysitter. I'm her father."

"Hey, Scout, come help me with these burgers, will ya?" Uncle Ray called, redirecting Scout's attention at just the right time.

Luke waited until Scout was out of earshot before speaking again. "What are you doing here?"

"I got out early for good behavior." Kim smiled.

"A couple days ago, you told me you weren't ready to leave. Are you sure you should be here?"

She scowled at him. "I did my time, Luke. Completed everything I was supposed to. Now I'm in a sober living house and trying to get my life back on track. I really don't need you giving me a hard time right now. It's tough enough just trying to get through a day at a time."

He drew in a breath and tamped down the riot of emotions in his chest. He'd known this day was going to come, of course, but it all seemed so sudden. He'd just started building a relationship with his daughter, and Kim was undoubtedly going to want to take Scout back with her. "I'm sorry, Kim. I don't mean to give you a hard time. I'm happy for you, truly." He sighed. "I also don't want to keep you from seeing Scout because I know she misses you. But I need to trust that she'll be okay if she's with you."

"Look at you, becoming an involved parent finally." She shook her head. "You were barely there for the first four years, and now you're making all the rules?"

"I deeply regret not being involved like I should have been. It was wrong. I had no idea what I was missing out on. I never should have dumped it all in your lap. I'm sorry, Kim."

Her eyes misted. "I...I didn't expect that. Thank you."

"We both love Scout to death, and I'm sure we both want what's best for her."

"And you don't think I'm what's best right now?"

"Do you think you are?"

She cursed and shook her head. "I'm here to see my daughter, not argue with you. You're just going to have to trust me."

Fighting with Kim would only make things more difficult for Scout, who had already been through enough. Luke pushed down his frustration and worry, deciding to extend an olive branch instead. "I'm just worried about you, Kim, and I'm sorry if it came out wrong. We were just about to have some burgers and hot dogs. Why don't you stay for lunch?"

"And then I can take Scout?"

He hesitated. Kim looked and sounded sober, but that didn't mean she wouldn't relapse again. He'd had a second chance to be a father to Scout, and for that he would forever be grateful. Maybe all Kim needed was a second chance to be the mother he knew she could be. "Let's play it by ear. Okay?"

Kim paused a second and then nodded. "I guess I earned that. I'm still trying to trust myself. I can't expect everyone else to trust me right away. Thanks for the lunch invite. I'd love to stay." Kim headed for her daughter. Scout broke away from Uncle Ray and ran over to her mother, talking nonstop about the bus she was helping her uncle "fix." Kim bent down to Scout's level. She brushed a lock of hair off her daughter's face while she was talking to her, and in that tender touch, Luke could see the deep love Kim had for their daughter.

Scout's life was about to change again. Luke could

only pray it would all work out for the best. This time, the stakes were higher than ever before.

❧❦❧❦

"You look like someone canceled your birthday party." Grandma opened her arms and welcomed Emma into a tight, much-needed hug. "What's wrong?"

Emma had stopped off at Grandma's house on her way home from work Monday night. She had managed to successfully avoid Luke for the last two days by putting in extra hours at the hotel—an easy thing to do as Sharon's wedding date, and her demand list, grew closer—and going for a run every morning the second she heard him stir. He'd invited her to have burgers with them tonight, but she'd claimed a bridal consult was keeping her late when, really, Emma was spending way too many hours thinking about her mistakes.

I think I love you. Those words alternately sang in her heart and made her want to run for the hills. A single sentence and everything she thought she could leave behind, as neat and easy as shutting a door, became ten times more complicated.

The weight of the past few weeks seemed ten times heavier now as the weekend loomed. Sunday was Sharon's wedding, Monday was the annulment hearing, and Tuesday...Emma had no idea what Tuesday would hold. Karl hadn't sent out any updates, nor had he returned her check, so any last-minute hope that the foundation would come through for her had been dashed. What on earth was she going to do now? "Everything's wrong, Grandma."

"Do you want to talk about it?"

In other words, did she want to tell her family that she'd made another stupid mistake? That she'd invested her savings in something that was just a scheme? That the big plans she'd been talking about for months were going exactly nowhere?

Not to mention the tumultuous feelings she was having for the man she was living with—and soon divorcing. Her life could be an episode of *Real Housewives* if it weren't so sad.

Emma read the concern and love in Grandma's face and couldn't bring herself to tell her grandmother the truth. "I'm just having a bad day. That's all. Work stress and stuff like that."

"Well, if you ever want to talk about what's going on, I'm here," Grandma said. "In the meantime, there's some vanilla bean cheesecake in the kitchen."

"Cheesecake? Not cookies?"

"Harry likes cheesecake, and I made one to thank him for doing me a favor."

"Really?" Emma took a second look at her grandmother, who was wearing a robe even though it was barely five o'clock, as if Emma had caught her in the middle of getting ready. "Grandma, are you wearing makeup? And perfume?"

Grandma ran a little water over the dishes in the sink. "I have plans this evening."

"With Harry?" Emma came around Grandma's side and leaned closer. She'd touched up her hair, put it up in a curly bun, and had even added lipstick. She was making special desserts, fixing her face, wearing perfume—that all added up to one conclusion. "Wait...are you officially *dating* Harry?"

Emma couldn't remember her grandmother ever dating

anyone. Grandpa had died shortly before Momma, and when the girls were little and consuming every spare second Eleanor had, it was understandable that she wouldn't date. But the girls had been grown-up for almost a decade now, and still Eleanor had avoided relationships. Harry, however, had been determined from day one to capture Grandma's heart. Maybe his one-man wooing campaign was working.

"I am going out with a person who just happens to be Harry," Grandma said, "but it's not a date. It's just two neighbors grabbing dinner."

"Sounds suspiciously like a date to me." Emma grinned. It made her heart happy to see her grandmother venturing out of her comfort zone. "And if it was a date, I would tell you to wear that blue dress that you bought at Gabby's shop. It brings out your eyes."

Grandma swiped the counters, rinsed the sponge, and then set it to dry in the basket at the back of the sink. "Maybe I will wear that. Only because I like how I look in it and the fact that it's comfortable." She glanced at the clock on the wall. "Oh, it's almost time to go. I have to change. If you don't want cheesecake, there are a couple of cookies left in the plastic container."

"Thanks. I was thinking I'd go up to the attic and dig through Momma's stuff. Is that okay?"

"Of course, dear. You never know what kind of treasure you'll find up there." She pressed a kiss to Emma's forehead and then headed out of the kitchen.

"Have fun with Harry!" Emma called after her. "And don't do anything I wouldn't do on a date!"

"It's not a date!" Grandma called back.

"Sure it's not." Emma laughed to herself as she snagged a cookie out of the container and took the back

stairs instead of the main staircase by the front door.
The narrow flight rose to the second floor where three
of the four bedrooms were located. A small door halfway down the hall opened to another staircase that then
led to the attic. The old Victorian was as full of nooks
and crannies as it was history, and Emma loved every
inch of it.

She flicked on the overhead light, which cast the
attic in a pale-yellow glow. A pair of faded upholstered
chairs sat against one wall, alongside several boxes
marked CHRISTMAS. A few others sat on the far wall,
each labeled carefully with the girls' names. Undoubtedly crammed with every single report card, favorite toy,
and rudimentary drawing the girls had ever made. Each
piece had had its turn on the fridge because Grandma
proclaimed all of the girls' artwork, no matter how bad,
her favorite and as far as Emma knew, her grandmother
never threw a single one away.

To the right were the boxes marked PENNY, stacked
neatly in one space. A few were still covered with a fine
layer of dust. A few months ago, the three girls had been
in this very spot, going through some of the same boxes,
looking for Momma's wedding dress for a special event
the town was having. During that hunt, they had come
across Grandma's trove of Dear Amelia letters and put the
pieces together about their grandmother's secret identity.
At the time, Grandma had seemed rather down and out
of sorts, so the three girls had banded together to nudge
Grandma's advice into becoming true. They'd matched
up some couples, meddled in Harry's relationship with
his son and grandson, and threw in some free babysitting
for a stressed-out neighbor. The mission to help Grandma
had done a lot to restore the bond between Emma and

her sisters. Even amid the sisterly squabbles, there'd been a few tears and a lot of laughs, and a common purpose that united the three of them for an all-too-brief moment.

Emma missed the times when her worst problem was failing a math test or being dumped by some cute guy. She missed the nights when the three Monroe girls would climb into Gabby's bed, eating cookies and talking until the wee hours of the morning. They'd been a team—the Monroe Musketeers, as Grandma dubbed them—and Emma had known that, no matter what, her sisters had her back.

She could use that support right now. Would Gabby and Margaret hug her and tell her it would all be okay? Would they be her cheerleaders, as they used to be, if they knew the truth about how far sideways everything had gone?

When are you going to stop being so irresponsible? Margaret's words echoed in her head.

Emma had a week to figure out her next move. For the first time in her life, though, her heart had no idea which direction to go. There were no cliffs calling to her, no amount of yoga that could calm the constant anxiety in her chest, and no meditation that would quiet her mind enough to hear the answers.

Maybe here, among her mother's things, she would find something to inspire her. That way, when she broke it to her family that the foundation was a bust, she could rebound with a new plan. Something that would show them she hadn't failed—she'd just taken a little backstep.

Emma started with the trunk, which had sat at the end of her mother's bed for years before someone, probably Dad, lugged it up to the attic. The lid creaked as she opened it. A couple of months ago, Momma's wedding dress had been the first thing inside the trunk. Right now that dress was at Gabby's house, waiting to be worn again as the beginning of a new love story.

Inside the trunk, Emma found the usual high school keepsakes—yearbook, prom corsage, cheerleader uniform. She picked up each thing, hoping to feel a kinship, a connection, but it was as if she were holding a stranger's memories. Emma closed the lid and sat back on the dusty floor.

She opened another box that was filled with Momma's clothes. Dresses and jeans, a few sweaters that had been chewed by moths. More than two decades had passed since Momma died, and anything that might still hold the scent of her perfume no longer did. She could have been sorting through a bin at Goodwill for all the connection the clothes evoked.

Two more boxes and still that disconnected feeling lingered. Emma had no memory of any of these things. Unlike her sisters, she couldn't remember sneaking into Momma's bedroom to sit at her vanity and brush her hair with a silver-plated brush. She couldn't remember the color of her mother's lipstick or how it felt to be hugged by her.

The last box in the pile was marked simply MISC. Emma tugged off the packing tape and then peeled open the cardboard panels. A stack of books, each with a bookmark somewhere in the middle, sat against one side, a sad reminder of a life cut too short, the ending yanked away before it was done being written. A pile of notebooks flanked the novels Momma had never finished reading. Emma picked up the top notebook and began leafing through it.

An entire plan for the community center unfurled before her in Momma's neat, tight cursive writing. There were pages of ideas, curricula, and services that the new center could offer to the children of the area. Emma could see Momma's degree in early childhood education and her love for children in every word.

This was what Margaret and Dad had been talking about. Momma's dream, cut off in the middle, just like all of those books.

If Harbor Cove had something like this program Momma had designed but on a far more regular basis than the handful of events Emma put on at the hotel, it could change the lives of so many children. They'd have a safe, nurturing place to go to when life got too hard or they just needed support.

Emma tucked the book under her arm, closed the box, and stowed it away. She headed downstairs just in time to catch Grandma fastening some earrings in place. She had, as promised, changed into the blue A-line dress Gabby had made. It outlined Grandma's hourglass figure and offset the silver in her hair. "You look gorgeous, Grandma."

"Not bad for an old lady, huh?"

"You're only as old as you think you are," Emma quipped. "Someone wiser than me once said that. I think it was...you."

"Actually, years ago I think I said the opposite to my daredevil, rule-breaking granddaughter—you're not as old as you think you are."

Emma laughed. Grandma had indeed said that every time a young Emma had wanted to go off on a river rafting or skydiving adventure. "Either way, I think Harry is going to be wowed."

"I'm nervous. Is that weird?" She shifted right and left, checking her appearance. She fussed with her hair and swiped at a smudge of lipstick. Grandma glanced over at Emma. "Oh! What did you find in the attic?"

"This." Emma handed her grandmother the faded composition book.

Grandma flipped through the first few pages. "Oh, I remember this now. It's such a shame it never happened. Your mother was so excited about it. I think she had even started to put together a committee of sorts, but without her to spearhead the team, it all kind of fizzled away."

"Too bad because this would have been great. Harbor Cove is one of those relatively affluent coastal towns, but there are still lots of kids here and in the neighboring towns who need a program like this." She took the book back and smoothed a hand over her mother's handwriting. "Is it okay if I take this home?"

"Of course, dear. You should—" The doorbell rang, and Grandma's entire face lit up. For all her protests, Eleanor Whitmore was clearly as enchanted with Harry as he was with her. "Harry's here. Right on time."

"Have a wonderful date." Emma pressed a kiss to her grandmother's cheek and then grabbed her coat and headed out the door, passing Harry as she did. "Treat her right or you'll have three girls to answer to."

Harry chuckled. He was an affable, good-natured man. The girls had liked him from the first time they'd met him, especially because his presence brought a reluctant but shy smile to Grandma's face every single time he was here. "Of course. She's the kind of woman every man should treat right."

"Good answer, Harry." Emma patted him on the shoulder before heading down the porch stairs and to her car.

She tossed the notebook onto the passenger seat, buckled her seat belt, and started the sedan. She lingered in the driveway for a moment, long enough to see Grandma and Harry leave for their date, while Emma wondered which direction she should go.

CHAPTER 14

On Tuesday afternoon, Luke sat back in his office chair and stretched the kinks out of his back. The Berry Circle project was humming along and looked like it would finish right on time.

He logged into the video chat software, and Hassan Ali's face popped up on his screen. They exchanged quick pleasantries, and then Luke's boss got straight to the point. "Where are we on Phase One?"

"Right on target for every single deadline. We were able to make up the time we had lost by shifting some crews around, which kept the overtime at a minimum. We should also come in a little under the revised budget."

Hassan looked impressed. "That is good to hear, Carter. I'm honestly surprised you were able to make up a full month of delays."

Luke didn't tell his boss that the key to improving efficiency was staying on top of the crew instead of taking three-hour lunches at a local bar, as his predecessor had been rumored to do. "I've also negotiated better pricing on the cabinets and flooring. I know the company that you're working with pretty well, and I told them there would be future projects, so they were very eager to work with us on cost." Yet another thing the previous project manager had neglected to do, maybe because he'd been stumbling back from lunch and too out of it to care about saving the company money.

"That's fantastic. Glad to hear it." Hassan gave Luke a nod. "You're doing a great job. I can see why Brandon recommended you. I'm very impressed with what you're doing over there."

"Thank you. I appreciate that."

"I know this may be a little premature, considering Berry Circle is still ten or so months out from being fully complete, but what do you think about overseeing a similar project in Springfield?"

"That's clear across the state." Luke thought of uprooting Scout again and plunking her down in a town where she didn't know anyone. He couldn't do that to her. Not now, not when everything in her life was still so fragile. "I have a daughter, sir, who will be in kindergarten in the fall. I don't think it's a good time to move."

"I'll throw in a pay raise, too," Hassan said. "You're saving me tens of thousands of dollars on Berry Circle, so throw a number at me, and I'll make it work. Don't say no until the negotiating is over." Hassan grinned and hung up.

Luke sat at the desk a while longer, thinking about the life he could provide for his daughter with a hefty pay raise and weighing that against the upheaval a cross-state move would create. He loved his job here but had to admit that a big part of him missed the renovation work he had done before. The puzzle of a renovation challenged him because no two jobs were ever the same. There was nothing wrong with pumping out a bunch of cookie-cutter houses, of course, but Luke had loved going into work each day not knowing whether he'd have a foundation problem to solve or a roof repair to tackle.

After the last crew member had gone home, Luke shut down his computer and called it a day. He had a couple of hours of daylight left. Just enough time to mow the yard and trim the shrubs and maybe spend a little time with his family before the day came to a close.

Emma had picked Scout up from daycare earlier and brought her to the house. Having Emma around was like having a whole team of childcare providers. She seemed to intuitively know how to get Scout to calm down, eat her vegetables, and go to bed on time.

And she managed to do it all while avoiding him.

He shouldn't be surprised. She had made it clear that she wasn't interested in anything other than a job and temporary housing until he left town. Disappointment lingered in his chest regardless. What had he expected? They could get married on the fly and make such a hasty decision work? That was the stuff of fairy tales and movies, not real life.

When Luke pulled into Ray's driveway, he saw Scout in a pair of jeans and a T-shirt, both covered in grease, standing on a little stepstool and peering into the engine of the bus. Uncle Ray was bent over, most of the upper half of his body hidden by the engine, talking to Scout as she handed him tools.

"You teaching my kid how to hot-wire a car, Uncle Ray?"

His uncle straightened, narrowly missing the hood with his head. He grabbed a nearby rag to wipe his hands. "Scout, tell your dad what you learned today."

Scout propped her fists on her hips. "The pistons go up and down, and they smush the air, and that makes a little fire—not a bad fire, Daddy, just enough for a plug—and that turns the cran...cran..."

"Crankshaft," Ray supplied.

"And that makes the bus go fast!"

Luke picked Scout up and settled her on his side, heedless of the dirt she was getting on his clothes. "Well, my little grease monkey, that is pretty impressive. I didn't know my girl was so smart."

"Wicked smaht," Scout said, doing her best imitation of a Boston accent, clearly something else she had learned from her uncle.

Luke laughed and hugged her tight. "Never a dull moment with you, Bean." He glanced at his uncle. "What made you start working on the bus?"

"Tired of it taking up space in my yard." Ray scowled, but Luke could tell his uncle was excited by the project. "Thought I'd try to get her running, at least once. My little helper wants us to take a road trip this summer."

"A road trip, huh? I think we could do that. You want to go camping with me and Uncle Ray, Scout?"

"And Emma! Emma has to go because she knows how to make my hair all pretty." Scout flipped one of her pony-tails. Her hair did, indeed, look a thousand times better when Emma was the one wielding the brush as opposed to Luke, who had never had to manage much more than an inch or two of hair.

Even the thought of Emma left a hollow feeling in his gut. She was living under the same roof but it might as well have been a distant planet. He missed her smile. Missed it a hell of a lot.

"I think Emma is going somewhere else," Luke said. "She's got a trip planned."

"Then we can go with her! Uncle Ray said his bus can drive everywhere."

Ray chuckled. "It doesn't drive at all right now, kiddo."

Scout tapped on his chest. "Let's go with Emma, Daddy. She's my friend. I like her a lot."

"We all do." He set Scout on the ground. "Anyway, that's a conversation for a different day."

Maybe a day when his heart stopped hurting and the space around him stopped feeling so hollow without Emma's smile.

❦❦❦

Luke left Scout with Uncle Ray, who was teaching her how spark plugs worked. He headed into the house, snagging a piece of leftover pizza on his way to the bathroom. Just as he approached the door, Emma emerged in a cloud of steam. She was wearing a thick white robe and had wrapped her wet hair in a dark-brown towel. "Luke. You're home."

"And so are you." She looked so beautiful with her face bare of makeup and a slight flush in her cheeks from the warm bathroom. The connection between them felt as fragile as a spiderweb, as if it might fall apart at any second. "Listen, I'm sorry about the other night. I shouldn't have pushed you."

"It's fine. All water under the bridge in a few more days, right?"

Even as she was telling him that she was moving on,

all he wanted to do was kiss her. He wanted to ask her to stay, to not get the annulment, to give their relationship a valid shot. "You're right."

She nodded, and for a second, he thought he saw sadness in her eyes. "Bathroom is all yours. If it's okay with you, I thought I'd take Scout down to the lake for a little bit. She was asking me earlier about it, and we have some time before the sun sets."

"There's a lake here?"

"Just through the trees. It's hard to see in the summer when the leaves are so thick. My friends and I used to sneak into these woods and party back in high school."

"So you're the hooligans Uncle Ray was always complaining about."

"Guilty as charged." She started to turn away and then stopped. "Why don't you come with us? In case you want to take Scout down there again after I'm gone."

Everything about Emma's words and body language said she was halfway out the door. And there was nothing Luke could do to change her mind.

᠅᠙᠙᠙᠅

The waters of Benson's Lake sparkled under the early-evening setting sun. The surface was smooth, broken only by the occasional bird diving for a snack. A pair of fishermen sat in a low silver boat on the other side of the lake. A majestic blue heron picked its way among the rocks of the banks, giving the three visitors a wary eye.

"Can we go swimming?" Scout asked. She was still wearing her grease-smeared clothes from earlier when she was working on the bus with her uncle. Emma thought she looked adorable but also knew bath time was going to be a bit of an ordeal.

"The water is still pretty cold," Emma said. "Too cold to swim right now. Anyway, you have to always swim with your dad."

Scout pouted. "I wanna be a big girl and go by myself."

Emma bent down to Scout's level. "You'll be one soon enough. Don't rush the future when the present is such a sweet gift. That's something my grandmother told me when I was a little older than you."

Scout considered that for a long moment. Then, like a typical preschooler, her mind skipped to a different topic. She glanced up at Luke. "Can I look for rocks?"

"Sure," Luke said. Scout happily dashed down to the waterfront, in the process scaring away the heron, who soared across to the other side of the lake. "Your grandmother sounds very wise."

"She is one of the smartest and kindest people I know. I'm so grateful she was there for me and my sisters after my mother died. She was the family we all needed."

"Family works differently for each person, doesn't it? Scout's upbringing isn't the stereotypical nuclear family, either. All I can do is hope that what she's got will be enough to raise her into a good adult."

"You might not have been the best dad before, but you're a great dad now. She adores you." Scout was singing to herself as she searched among the rocks, pocketing one or two.

"I wouldn't call her throwing herself onto the floor and screaming at the top of her lungs adoring me."

"Come on, when was the last time she did that?"

He thought for a second. "Has to be at least a couple of weeks."

"See? You and Scout are building a bond, and she's learning she can trust you to be there for her."

"Which also happens to be around the same time you came into Scout's life. You're the kid whisperer, Emma. Not me."

It might have taken some time, but there was no doubt in Emma's mind that Luke had figured out how to be a parent to Scout. He had become more patient and more understanding, and had made space in every single day to spend one-on-one time with his daughter. Emma would lie in her room at night and listen to Luke read books to Scout. He'd do all the voices and make the entire experience magical. The last few nights, Scout had actually asked to go to bed early just to have her dad read to her. Maybe it was the return of Scout's mom that had Luke feeling so insecure about his parenting.

"That feather I gave Scout that day in front of the diner wasn't just for her, you know. It was also for you." She smiled. "When Dumbo gets that feather from the crow, he believes he can fly when he's holding it. Then he loses the feather and panics because he thinks the feather held all the magic. Turns out Dumbo had everything he needed already, and the feather was the thing he used to give himself courage." Emma sat down on an overturned log and rested her arms on her knees. "I'm just the feather for you, Luke. You've got everything you need to be the parent that Scout needs."

"You're much more than a feather to me, Emma." Luke perched on the log beside her and took her hand in his. She loved the way his strong hand felt against hers. The air was hushed back here in the woods by the lake, almost as if they were on a planet with just the three of them.

"These last two weeks, with you living at Uncle Ray's, have been some of the best weeks of my life."

"Luke, I…"

"I could be wrong, but I thought I felt something when you kissed me back. You might not want to admit it, Emma Monroe, but I think you kinda like your husband."

She laughed. "You're a dork. And for the record…"

"For the record what?" he prompted when her voice trailed off.

She drew in a deep breath. "I was going to say I don't like you but I'd be lying, and I'm tired of lying to myself. All that's done is get me into messes I have no idea how to get out of," she said. "So for the record, I do like you. A lot."

"Let's table the fact that you like me for later." He grinned and shifted closer to her. "What kind of messes are you talking about?"

"Nothing you can fix, so don't worry about it."

"I'm not trying to fix your problems, Emma, just trying to be your friend." Scout was still at the water's edge, darting back and forth between the sandy shore and the grass. "What I'm saying is, if you want to talk about it with someone who won't judge you, because I have made plenty of messes myself, I'm here."

She stared out at the water for a long time. It didn't hold any answers for her, just a calmness that seemed to whisper advice. That it was okay to trust Luke. To open up to him. "You know that trip I'm supposed to be going on soon?"

He nodded.

"Well, turns out the whole thing was either a scam or a disappointment. I'm not sure which. All I do know is that

I invested my savings and my future into a foundation that so far hasn't set up any of what it promised."

"So you're not going?"

She shrugged. "I can't stay here in Harbor Cove, tell my family that I made another foolish, impulsive decision that backfired, and crawl back to the job I hate. No, I can't do that. My family will never let me live that down."

"They can't be that bad."

Emma scoffed. "You've barely met my family, and I love them, I do. But they have this saying for my screwups. It's called an 'Emma Move.'" She put air quotes around the words. "As in, I do it so often, it's become slang in my house."

Scout called out for her father, waving a handful of rocks. He gave her a thumbs-up before turning back to Emma. "What if that's not judgment talking but rather envy?"

"Are you nuts? They're not jealous of me."

"I was. When I first met you and you told me about the cliff diving and the silent retreat and that hike along the Appalachian Trail, I thought, *Here's a girl who has lived more in the last six months than I have in my entire life*. You said yes to every opportunity that came along, including marrying me. When I saw you again in Nevada, I wanted to be just as impulsive as you, and when Yogi Brown started marrying people off, I asked you to do it with me. You made me brave enough to do that."

"And look at the mess we created, Luke." She waved her arms as if she could encompass cousin George and the courts and the last couple of months in a single circle. "We had to get lawyers and a judge, and it's a whole thing to undo."

"But it's also part of what brought me here, back to

you, to the one person who could help me find a way to talk to my daughter and show her how much I love her, right when she needed me to be a parent the most. A lot of good has come out of what you call a mistake."

"Maybe."

"And maybe some good can come out of this mistake with the foundation. You just have to look a little deeper, Emma."

"Trust me, there is no good to be found in this situation. Other than the fact that I'll be out of this town in two more weeks." She got to her feet and brushed off the back of her jeans. "I'll see you back at the house."

CHAPTER 15

The next night, Emma was heading up the walkway toward Grandma's house as Margaret was coming down the porch stairs. It was Wednesday night, family dinner night, and Emma had brought another store-bought pie. This might be the last family dinner Emma would enjoy, since her last day at work was this Sunday. She didn't have to attend the annulment hearing on Monday but it was a final detail she should probably make sure was taken care of before she left town.

She had yet to figure out what she was going to do come Tuesday, the day she was supposed to be flying for parts unknown. She could stay here as Luke had said, but where? She'd given up her apartment at Margaret's, quit her job, and blown her savings on a fraudulent foundation. She couldn't keep on living with the man who was no longer her husband. That had been a temporary thing.

Starting over meant quite literally starting from nothing. Maybe it was better to just catch the first flight to

Anywhere-But-Here and do all that far from the well-meaning judgment of her family.

Emma stopped beside her sister. "Where are you going, Meggy?"

"I have some work to finish up. Tell Grandma I'm sorry I'm missing dinner."

Again? Margaret had been gone more often than she had been here. "It's after five. Why are you going back to the store?"

"Because..." Mike's car swung into the driveway, and for just a second his headlights illuminated Margaret, like a ghost in the center of the walkway. "Because I have to. Mike will be here so you get half of us."

Mike got out of his car as Margaret came down the walkway. Margaret's husband of ten years was a tall man with a muscular build. He played tennis several times a week and had started golfing a few months ago, which seemed so out of character, but here he was, fresh from the links and at a family dinner.

Margaret paused by her car. She and Mike exchanged a few words that could have been a conversation in the checkout line for all the emotion in their faces. After a moment, Mike shook his head, told her goodbye, then returned to grab a bag out of his car. He turned and watched his wife's car head down the street. "Here, Emma, you take these." He pressed a bag of warm biscuits from the local bakery into her hand. "I don't really feel like being here tonight. I'll just do the Lean-Cuisine-for-one thing. Again."

"Are you sure you don't want to visit the family? Grandma will be so disappointed." Emma adored her brother-in-law. He was a little nerdy and distracted, but also affable and pleasant. He did, however, need Garanimals tags to match his clothing, but what CPA wasn't like that? Tonight, Mike's teal polo shirt clashed with the dark-green khakis he had on, all paired with white golf shoes that looked like sneakers.

"I love your family, I really do," he said, "but I'm just not in the mood for answering questions."

"I get that." Poor guy. What he had in common with judgy, grumpy Margaret, Emma would never know.

Emma wasn't quite sure how to—or if she should—bring up the subject of his struggling marriage. She opted not to say anything because it wasn't her business or her marriage. And she was the last person who should give anyone marital advice, considering her own marriage was going to be over before the ink dried on the license.

"So, you're golfing now," Emma said. Small talk was clearly not her forte.

"Not really." He leaned against his car and drew in a deep breath. "I'm more just avoiding going home. Things are bad between Margaret and me."

"We know." Emma said and then rushed to recover. She didn't want Mike to think that the girls talked about the state of the Brentwood marriage all the time, even if they did. "I mean . . . I mean, *I* know."

"It's okay, Emma, really. Your family is so close, I know they have realized that Margaret and I are having some issues," Mike said. He nodded toward the Victorian on Bayberry Lane where Gabby and Jake were inside, helping Grandma and Harry put the finishing touches on dinner. "I've always been envious of your family. Mine's nothing like that. I think they're half the reason I married Margaret. I wanted to have that kind of family so badly when I was growing up. People who were close, who had family dinners once a week, and who had all these inside jokes and happy memories. I mean, I know not all your memories are happy because your mom died, but..." He seemed flustered. "You know what I mean."

"Well, you do have us, Mike. You've had our family since the day you married my sister." It was true—all of the Monroe girls had welcomed Mike with open arms. He was sweet to Margaret when they were dating, and she'd seemed happy, so the family had been quick to embrace him, just as they had Jake. "And you have Margaret in your little family of two."

"Yeah, but that closeness you and your sisters have with each other and your grandmother, that's not the kind of closeness Margaret and I have. We got married so young, and I guess I thought we would eventually become close like that, but if anything"—he let out a long sigh—"We've drifted farther apart. I was hoping a baby might help, but Margaret wants no part of having kids, and I...I don't know what to do anymore."

"I'm sorry, Mike. I don't know what to say." Two workaholics with a struggling marriage. Emma wasn't surprised, especially since Margaret had said much the same thing at lunch a few weeks ago. Putting a Type A with a Type A+ was a recipe for disaster, she was sure. "Have you tried talking to Margaret about how you feel?"

"Of course. But...it's complicated." He glanced up at the house again and then looked down at his watch. "Anyway, I'm not here to dump my problems on you. And I don't want to put a damper on dinner by just moaning about my issues all night."

"It's okay. I just don't have any advice to give you. Relationships aren't really my jam, unless they're temporary." She said it like a joke, but neither of them laughed.

"I'm beginning to think they're not mine, either." He tried a smile, but it fell flat. "Hey, I met that guy of yours the other day. Luke."

For a second, she liked those words together—*that guy of yours*—but then she reminded herself that, despite how much she thought about Luke (which was way too much) and how much she liked him and the way he kissed, they were just a momentary thing that was in the past, or would be as soon as the judge signed the annulment papers. *I'm falling in love with you.* "He's not really my guy. I mean...it's complicated."

Mike chuckled. "I get that. Anyway, he seems like a nice guy. I do the books for the company he works for. He came in to get last year's numbers from the developer's books so he could do some budgeting analyses for this project. We ended up talking for a while. He's smart, knows his stuff. I've met his boss, and if you ask me, Luke would be far better running that company."

"How come?"

"He's invested. Hassan is smart, driven, and has the money to take that company where it wants to go, but Luke has the passion for the work, for doing a good job. He treats that company like it's his own. I've worked with a lot of businesses, and I tell you, that's a rare trait in an employee."

She wasn't sure if she was supposed to be proud or impressed. After all, Luke was her...husband. No, that word still sounded wrong. *Friend* seemed too blah. Were they more than that? Did she want them to be more than that?

No, definitely no. She was leaving town in a few days, and turning whatever this was into a relationship would only muddle things.

And what did you think moving in with him was going to do?

After a little more small talk, Mike said goodbye and got in his car. Emma watched him go, her heart breaking for her sister and brother-in-law. Hopefully, they would figure it out.

Emma carried the bag of rolls into Grandma's house. Grandma, Harry, Gabby, and Jake were bustling between the kitchen and dining room, getting dishes and food on the table. A wonderful hum of conversation and laughter flowed among the four of them. For a moment, Emma stood in the hall to watch and listen.

As much as she wanted to leave Harbor Cove, she knew she was going to miss her family dearly. Every time she walked into Grandma's house, it was like coming home. More so than her apartment had ever felt. Maybe because she'd never really done anything to personalize the space. Margaret had highlighted and underlined the parts of the lease that told Emma the apartment was to be left in the exact condition she'd moved into—with the plain taupe walls and boring beige carpet. Emma had hung a couple of photos from her trips but, other than that, left the apartment untouched.

Grandma's house, however, with the sitting room full of antiques where Emma and her sisters had done their homework every afternoon and the swing in the backyard where Emma had spent many a lazy summer afternoon, embodied the very essence of home. Leaving it would mean leaving a part of herself back here in Harbor Cove.

But how could she stay and go back to living the same life that had felt so suffocating? That was an answer she didn't have. At least not yet.

"I've got rolls!" Emma announced as she entered the kitchen.

"I thought Mike and Margaret were bringing those," Grandma said.

"Margaret went back to work, and Mike went home. I think he didn't want to be here and pretend to be happy when things are anything but with Margaret right now."

Grandma sighed. "I wish the two of them would work out whatever problems they have."

"They will, I'm sure of it." But it was a lie, the kind of thing Emma said to try to erase the worry from her grandmother's features. "So, what's for dinner?"

"Lasagna. *Someone* said that the lasagna at Bella Vita was the best, and I decided to prove him wrong." Grandma smiled at Harry, and he gave her a quick peck on the cheek.

"Everything you make is the best, Ella Bella."

Looked like their date had gone well. In fact, everything between Grandma and Harry seemed to be going well. Fifty percent of the Monroe/Whitmore family was happily ensconced in relationships while the other half had no idea what the hell they were doing.

"Well, I brought dessert. Bought from the store, of course, because we all know I can't cook." Emma placed the bag of rolls and her store-bought pie on the counter. "Let's eat. I'm starving."

"We're waiting for two more guests to arrive," Grandma said. "They should be here any minute."

Emma shrugged out of her sweater and stowed it on a kitchen chair. "Grandma, I told you, Margaret and Mike both left. I don't think they're coming back."

"I'm not waiting for them." A mysterious smile filled Grandma's face. A smile Emma knew well, because it meant Grandma had something cooking. She thought of the Dear Amelia column. The Father-Daughter Dance and her grandmother's insistence on chatting with Luke. "Grandma, what did you do?"

※❧❧※

Luke knew the second he saw Emma's face that she didn't know he'd been invited to dinner a second time. Although she put on a smile and greeted him and Scout with a little hug, the stiffness of her spine and set of her jaw gave it away.

They sat on opposite sides of the table, with Scout on his right and Jake on his left. Maybe to give him another male ally? Luke wasn't sure. Jake gave him a warm welcome and then whispered something like, "Welcome to the jungle," as he sat down.

The family slipped into an easy patter of teasing conversation. As they passed the rolls and dished up portions of lasagna, the sisters caught their grandmother up on the cake tasting and a possible wedding date for Gabby and Jake.

"Congrats, man," Luke said to Jake.

"I should say the same to you." Jake grinned. "You two beat us to the altar."

"A temporary situation," Emma said. "Now, can we talk about something other than that blip in my personal history? We have a little teapot at the table with big ears."

"Well, if you two would just make it permanent, we could talk about your M-A-R-R-I-A-G-E at dinner," Eleanor said as she buttered a piece of bread.

Emma shot her grandmother a glare and then whipped her attention back to Luke. "I heard you met my other brother-in-law, Mike."

"I did. I forgot to mention it to you." Because she'd done her best to avoid him all week. "Nice guy. Is he coming tonight?"

"No," Emma said.

"Soon," Eleanor said. "We will all be back together soon. Now, who wants more bread?"

"I just want more of this lasagna," Harry said. "You were right, Ella Bella. This is much better than Bella Vita's."

"Don't tell Frank that," Jake said. "He's already anxious enough about his advertising."

Harry made a gesture like he was zipping his lips and then unzipped them to eat another bite of lasagna. Eleanor laughed, and a tender look extended across the table.

Luke had never known a family quite like this. His own family was distant and cold, his father a judgmental man who rarely had a kind word for anyone. The Monroe clan, however, was straight out of a holiday coffee commercial. Warm, inviting, friendly, and everything he'd ever imagined a family could be.

Once she got comfortable with everyone, Scout opened up and became the darling of the room, charming every single person at the table, as she often did with people she met. She talked nonstop about everything from her teddy bear to the bus project. "I'm gonna be a bus fixer when I grow up. Uncle Ray and Daddy are showing me how."

"Yesterday you wanted to be an artist," Luke said.

Scout propped a fist on her hip. "Daddy, I can be a bus fixer *and* an artist. Miss Emma says I can be anything I put my brain to."

"That's right, Scout." Emma tapped Scout's nose. "And I think being a bus fixer is an awesome job."

"Bus fixer?" Gabby asked. "I thought you built houses, Luke."

"I do, but I also like rebuilding things. My uncle has this bus that he bought many years ago at an auction. He'd planned to restore it so that he and his wife could travel the country. But then he got injured in the war and they broke up, and the bus has just been sitting in the yard. Scout discovered it and convinced her uncle Ray that it needs to be running again."

"'Cuz then we can take it on vacations, Daddy, and go see Mickey Mouse."

"That's a mighty long drive from here, but maybe, Bean." He scooped some more lasagna onto his plate. Every cheesy layer was better than the one before. "It's been a great learning experience for Scout. Kids are natural-born scientists, and she's loved seeing how things work."

"That's a program I always wanted to start at the hotel but never got a chance to." Emma dished up some of the cucumber salad that everyone else had ignored in favor of pasta and cheese. "Sometimes the lumber store does a little kids' workshop where they get to build stuff and use handsaws and hammers. My mother had the same idea years ago for skills programs for kids to replace the things that have been cut from school funding like shop and home ec."

"That sounds like a great idea," Gabby said. "I didn't know Momma was working on that."

Emma nodded. "I found this notebook of hers up in the attic. She had all kinds of ideas and plans."

"Such a shame it never happened," Gabby said.

"Why not do it yourself?" Luke took a bite of lasagna.

"That's a lot of overhead," Emma said. "And I don't really have that kind of money."

"True. Building rental, materials, electricity." He thought for a minute. "I could help you find a building and fix it up. And maybe you could do a fundraiser for the rest."

"What, in the five days before I leave?"

"You could stay," her grandmother said gently, reaching a hand out to cover Emma's. "And use that inheritance from your mother to set it up."

Emma's gaze dropped to her plate. "I...uh, don't have that anymore."

Gabby gasped. "What?"

There was a long moment of tense silence before Emma spoke again. "I...well, I invested it in the Atlas Foundation because I really believed in what they were doing and they needed the seed money."

"All of it?" Eleanor asked.

A palpable tension hung over the table. Jake shot Luke a look that said, *Sorry you're in the middle of this.* Luke willed Emma to look up at him, for her to see that he had her back and that they could get through this tough moment together, no matter what.

But Emma kept her gaze on her lap. "Yes."

"Well, that might not have been your wisest decision," her grandmother said, "but at least it's for a good cause." She forked up a piece of lasagna. "Where's your first assignment? Where are you flying to on Tuesday?"

"I'm uh...not flying anywhere on Tuesday."

Silence. A clock in another room chimed the hour. A gust of wind rattled a windowpane. The candles on the table crackled as the wax melted. Luke thought of pushing away from the table and going over to Emma's side. He was halfway out of his chair when she caught his eye and shook her head. *Thank you,* she mouthed. *I've got this.*

"What happened?" Gabby asked.

Emma bit her bottom lip. "The foundation hasn't gotten their act together yet. They don't have a destination for any of us. And to be honest, I don't know if they ever will."

"What were you thinking? Giving Momma's money to them?" Gabby asked.

"Gabriella, be nice. Emma didn't think—"

"No, Grandma, she didn't. That's the problem with Emma. She never thinks things through." Gabby sighed. "This is what happens when you jump without looking. Sometimes you crash to the ground."

CHAPTER 16

I can't believe this is your last event at the hotel," Diana said.

Emma straightened a bouquet that had started to wilt, brushing the fallen petals off the table and into her hand before the bride saw a single drooping rose and threw yet another temper tantrum. Four-year-old Scout had been easier to handle than this bride from hell. "Seems fitting that my last event is Sharon's wedding. That right there is a message from the universe. Never ever work with bridezillas again."

Diana laughed. "She wasn't that bad, was she?"

Emma just arched a brow. Across the room, Sharon was dancing with her father. The wedding itself had gone off more or less without a hitch, save for a last-minute Sharon crisis about the red carpet that was shorter than she'd expected between the hotel and her limo. She'd sat in the limo for a solid two minutes, expecting Emma to somehow lengthen the rug to close the two-foot gap between the curb and Sharon's first step. Emma finally pulled the carpet down to the car and then messaged the bellhop to grab the small red entry carpet from the foyer to fill the resulting gap at the top of the path. "Thank God it all went well. I've had the staff keep her champagne glass filled so that hopefully she gets too tipsy to complain."

Diana grabbed Emma in an impulsive, tight hug. "I'm going to miss you so much, Emma. Do you really have to go?"

A part of Emma didn't want to leave her friends, her family, and everything that was familiar. Nevertheless, this morning, she'd bought a plane ticket to Haiti and written to a charity in Port-au-Prince about volunteering there. She had enough money to get by for a few weeks, and maybe she could pick up a job at a school or something. "Even if I wasn't going away, I couldn't stay in this job, Diana. I hate planning weddings."

"But you're great at event planning." Diana gave Emma's hands a squeeze. "I don't know what the hotel will do without you."

True. Emma did enjoy the jigsaw puzzle of creating an event and the challenge of making it unique. "It's too bad Larry wouldn't make that part of my job a full-time thing. I love doing the kids' events."

Diana scoffed. "I can barely get Larry to pay for two-ply toilet paper in the staff ladies' room. There's no way he'd make that a full-time position."

Emma laughed. Their penny-pinching boss was well known for his crazy cost-saving ideas. "Well, at least this event has finally moved forward without a hitch."

"Don't say that," Diana whispered. "You're going to curse it."

As if Diana's words had been the match to a flame, Sharon's wedding began to fall apart right in front of Emma's eyes. Someone stepped on Marshmallow's tail, which sent the little dog running for the safety of the banquet table. A man on his way to the bar dodged the dog and ended up stumbling and hitting the table. The five-tier cake and twin dog-shaped ice sculptures flanking it began to wobble.

For one brief second, Emma thought it would all be okay. Then the man—who had probably already been to the bar one too many times—took a second stumbling step into the table, causing it to tip. In slow motion, Emma watched the ice sculptures slide off their bases and the cake tumble, one tier after another, onto the floor.

Sharon began to shout at everyone in a twenty-foot radius while Marshmallow spied his opportunity to duck in there and begin licking the frosting off the floor. "Whose fault is this?" she screamed. "Someone needs to fix this! I want a new cake. Right now!"

Emma dashed over to Sharon, scooping up Marshmallow as she did. Emma didn't know much about dogs but she doubted two pounds of buttercream frosting was good for Marshmallow's belly. "Sharon, I'm so sorry. It was an acci—"

"This is the hotel's fault. You should have anchored the cake and the table better. What kind of shoddy operation is this?" She took two steps forward, coming almost nose-to-nose with Emma and ignoring her dog, who was terrified by his owner's angry outburst and shaking in Emma's arms. "I want a new cake."

"Honey, it's not her fault." Sharon's groom took her arm and tried to tug her back. "Like she said, it was an accident."

Sharon wheeled on him. "Everything was supposed to be perfect. My parents paid fifty thousand dollars for this wedding, and look at what cheap construction this hotel has. That table was not sturdy enough. And now I want the cake we paid for."

"Sharon, you're being unreasonable," her husband said. "Cakes take time to make, and—"

"Kevin, you better go to management right now and tell them I want my cake." She pointed at Larry, who was cowering in the corner, looking like he'd rather die than have a conversation with Sharon or her groom.

"I'm sure the chef has another dessert he can whip up," Emma said, hoping to God that Chef Tyler had enough of some kind of dessert for 250 people. "You'll just need to give him a minute."

"I paid for the five-tier French vanilla cake with lavender mousse," Sharon said. "And that is what I want. Not some pudding he has in the back of the walk-in."

"Sharon, you're being unreasonable—"

She wheeled on her husband, her face tight with controlled rage. "This is my wedding, Kevin. My special day, and now it's ruined."

"Honey, it's not about the cake, or just about you. It's supposed to be about our marriage. And I'm part of the wedding, too." He let out a little laugh and held up his left hand. "In case you didn't notice."

"No, Kevin. This is my day!" she repeated. "And this horrible hotel has destroyed it."

Kevin stared at her for a long moment. The rest of the room had gone silent. The DJ had stopped playing music. The guests had stopped eating. Even Marshmallow had tucked his little head under Emma's arm, his tiny body quivering.

"I guess I'm just another accessory then," Kevin said. "Ranking right up there with the bouquet and your"—he waved at her head—"two-thousand-dollar tiara."

Sharon snorted. "The tiara is worth more than that, and I deserve much more than this shoddy wedding in this run-down, godforsaken small town where you grew up. If you were a real man, Kevin, you would do something and save my wedding. I will not be humiliated like this."

Kevin shook his head, a wry smile on his face. "You know, my mother told me not to marry you. She said you were selfish and self-centered and that you were only after my money. I told her you had a good heart and that you truly loved me. I can see which one of us was wrong now."

"Of course, baby," Sharon crooned. She reached for his shoulder and gave it a little pat. "Let me just fix this cake issue, and then we will get back to my"—she laughed—"our day."

"Don't bother, Sharon." Kevin slid off the ring that he had put on his finger less than two hours ago and dropped it into his new bride's palm. "I'm done with this wedding, and I'm done with you."

"But…but…but…you can't walk out," she sputtered. "We're married!"

"Since we didn't even make it to the wedding night, I don't think this is even legal. Either way, Sharon dear, you will be hearing from my lawyer. Enjoy the cordon bleu." Then he spun on his heel and stomped out the door. The room erupted into applause, and Sharon burst into tears.

"That's what I get for jinxing it by saying everything was going well," Emma muttered to Diana as the two of them crossed the room, leaving a hysterical Sharon behind. Marshmallow stayed tightly wedged in Emma's arms. "Happy last day to me."

❧❧❧❧

On Sunday afternoon, Luke stood at the edge of the playground and watched his daughter and her mother play tag. Kim would peek around a corner, spy Scout, and then run to tag her, but every time, Scout managed to slip away, running to the next hiding spot in an endless stream of giggles. Clearly, she was happier with her mother back in her life.

Scout would probably bounce back from this interruption in her childhood pretty quickly, if Kim stayed on track and Luke found a way to balance parenthood and work. From here on out, his daughter was his priority. He couldn't imagine a day without Scout's smile.

A couple other kids Scout's age asked her if she wanted to play with them in the tunnels that ran over the top of the Harbor Cove playground. Scout nodded and ran off with them, scrambling up the ladder in an instant. Kim wandered over to where Luke was standing. "Phew. I forgot how exhausting it is to keep up with a four-year-old."

"Tell me about it. My bedtime gets earlier every week. She wears me and Uncle Ray out."

"But she's worth it." Kim smiled as she watched their daughter laugh and chat with the other children. Scout peeked her head out of one of the tunnel holes, waved at her parents, and then ducked back inside. "I was kind of mean to you when I came back. I'm sorry."

"It's okay." Luke shifted over to make room for Kim

on the shaded half of the bleacher seating where several other parents were sitting. "Our relationship hasn't exactly been smooth. You were right to have resentment toward me. I was a drive-by parent who did the fun stuff and none of the hard work."

"But when it mattered, Luke, you stepped up to the plate," Kim said. "I can't tell you how much I appreciate you taking Scout while I went and got my act together."

"Of course. She's my daughter, and you are her mother. If you ever need anything, Kim, I'm here for you."

"I appreciate that." She gave him a weak smile. "The road ahead will undoubtedly be a little rocky. I'm not fooling myself and thinking sobriety will be a walk in the park. As the therapists at the center reminded me, it took time to get here, and it'll take time to get to where I want to be."

"Take all the time you need."

"Because of that, I know I can't be the mom I should be." She put up a hand to ward off his protests. "I love my daughter enough to know when to say I'm not the best primary parent. I'm hoping that you'll keep full custody of Scout for a while longer. I need to stay in the sober living house and concentrate on my sobriety until I have a really solid foundation and a concrete plan for maintaining my sobriety for a lifetime. I still want to see Scout, of course, as much as I can, but taking on the responsibility of working, paying bills, and being a full-time parent...I..."

"Kim, of course I will."

"It would mean staying put for a while. Putting down roots." Her gaze met his and held. All the history between them, the weeks he spent on the road, the promises he broke, the fights that had occurred, flowed in that tense moment when she questioned his commitment without saying a word. "I want that for our daughter, Luke."

"I do, too. Believe me."

"I hope so." She shifted her attention to the child they shared. He and Kim might never agree completely, but Luke had no doubt they could figure out a way to co-parent. There was no *if* about that—Scout was too important to not make that work.

"Do you think I'm a bad mother?" she said softly.

He thought about his answer for a second. Kim was nothing like his father had been. She had her struggles as Dad had, but unlike Luke's father, Kim was deeply invested in being a better parent, and he could see the difference those weeks in rehab had made. When it came down to it, Kim had accepted the help she had been offered and that was what mattered. "From the minute Scout was born, I thought you were an amazing mother. You knew just what to do when she cried and how to calm her down. Yeah, you got off track there for a little while, but I think it'll all be okay because I know you love our daughter more than anything in the world and want to be the mother she needs. You have this bond with Scout that is ... enviable. I never thought I could have that with her."

"But you do now."

"It took some work." He chuckled at the word *some*. "And a lot of lessons from you and from Emma. I had to be a fast learner."

"I'm sorry about that."

Luke could see the regret in her eyes, the guilt she still carried. How he wished he could make that easier for her. "Don't apologize for putting your health first, Kim. That's part of what makes you such a great mother. You weren't afraid to say, *I need to do this to be the best possible version of myself.*"

"Are you kidding me?" She shook her head. "I was terrified. Terrified I'd lose Scout forever. Terrified I'd fail. Terrified I couldn't handle life when I got out."

He took her hands in his and held them tight, two friends who had a shared love for an incredible little girl. "I'll be right here, Kim. I'm not going anywhere ever again."

CHAPTER 17

Emma pulled into Ray's driveway an hour after the debacle that had been Sharon's wedding. The bride had stormed out shortly after her husband, telling Emma she could keep the little dog who had "ruined everything." Emma swore she heard Marshmallow sigh in relief.

The old Toyota that had been Emma's reliable ride to and from work for the past six years ticked as the engine cooled. This part of Harbor Cove was nearly silent, filled only with the sounds of nature hiding in the woods ringing the lake. Emma could imagine herself unrolling her yoga mat in front of the water and doing poses while the sun set at the end of the day. All the time she'd lived here, she hadn't done that. Hadn't, in fact, shown up for a single yoga class. In the past month, there'd been far too much work and worry and far too little meditating and calming.

Inside Ray's house, Emma could see Scout and Luke at the kitchen table, working on something together. On the far side of the yard, Ray's head was buried in the engine of the bus. He glanced up, saw Emma, and headed toward her car.

She clipped the leash she'd bought on her way home onto Marshmallow's collar and then got out of the car. The dog seemed stunned to be surrounded by so much nature, instead of the modern upscale apartment in Boston where Sharon lived. "Hey, Ray, how's the bus coming?"

He pulled a rag from his back pocket and wiped the worst of the grease off his hands. "She's getting there. It's going to take some work and a lot of hoping and praying, but that's okay. Anything worth having is worth working for."

"Very true." Marshmallow sniffed at the ground, her tail moving a mile a minute. Emma trailed along behind the dog while Ray walked beside her.

"Where'd the dog come from?" Ray asked.

"The bride I was working with today threw a fit and refused to take her dog home. Marshmallow is the cutest little thing, and I couldn't let her go to the shelter, so..." Emma shrugged.

"Aren't you leaving town soon? Doesn't a dog kind of complicate that?"

Emma let out a sharp laugh. "What about my life isn't complicated? I really can't take Marshmallow where I'm going so I need to find her a home before Tuesday."

Ray bent down and scratched Marshmallow's ears. The dog practically climbed into his lap in joy. "I'm sure you'll find her a good place to live. She's a sweet little thing. I bet she's going to be hard to leave behind."

A rush of tears sprang to Emma's eyes, and her throat got thick. Maybe it was the emotion of her last day at work or the stress of the last few weeks but it seemed like she was always on the verge of tears. "A lot of things are going to be hard to leave behind."

"I get that," Ray said. In the weeks since Emma had moved in, the war vet had seemed to have become more engaged, happier about his life, and less depressed. She had no doubt that having his nephew and great-niece here had a lot to do with that change in attitude. "When I was in Iraq, part of my job was working with the locals in the village." He kept petting the dog as he talked, as if the distraction made it easier to bring up the past. "Building relationships and trust, helping them see that we were just trying to protect them. It's a tough job because the army is the very same people that are shooting at their neighbors for being on the side of the enemy."

"I can't even imagine how difficult that was," Emma said.

"I made friends with this family. The wife thought I was too skinny, and she was always inviting me over for dinner. They had this dog, a mangy mutt they found on the streets, which is what made me think of them just now." He gave Marshmallow a final pat before straightening. His face grew serious. "I have done my level best to forget everything that happened in that country, but I think it's time I remembered and dealt with it."

What Ray had seen overseas was something no one could understand unless they'd been there, Emma knew. She had seen the pain in his face many times, and more often than not, he avoided any discussion of his army career. No wonder. "You went through a lot. It's understandable that you would want to put that out of your mind."

"It's more the regret, Emma. This family loved and accepted me, even though a lot of people in that village hated the Americans. But I never told them how much their friendship meant to me. I kept up that tough soldier bravado the whole time, thinking it would hurt less when I left. When my deployment ended, I didn't even go say goodbye. I just got on the plane and closed my eyes so I didn't have to watch what I was leaving behind. And then..." He let out a deep breath, hauled another one in. "As soon as I landed in the States, I learned that village had been bombed and everyone in it was killed."

"Oh God, Ray. That's horrible."

He closed his eyes for a second as if the memory was too much even now. "I've spent six years of my life as a hermit, unable to forgive myself for not being there. Not telling them how much I appreciated them. For running away instead of opening up. I've chased away everyone that ever cared about me because I was a coward. I could jump out of an airplane, face a sniper, drive a convoy, but I couldn't tell a single person I loved them. Until that little girl came along." Ray pointed at the window. Inside, Scout was hanging a freshly glittered picture on the fridge. "She accepted me, warts and all, and invited me to her tea parties and had me hold her teddy bear. She saved me, Emma, because I was finally brave enough to love her back."

Emma wasn't surprised. Everyone who met Scout instantly fell in love with her. She had this irrepressible spirit and generous heart that seemed to light up a room. In all the time Emma had lived here, though, her conversations with Ray had been mainly small talk. Now, two days before she was supposed to leave, he was telling her stories of the past? "Is there some kind of message in all that?"

"I'm not one to give advice. Hell, I barely know how

to live my own life. I'm just saying, don't let fear be your guide, because all it does is lead you down dark paths." Ray tucked the rag back into his pocket, gave Marshmallow a final pat, and then headed back to the bus.

At the same time, Scout noticed Marshmallow through the window and, a second later, came bounding out of the house, dragging her father along. "A puppy! You got me a puppy, Emma?"

Emma laughed at the little girl's overabundance of joy and excitement. "Right now, I'm just babysitting Marshmallow. But I know she'd love to play with you. I don't think she's had a little girl as a friend before. So if you promise to be very careful, I'll let you hold her leash and take her for a walk around the yard."

Scout's exuberance immediately stilled into a stone-serious face. "I will. I promise." She accepted the leash from Emma and allowed the dog's insatiable need to sniff every bit of this unfamiliar ground to lead them across the yard.

"Isn't that the dog owned by that woman who stormed out of your office a few weeks ago?" Luke said.

Damn he looked good, even with glitter on his hands and dusting the front of his shirt. He was wearing jeans and a T-shirt, which on any other man would look ordinary but on Luke looked...delicious. "Yup. Today was her wedding, and it was a disaster, and now I have her dog. It's a long story."

Luke chuckled. "I bet. You wanna talk about it?"

"Not really." She was suddenly exhausted by the whole day and everything that had happened. "I just want to enjoy the time I have left in Harbor Cove."

"You're really leaving?"

She nodded and tried to ignore the hurt in his eyes.

He'd forget her as soon as she was gone, Emma told herself. He'd move on, find a woman who wanted to settle down, and walk down to the lake with her to watch the sunsets. If that was what Emma wanted, why did it hurt so damn much? "I, uh, connected with a charity in Haiti, and I'm heading there on Tuesday. I'll find a job in a school or something and carry on the Atlas Foundation's mission without the Atlas behind it."

"I have no doubt the children of Haiti could use your gifts, Emma. But the kids here in Harbor Cove need them, too. I've seen firsthand how you've transformed a child's life. Why not stay here and do the same work?"

"And admit that I failed at pursuing my big huge goals that I've been talking about forever?" She shook her head. "I'll always be labeled as the family mess."

"Your dream is to help children," he said. "I don't think it matters where you do that. To me, that's not failure. That's daring to dream in a different direction."

She scowled. "You sound like a TED Talk."

He chuckled. "Maybe so. I've been reading a lot of books about relationships since I got Scout and since..."

She turned to look at him when he didn't finish. "Since what?"

"Since we got married." He shrugged. "I went to the retreat in the first place to figure out how to have a better relationship with my daughter. Hell, how to have better relationships with people in general. Learning how to be a better parent has taught me a lot about how to be a better human being. But not necessarily how to be a better husband."

"You don't have to learn that, Luke. By Tuesday—"

"Will you forget the annulment for one second, Emma? We started something in Nevada, and it's never felt quite finished to me. I think that's because it's meant to keep going." He took her hand in his. "You can't tell me that you didn't feel anything for me in these last few weeks or when I kissed you or when we danced together."

How could she possibly explain the confusing tangle of feelings that had been running through her ever since they'd decided to go along with the marriage thing? If she told him that she thought about his kisses and how it felt to be in his arms all the time, he'd see hope in that. A future. Emma couldn't give him that.

"I felt a lot, Luke." She toed at the ground. Her heart raced, full of nerves and vulnerability and fear. So much fear. What if she did what he said and dared to dream in a different direction...and failed all over again? What if she opened her heart to him and told him the truth, that she was falling in love with him, too? But those words remained locked inside her by the insistent patter in her brain telling her to run away before she got hurt. "With you, I've felt so many things I've never felt before with anyone else."

"It's the same for me, Emma. In fact, I love—"

She put her fingers over his lips. "Don't say it. Don't change things. Don't make this harder."

He gently reached up and pulled her hand away. "It's the hard stuff that makes us stronger, Emma. And I can't let you leave without telling you that I love you one more time."

Joy leaped in her heart, flushed her skin, and filled her stomach with butterflies. She ached to say the words back, to just take that leap. *I love you, too.* But she couldn't get those words past her panicked heart. "I'm scared, Luke."

"Me too." In his eyes, she could see an echo of her own fear. "But I'm more scared of losing you."

"We're getting an annulment tomorrow." Maybe if she said it enough, that fact would stop hurting. The paperwork was filed, the annulment a signature away from being final. Then she could leave this town before she became any more attached to the handsome builder and his adorable daughter.

"We don't have to, Emma." He brushed a tendril of hair off her cheek, the touch so tender, so gentle, she felt as fragile as a robin's egg. "Stay here. Stay with me. Take a chance."

She closed her eyes before the tears that had been threatening all day could spill over. This was the hard part, she told herself, saying goodbye. It would all be easier once she put a few thousand miles between herself and this town.

Or at least that was the lie she kept telling herself. "What we did was a spur-of-the-moment decision, Luke. We can't make that work. It's not how it's supposed to be."

"And when have you ever played by other people's rules, Emma Monroe?"

❧❦❧

The corridor of the Essex County courthouse stretched in an endless sea of pale tile and marble walls. The historical design, part of a massive renovation he'd read about on a placard in the lobby, seemed imposing and stern. Maybe because there weren't a lot of happy things happening in a courthouse. For every adoption and elopement, there were probably a hundred criminal cases, arraignments, and...

Annulments.

Luke had debated long and hard about going to the courthouse. He had no intentions of contesting the annulment—if Emma wanted him out of her life, then he would certainly grant her that—but he couldn't just let the event pass by in the background, a stamped sheet of paper that canceled the word *husband*.

Last night, she'd left the dog with him and Scout while she went to her grandmother's house for one last family dinner. Emma hadn't come home until late in the evening, long after everyone had gone to bed. Luke had debated going down the hall to knock on her door, but he'd already said everything that was in his heart. The ball was in Emma's court.

Luke checked in at the front desk of the courthouse. "Carter annulment is in ten minutes," the receptionist said. "If you're not contesting, the judge will just sign the decree, sir, and we'll mail it to you. You don't have to be here."

"Yeah, I do. If only to see this all the way through." He took a seat on the wooden bench in the hall and hoped like hell that the other half of the Carter union would walk through that door.

❧❧❧

Emma was standing in the lobby of the courthouse, reading the confusing list of offices and locations, when she heard the chatter of two familiar voices behind her. She turned and saw Grandma and Gabby striding down the hall. "What are you two doing here?"

"Moral support," Gabby said as she threw one arm around Emma's shoulders. Gabby was wearing one of her Momma-inspired designs, a crimson dress with pockets that had a square neck and little cap sleeves. Ever since Gabby had taken the risk of switching her inventory to her own spin on retro classics, business at her shop had been booming, and Gabby's designs were being worn by women all over town. "You said last night that you were going to go to the hearing, and we thought we should be here for you."

"No matter what you decide," Grandma said, taking Emma's hand. "We're not here to sway you either way."

Emma had to admit she was glad to see them. When she'd been at dinner last night with her family, they'd talked briefly about the annulment, but Emma hadn't wanted to tell them that the closer the hearing loomed, the more lonely she felt. She supposed a divorce of any kind was a lonely venture, and Emma had been purposely distancing herself from Luke over the last week, maybe to make the whole process easier. She'd been so tempted last night when she came back to his house to knock on his bedroom door and have one last conversation.

Emma shook off the thoughts. The annulment was the right thing to do. Luke could move on with his life, and Emma could leave town without regrets. She hoped. "You mean Dear Amelia doesn't have some advice about a last-minute pitch to save my marriage?" she said to her grandmother.

"Oh, she has plenty of advice." A mischievous smile filled Grandma's face. "But for once, Dear Amelia thinks you should listen to your heart instead of to her."

"Grandma, I have no idea what my heart is saying. It's pounding too loud." Emma had tossed and turned all night, torn between going to Luke and letting him go. That nagging feeling of missing something, the feeling that had been with her all her life and had spurred her into saying yes in the ballroom, had only grown louder and deeper the closer she got to ending her marriage.

"Just a couple of months ago when I was terrified of losing Jake, somebody very wise and looking a lot like you, Emma, told me to do what makes me happy," Gabby said. "Whether that was falling in love, getting married, or running off to Paris to eat my body weight in croissants."

Emma remembered that conversation very well. She and Margaret had gone to Gabby's store after hours for a sister comfort session with cookies and wine. After Margaret left, Emma had lingered to give Gabby advice and extra hugs. The Monroe sisters had always been each other's biggest allies—and most honest advisers. Emma laughed at their meddling even as tears came to her eyes because of their love for her. "You guys suck, you know that, right?"

"That's what families are for." Grandma drew the two girls into a hug. They held each other for one long moment before Emma pulled away.

"I've got this," she said as she straightened the skirt on her dress and ran a hand over her hair to tame any flyaways. "I appreciate you guys being here, but I think this is something I need to do alone."

"Are you sure?" Grandma asked. The same concern that Emma had seen in Grandma's face when she'd fallen off the monkey bars in third grade filled her grandmother's eyes now, even though Emma was long past needing someone to worry about her. For a second, Emma wondered if she would look at Scout the same way twenty years from now.

No. There was no sense dwelling on that. She'd made her decision, bought her plane ticket, and packed her bag. This was what she should do.

But does it make you happy? that annoying voice in her gut asked.

"I'm not sure about a lot of things, but I am sure about this. I love you both." Emma swiped away the tears that were now spilling onto her cheeks. "How about I meet you both for lunch after all this is done?"

Grandma shook her head. "I'm sorry, Emma, I can't. I have a lunch something with Harry."

"And Jake and I are meeting with a DJ over at Bella Vita," Gabby said.

Grandma's dating life was moving in some kind of direction, Gabby's wedding plans were moving forward, and Emma felt like she was the only one stuck in the mud of indecision. "Things are changing all around me," Emma said.

"Maybe this little town isn't as boring as you think it is." Grandma pressed a kiss to her cheek. "And I hope it's always your sanctuary, no matter how far you roam."

After Gabby and Grandma left, Emma headed down the hall toward the judge's chambers. She checked in with the receptionist and was surprised to find Luke sitting on the bench outside the closed office door. She'd expected him to wait for the paper in the mail. Was he planning to contest it? "What are you doing here?"

"It seemed wrong not to show up," he said. "I'm not going to contest the annulment, if that's what you're worried about."

"But I thought you wanted to stay married."

"I do. But I'm not going to try to convince you to do that. You have a life planned, Emma, and I'm not part of that. It's okay. Or... it will be."

She put her little white wristlet on the empty seat beside her and thought of that morning in Nevada when she had woken up beside Luke. For one brief second when she was caught between dreaming and waking, she'd considered lingering in that bed with him. She'd been so cozy and warm, tucked under his arm and against his chest. As if that was exactly where she was meant to be. A part of her wished she could go back to that twilight moment and do all of this all over again. Would she have stayed with him and gone to the retreat? Or would she have ended up right back in this courthouse?

Emma sighed. "All my life, I've looked for signs of where I should go and who I should be instead of listening to what my gut told me. I guess I wanted validation or a neon billboard, but deep down I knew those signs and answers were already inside me. I was scared to follow what my gut was saying."

"And what is your gut saying right now?"

The door to the chambers opened, and a woman stepped out. She glanced up from her clipboard at them. "Mr. and Mrs. Carter? The judge is ready for you now."

Emma and Luke got to their feet and crossed to the open door. Just before they crossed the threshold, Luke caught Emma's hand and stopped her. "In the spirit of listening to your gut, I did something crazy this morning, and I bought a piece of property on the outskirts of Harbor Cove. It used to be owned by a church so there's a chapel and a rec hall and a house that used to be for the minister. It's been vacant for years, and they sold it to me really cheap. I decided I'm going to stay in Harbor Cove after I'm done with the Berry Circle project and open up my own business renovating homes, starting with that one."

He was staying? That meant Luke would be here when she came home for Gabby's wedding and Diana's wedding. It meant he would put down some roots, maybe find someone else, and build a life. Why did the thought of that hurt so much? Wasn't that what she wanted for him? "Why are you telling me this?"

"Because I'm done running from my responsibilities and the life I truly want. I'm going to stay here with Scout so she can make friends and build memories and be happy."

The assistant shifted her weight. "Mr. and Mrs. Carter—"

"And I bought it because I'm an optimist, Emma," Luke went on, ignoring the impatience of the other woman. "I thought that rec hall would be perfect for the community center that your mother dreamed of and that you should someday run. That hall will be there waiting for you to change some lives when you come back to Harbor Cove."

She shook her head. "I'm not planning to come back." She was going to run far, far from this town and the look of hope in Luke's eyes and the dreams he had just put on the table.

"Mr. and Mrs. Carter, we cannot keep the judge waiting." The woman ushered them inside the office and gestured toward two chairs sitting across from an older woman in a black robe.

They sat down and waited while the judge skimmed the file before her and then looked up at them. "Mr. and Mrs. Carter, it is my understanding that you are here to annul this marriage?"

All Emma had to do was say one word and everything that she had been through with Luke would be erased, as if it never happened. She would be free to leave this town, this life, and every memory of him and Scout. Free to run. Again.

Do what makes you happy.

"Mr. Carter?" the judge asked. "Is that why you're here?"

"Yes, Your Honor," Luke said. "If that's what Mrs. Carter wants, too."

The judge shifted her attention. "Mrs. Carter?"

Emma thought of the plane she was scheduled to board tomorrow. The bag that was packed and waiting by the door. And for the first time in her life, the thought of leaving sat like a lump of lead in her stomach. She wasn't excited about starting over. She wasn't dreaming of a new beginning.

She was, in fact, heartbroken at the thought of getting on that plane and leaving everything she knew—and loved—behind. Her conversation with Ray came back, and she decided there was no way she was going to pack a load of regrets in her suitcase, too.

Emma turned away from the judge and toward Luke. His brown eyes locked on hers, familiar and warm, and she knew what she was going to do. What she absolutely had to do. "Two months ago, if you asked me what would make me happy, I would have said traveling the world, without having to worry about a mortgage or what to make for dinner or who was going to take out the trash. But now…"

"Mrs. Carter, the court is running behind. Can you just answer the question so I can issue you the final decree?" The judge leaned across her desk and met Emma's gaze. "Do you want to annul your marriage to this man?"

Emma's gaze stayed on Luke. The butterflies in her stomach were rioting, but as she spoke the next word, it seemed like everything within her stilled. "No. I do not."

"And Mr. Carter?"

A smile curved across his face. He took Emma's hands in his, his thumb skating over the wedding band that Emma had somehow never removed. "I don't want to lose this woman, Your Honor."

"Then get out of my chambers." The judge shook her head and waved at the both of them to go. "Silly romantics," she muttered under her breath.

In the hall, people passed by Luke and Emma, lawyers on their way to hearings, plaintiffs off to plead their cases, assistants hurrying to juggle a heavy workload. But all of that dropped away into background noise as Emma stood in front of Luke and finally told him the truth. "I love you, too."

"I feel like I've waited a lifetime to hear you say that." He put his hands on her waist and pulled her to him.

She laughed. "We've only been married for a couple of months."

"What can I say? I'm an impatient man." He grinned, leaned in, and kissed her, long and slow and sweet. She wrapped her arms around her husband's back and finally realized what her grandmother meant about coming home.

EPILOGUE

S it, Marshmallow!" Scout made the hand gesture she'd learned at the puppy obedience class last week, and Marshmallow plopped her bottom on the grass. Scout squealed with joy and fed the dog a treat. "My puppy learned how to sit, Emma!"

"That's because you're such a good teacher." Emma swooped Scout into a hug. "And Marshmallow is such a hungry student."

Scout giggled and then scrambled down to dash across the parking lot with Marshmallow hot on her heels but trotting nicely on the leash. Uncle Ray handed Scout a square of cloth and the two of them polished the handprints on the outside of the rehabilitated bus that had, indeed, been painted a very pale shade of pink and had just made its first successful journey across town with Ray at the wheel and Scout riding shotgun. In a week, the four of them were going to take the bus up to a campground in Nashua for Labor Day weekend, an

end of the summer hurrah before Scout started kindergarten.

Luke came up behind Emma and wrapped his arms
around her. "How are you today, Mrs. Carter?"

She leaned into his chest and smiled up at him.
In the weeks since they had called off the annulment,
Luke and Emma had settled into life together. She'd
been working part-time at the hotel doing kids' events,
and in the evenings, the two of them spent time working on the building while Scout "helped" and mostly
made a mess. Life was happy and good, and all the
panicked chatter in Emma's gut had finally, completely
stopped because she had stopped trying to run from what
she truly wanted. "I still can't get used to you calling
me that."

"Which is why I'm going to do it all the time." He
grinned and ducked as she pretended to swat at him. "So,
Mrs. Carter, are you ready?"

She nodded and stepped out of his arms. She gnawed on
her bottom lip and looked at the people waiting for them
a couple hundred yards away. "I'm nervous, though."

"It'll be okay. I'll be right beside you." He took her hand
in his, and together, they crossed the parking lot. This fall,
the weedy, cracked lot would need to be repaved, and the
landscaping would need to be replaced, but hopefully the
bright banner hanging across the front door of the former
rec hall would draw everyone's attention away from the
to-do list still left on this place.

The assembled crowd outside the building was small.
Just a handful of people, including Leroy from the
Gazette and Emma's family. Maybe it would have been
smarter marketing-wise to make a big splash with the
grand opening, but to Emma, this whole dream was

a family affair started by her mother. Later, after the ribbon was cut and the cake was gone, she would start advertising and sharing the Penny Monroe Community Center with the rest of the world. For now, it was just Momma's notes and the people who had loved her the most.

Dad was the first to cross to Emma. He said hello to Luke and then drew his daughter into a quick hug. "I'm so proud of you, Emma."

"Thank you, Dad. I couldn't have done it without you."

He drew back. "I still don't understand why you wouldn't take my money as a gift and insisted on it being a loan."

Shortly after she'd come home from the courthouse, Emma had told her family of her plan to join Luke in creating the community center her mother had once dreamed of building. It wasn't a charity in some far-flung locale, but that was okay because Emma knew that Luke was right. There were children all around her, and parents too, who needed support, just as Luke and Scout had.

Emma had thought long and hard about her family's offer to help, finally deciding that, if she wanted to run a charity, then she had to do it 100 percent like a regular business, not a handout. "Because if I'm going to make this work, Dad, I'm going to do it like a responsible adult."

"You were already one of those, honey." Dad smiled at her and then stepped to the side to make room for her sisters and Grandma.

Margaret crossed her arms over her chest and gave the building an assessing look. "Well, I think, after this, we're going to have to redefine what an Emma Move is." She put up a hand to stop Emma's protest. "To mean something really, really brave. You pulled it off, Em, despite all the odds against you. I might not say it that often, but I'm proud of you, too."

"I had a little help." She glanced at Luke and then her family before casting her gaze to the sky. She had no doubt her mother was watching the whole thing, overjoyed to see her dream take physical form. There'd been sketches in the notebook, designs for the community spaces and the individual classrooms. Luke and Emma had replicated those ideas as best they could when they did the renovations. Thankfully, the rec hall had been in pretty good shape, and there were no major construction issues. They'd only redone half of it so far with a plan to redo the rest as enrollment in the center went up and donations began coming in.

Emma's phone buzzed, and she pulled it out to look at the incoming text. Karl's name lit up her screen. She'd kept in contact with him even after the foundation crumbled, a charity started with good intentions and no experience, which had overwhelmed Karl and cost him a lot of his own money. He'd managed to recoup some of the investment by pulling the plug. *I wired your donation to your bank today*, Karl had written in his text. *I'm sorry Atlas didn't work out. Thank you for believing in it.*

Thank you, Emma texted back. *And if you're looking to give back in a smaller way, there's a new charity in Harbor Cove that could use some people excited about helping kids.* She added the address of the hall and sent the message. She knew what it was like to screw up something important and need someone to nudge you with a second chance.

Luke handed her a giant pair of scissors. "Here you go, Mrs. Carter."

She laughed and gave her husband a quick kiss before snipping the bright-pink ribbon in front of the door to the future she couldn't wait to start. Then Luke and Emma each took one of Scout's hands and walked inside a bright, beautiful beginning.

READING GROUP
GUIDE

Dear Reader,

A reader once asked me what I thought my novels all had in common. My answer was simple—hope. Hope that we can muddle through our problems and setbacks, hope that broken families can be mended, and hope that we will all find our one true love.

I know that those things don't always happen and that not everything works out with a happy ending; our life journeys are rarely, if ever, smooth. Ironically when I started writing The Forever Family, *I had no idea that I would end up getting engaged myself while working on Emma's story. I've spent my life writing romance novels, imagining the perfect man. But to be honest, I never quite believed that man existed in real life. Then I met my husband, and as I sit here writing this letter to my readers, I am also working on my vows, telling him how blessed I am that my search for forever led to him.*

When I started dating the man who would become my second husband, one of my friends told me she admired me. I asked her why. She said, "Because you've been divorced and gone through painful breakups, yet you keep hoping and believing in true love." Call me a sappy romantic but that is, indeed, true. I never gave up hope that the perfect person for me was somewhere out there.

As we blend our families and build our lives together, I see echoes of our loved ones in the Monroe and Whitmore families. I know we'll face bumps in the road and detours from our path, but I'm confident that the two most important ingredients in life—hope and love—will carry us through whatever comes our way.

I wanted to mention one other little nod to Gabby from The Marvelous Monroe Girls. *I lost my mother when I was in my thirties, much older than the Monroe girls, but to me, that's a hole in life that never quite closes. On my wedding day, I took the bow from her wedding dress and used it to hold my bouquet, bringing a little bit of my own Momma to this new beginning.*

Wishing you hope and love,

DISCUSSION QUESTIONS

1. This novel explores the emotional wounds that hold people back in life. Are Emma's wounds understandable at this point in her life? Are they motivating her forward or holding her back?

2. What are some of Luke's wounds? How do his wounds differ from Emma's? In what ways are his coping mechanisms more effective than hers?

3. Emma's family is a strong influence in this story. What do her sisters try to teach Emma? How does her grandmother influence her? What does she offer Emma that her own father does not?

4. Emma suffered a major loss at a young age. She learned that nothing is permanent and is afraid of commitment. Her coping mechanism of running away has kept her from fully embracing life. Do you believe she has learned better coping skills by the end of the story? Her sisters also experienced this same loss. Do they have better coping skills?

5. *The Forever Family* teaches us that it is possible to heal old wounds. Through loving Luke and Scout, Emma comes to understand the loss of her mother better, and she is able to take steps toward bridging the gap between her and her sisters. What has this novel shown us about love, belonging, forgiveness, and healing?

6. The three sisters couldn't be more different. Margaret is pragmatic and career-driven, Gabby is cheerful and well balanced between her store and her fiancé, and Emma is impulsive and unfocused.

Yet if you look more closely, you'll find that they have more in common than meets the eye. What characteristics do they share?

7. When did you know that Luke was the right man for Emma? Was it right away, when he tries to calm her the morning after their marriage, or was it when she confesses to him about donating her life savings to the foundation? Or was there another moment?

8. Margaret is very tightly wound. She's very controlled in certain aspects of her life but appears to have no control over her marriage. Sometimes people create their own obstacles to happiness, whether it's out of a belief that they don't deserve happiness or because they're just not ready to be happy. Have you ever felt this way? Do you think that Margaret's marriage can be saved? Do you think that it should be saved?

9. At the beginning of the story, Emma doesn't appear to have the commitment necessary to be a good mother. And yet she's surprisingly comfortable around Scout. Do you think she will be a good stepmother in the long run?

10. What did you think of the way Emma related to her grandmother and sisters? What about her father? They clearly tried to help her when the going got rough. But did they hinder her ability to cope in any way?

11. Luke gave up a lot of freedom when he brought Scout into his life. What motivated him? We get just a glimpse of his family life, but what can you tell about his parents? Is Luke a good parent?

12. Sharon as a bridezilla brings some humor to the

story. If you're married, did you find yourself being a perfectionist about your wedding? Do you wish that you could have enjoyed the planning more? If you're not married, do you have a mental image of what the big day should look like?

13. Eleanor acts a bit embarrassed as Harry is courting her. Do you think that she really feels this way? Did you find their love story realistic? Did you feel happy as they both got their second chance at love?

14. Uncle Ray's life continues to be affected by his military service many years ago. Do you know anyone impacted by war? Luke finally convinces his uncle that he needs professional help to fully recover. Is there someone in your life that you need to encourage to seek mental health assistance? What will be the best way to go about that?

15. Emma doesn't trust her feelings for Luke, but she's drawn to him anyway. How does her trust in him grow? What does she bring to the relationship? What do you suppose their life will be like in a few years?

ABOUT THE AUTHOR

When she's not writing books, *New York Times* and *USA Today* bestselling author Shirley Jump competes in triathlons, mostly because all that training lets her justify midday naps and a second slice of chocolate cake. She's published more than seventy-five books in twenty-four languages, although she's too geographically challenged to find any of those countries on a map.

Looking for more second chances and small towns?
Check out Forever's heartwarming
contemporary romances!

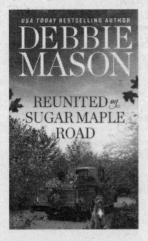

REUNITED ON
SUGAR MAPLE ROAD
by Debbie Mason

Ever since her fiancé's death over a year ago, Emma Scott's been sleep-walking through life, and her family is growing increasingly worried about her. Enter Josh Callahan, high school football coach and her brother's best friend. Though he may drive her crazy, his suggestion to fake-date is brilliant because there are no feelings involved. And his plan works… until Josh realizes that the feelings he has for Emma are all too real. But is Emma ready to share her heart again?

THE CORNER OF
HOLLY AND IVY
by Debbie Mason

Arianna Bell isn't expecting a holly jolly Christmas. That is, until her high school sweetheart, Connor Gallagher, returns to town. But just as she starts dreaming of kisses under the mistletoe, Connor announces that he will be her opponent in the upcoming mayoral race…even if it means running against the only woman he's ever loved. But with a little help from Harmony Harbor's matchmakers and a lot of holiday cheer, both may just get the happi-ly-ever-after they deserve.

Discover bonus content and more on
read-forever.com

THE HOUSE ON FIREFLY BEACH
by Jenny Hale

Sydney Flynn can't wait to start fresh with her son at her sanctuary: Starlight Cottage at Firefly Beach. That is, until she spies her childhood sweetheart. Nate Henderson ended their relationship with no explanation and left town to become a successful songwriter—only now he wants to make amends. But when a new development threatens her beloved cottage, can Sydney forgive him and accept his help? Or will the town they adore, and the love they had for each other, be lost forever?

THE INN AT TANSY FALLS
by Cate Woods

When her best friend dies and sends her on a scavenger hunt from beyond the grave, Nell Swift finds herself setting off for a charming little Vermont town, where she's welcomed by friendly locals, including an adorable Labrador and a grumpy but attractive forester and his six-year-old son. Is Nell willing to start her life all over again and make this new town her forever home? Includes a reading group guide!

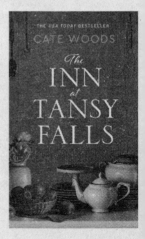

Meet your next favorite book with @ReadForeverPub on TikTok

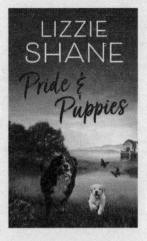

PRIDE & PUPPIES
by Lizzie Shane

After years of failing to find her own Mr. Darcy, Dr. Charlotte Rodriguez swears off dating in favor of her new puppy, Bingley. And there's no one better to give her pet advice than her neighbor and fellow dog owner George. When their friendly banter turns flirtatious, Charlotte finds herself catching *feelings*. But will Charlotte take one last chance with her heart before they miss out on happily-ever-after?

A CAT CAFE CHRISTMAS
by Codi Gary

In this laugh-out-loud, opposites-attract romance, veterinarian and animal lover Kara Ingalls needs a Christmas miracle. If Kara can't figure out some way to get her café out of the red, it won't last past the holidays. Marketing guru Ben Reese hatches a plan to put the café in the "green" by Christmas, but they will need to set aside their differences— and find homes for all the cats—to have their own *purr*-fect holiday… together.

THE FOREVER FAMILY
by Shirley Jump

The youngest of three close-knit sisters, Emma Monroe is the family wild child. Maybe that's why a yoga retreat leads to a spur-of-the-moment decision to marry Luke Carter, a man she's met exactly three times. The next morning, Emma sneaks back home, where she should have nama-*stayed* in the first place. When her brand new husband arrives to convince her to give their marriage a chance, can she envision a future where her biggest adventures come not from running away but from staying?

SWEET PEA SUMMER
by Alys Murray

May Anderson made the biggest mistake of her life when she broke up with her high school sweetheart, Tom Riley. Now he's back in Hillsboro, California, to take over his family's winery—and wants nothing to do with her. But when they're forced to partner for the prestigious Northwest Food and Wine Festival, their plans to avoid each other fall apart. When working side by side causes old feelings to surface, can they find the courage to face the fears that once kept them apart?